ADVANCE PRAISE FOR ONCE UPON A TIME IN WEST TORONTO

Terri Favro's novel *Once Upon a Time in West Toronto* is a brilliant follow-up to her award-winning novella *The Proxy Bride*. This novel dives into the lives of the endearing Ida, Marcello, and Bum Bum and vividly reveals their experiences of trying to redefine themselves and move from painful pasts to hopeful futures. Moments of joy and love collide with sadness and tragedy. With insight and boldness, Favro evokes the Italian experience from confessional boxes to the emotions accompanying new immigrants and the longing to move forward even when familial secrets and betrayals try to unravel new lives. Favro explores the themes of sexual desire, women's solidarity, and family obligation and weaves the reader through mystical and hypnotic passages. Honest, moving, and gutsy, Favro's dazzling novel drifts between flashbacks and compelling present scenes, providing deep empathy for the unforgettable characters. Favro's craft and skill at storytelling shape *Once Upon a Time in West Toronto* into an engaging novel.
—Sonia Saikaley, author of *The Lebanese Dishwasher*

Ida and Marcello must run away from church, family, and the hoodlums that threaten their bodies and souls. Can they reinvent themselves and escape the bleakness of their respective pasts? *Once Upon a Time in West Toronto* is a hip, original take on the immigrant story, as well as a satisfying love story, a well told tale, and a slice of reality. Terri Favro's witty, supple prose is a discovery and a delight.
—Caterina Edwards, author of *The Sicilian Wife*

A sinewy and sensuous modern tale complete with compelling characters—a few bad guys and several lost souls—a wonderful addition to the stories about Italian Canadians and the trials of immigration. Favro puts her writing gifts to great use here, holding up a mirror to the troublesome past and shining a light on the difficult truths with sharply skilled prose.
—Eufemia Fantetti, author of *A Recipe For Disaster and Other Unlikely Tales of Love*

Once Upon A Time in West Toronto is a story about the power of family—those we are born into and those we make. It is also a story about the power of place— the land we come from and the country

we call home. But above all, it is a story about the irresistible, unrelenting, often treacherous, and ultimately transformative power of love. It is one of those rare novels that manage to be simultaneously epic and intimate, romantic and violent, tragic and hopeful.
—Ian French (IF The Poet), Canadian Individual Poetry Slam Championship Winner and World Cup of Slam Poetry Finalist

In *Once Upon a Time in West Toronto*, Terri Favro deftly weaves together multiple spellbinding narratives over the span of six decades, expertly covering the full spectrum of human experience from love and revenge to loyalty, honour, and forgiveness. Set during Toronto's coming of age—against the political backdrop of the rise of feminism and the immigrant experience—*Once Upon a Time in West Toronto* is a novel filled with wry humour, unflinching honesty, and unforgettable characters. Terri Favro is a wonderful storyteller who knows how to wring every last drop of emotion from each sentence. Filled with action and suspense, as well as heartbreak and insight, this novel is a page-turning delight.
—Bianca Marais, author of *Hum If You Don't Know The Words*

An utterly captivating and beautiful book. Ida, Marcello, and Bum Bum's lives overlap, interconnect, and tangle in a way that will have you exclaiming in delight and weeping in sorrow. Few writers capture the complex Catholic experience as masterfully as Terri Favro, who paints a poignant picture of the complicated clash of religion and love. Mapping lives from 1969 to 2013, the story brings to life the women's rights movement of the '70s and the pain brought about by the emergence of AIDS in the '80s. The story is also a love story to Toronto's West End, and it is so wonderfully written that you can taste the Asagio and smell the freshly ground espressos. Favro's writing is also so touching and funny that you will find yourself smiling at the originality of a perfect simile and graceful metaphor. This book is like the perfect snow globe of so many lives—lives we have lived, lives we are living, or might have lived. Tragedy meets the redemption of the human spirit and, as we move from Venice to Shipman's Corners, from love to loss and back to love, we realize that, with all its ugliness and hardship, the world truly is a beautiful and mysterious place.
—Lisa de Nikolits, author of *The Nearly Girl* and *No Fury Like That*

Once Upon a Time in West Toronto

a novel by
Terri Favro

inanna poetry & fiction series

INANNA PUBLICATIONS AND EDUCATION INC.
TORONTO, CANADA

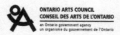 

We gratefully acknowledge the support of the Canada Council for the Arts and the Ontario Arts Council for our publishing program. We also acknowledge the financial support of the Government of Canada.

Cover design: Val Fullard

Once Upon a Time in West Toronto is a work of fiction. All the characters, situations, and locations portrayed in this book are fictitious and any resemblance to persons living or dead, or actual locations, is purely coincidental.

Library and Archives Canada Cataloguing in Publication

Favro, Terri, author
     Once upon a time in West Toronto / a novel by Terri Favro.

(Inanna poetry & fiction series)
Companion to: The proxy bride.
Issued in print and electronic formats.
ISBN 978-1-77133-417-4 (softcover).— ISBN 978-1-77133-418-1 (epub).—
ISBN 978-1-77133-419-8 (Kindle).— ISBN 978-1-77133-420-4 (pdf)

     I. Title. II. Series: Inanna poetry and fiction series

PS8611.A93O53 2017   C813'.6   C2017-905373-6
                                                   C2017-905374-4

Printed and bound in Canada

Inanna Publications and Education Inc.
210 Founders College, York University
4700 Keele Street, Toronto, Ontario, Canada M3J 1P3
Telephone: (416) 736-5356 Fax: (416) 736-5765
Email: inanna.publications@inanna.ca Website: www.inanna.ca

The adventures of
Ida, a liberated Proxy Bride
her lover, *Marcello*, a Ditch Digger;
Bum Bum, a Virtuous Thief;
and assorted *Villains*, *Hustlers*, and *Whores*.

ALSO BY TERRI FAVRO

Sputnik's Children
The Proxy Bride

For Ron

I can't see America any other way than with a European's eyes. It fascinates me and terrifies me at the same time.
—Sergio Leone, filmmaker

Lookin' back is a bad habit.
—Charles Portis, *True Grit*

CONTENTS

1. GENESIS

CHURCH OF ST. ROCCO, VENICE, MAY 1952

ZARA SAILS INTO Ca'San Rocco carrying her pregnancy like the prow of a ship, the *click-click-click* of her heels on the marble floor panicking the pigeons in the rafters. Ferragamo pumps are too dressy for a Saturday afternoon, but Zara is a firm believer in *la bella figura*. Always look good, especially when under attack. Tugging two-year-old Riccardo by the hand, she clatters past Tintoretto masterpieces so grimy with smoke that you can no longer tell San Rocco from the plague victims he's curing.

In a back pew kneels Leona Bellini, her righteous black curls bobbing over her rosary beads. Barely twenty years old, she has already turned herself into a respectable housewife. She comes to confession once a week to scrub her pristine soul as spotless as her kitchen floor. You could eat off either one.

Refusing to give this sanctimonious bitch the satisfaction of shaming her, Zara stands next to the pew where Leona pretends to be concentrating on her Hail Marys. "*Signora* Bellini, you are a good Catholic." Zara is careful to address Leona in proper Italian rather than the crude *Veneziano* dialect. She doesn't want to sound untutored.

Leona looks up suspiciously. "I'm on my knees cleansing my soul, aren't I?"

"*Giusto!* That's why I know you won't mind looking after my little boy while Father Paolo dabs at my sins a little," says Zara, failing to keep the sarcasm out of her voice. She pushes the boy into the pew beside her odious, but trust-worthy, neighbour. "Here, Rico, go say your prayers with Signora Bellini."

Riccardo, a heartbreaker with eyes as blue as the Adriatic and a bush of white curls covered by a cowboy hat, offers the woman a broad grin before scooting into the dust beneath the pew.

"Well, I..." Leona starts to object, but Zara has already pushed aside the velvet curtain. The box is dark and stuffy; the dust makes her sneeze, which has the desired effect of causing the interior door to slide open and the priest to begin mumbling a Latin blessing through the grillwork.

"Doesn't anyone ever clean in here?" she complains.

The blessing stops.

"Zara?" asks the deep voice. "Is Rico in there with you?"

"He's in the church with Bellini the Busybody."

"You are well?"

Zara shifts her weight on the rock-hard kneeler; the baby is starting to kick, hammering its tiny heels against her bladder. This pregnancy is very different than her first, the baby objecting strenuously every time Zara gets down on her knees. Probably a little heretic. She feels an intense desire to urinate.

"I'm well enough," Zara allows.

Silence. "Have you come to confess?"

Zara snuffles a bit, trying not to sneeze again. "I've come for absolution, but I don't need to confess. You already know everything. Just give me my penance and be done with it."

A deep sigh. "You have to say your sins out loud so they reach God's ear."

Zara feels a sudden annoyance with the priest; she's tempted to storm out, but who wants the worry of going into labour with a sin on her soul? More than one of the girls at Ca'Rosa has been carried off by childbed fever to purgatory or worse, because a priest didn't want to give last rites in a brothel, even one officially sanctioned by the government.

"God is everywhere, no? He already knows my sin. And yours. Am I supposed to confess for us both?" Zara pauses. "You were a nicer man when you were a seminarian, Paolo."

The priest clears his throat. "When I'm in here, I'm not 'Paolo.' In fact, I'm not a man at all. I'm God's ears and God's mouth. And Zara, God is telling you to leave this child at the front gate of the foundling home."

Zara is astonished. "Sitting alone in this box has hardened your heart. You want me to give Rico to the nuns, too?"

The priest gives a heavy sigh. "Of course not, but we must be careful. One child can be taken to the cinema or a sweet shop from time to time without arousing suspicion. Two, starts to look like a family outing. If you give this one to the Sisters, you could go back to running Ca'Rosa."

"Just like you could go back to being a man," points out Zara.

She can hear him shifting in his seat, checking the other door, nervous about being overheard. What a shame to shut up a man so young and beautiful in the darkness of a confessional. Zara fears that sitting in this stuffy box, listening to people's filthy sins, has turned him into a *testadura*—a man hard of head and heart. When he speaks again, his tone has softened so that he sounds less authoritarian and more like the twenty-three-year-old he actually is.

"Zara, I have a calling."

"So do I," she points out.

"You call what you do at Ca'Rosa a calling?"

"I started out on my back; now I run the place. I'm a businesswoman. You don't think that's a calling?"

He pauses. "If I acknowledge the children, it would kill my mother."

Allora! Now we get to the heart of the matter, thinks Zara. The child inside gives her another swift kick as if to say: *Up off your knees, Mamma!* Zara hoists herself unsteadily to her feet.

"Where are you going? I haven't given you absolution yet!"

"Absolve yourself!" shoots back Zara, pushing aside the velvet curtain. Out in the church she can see Riccardo peering at her over the back of the pew. Leona has removed his cowboy hat and is trying to show him how to make the sign of the cross.

Zara feels a warm trickle down her leg. *Uh-oh*, she thinks. *My bladder is too weak for all this kneeling.* That's when the trickle turns into a gush. There's a gentle plop in her underwear as the mucous plug inside her womb lets go. Even in the dim light she can see blood dripping onto the five-hundred-year-old marble floor. The first stab of pain comes, doubling her over.

Zara seizes the curtain to steady herself. *The little heretic is on its way.*

2. SPAGHETTI WESTERN

IDA CROUCHES IN THE FIELD, paring knife in one hand, battered metal bowl in the other. Resting her elbows on the knees of her sagging pedal pushers, she digs around the base of the plant, yanking the stem and roots out of the ground; it's easier to take the whole weed and clean it later, even though all she needs are the leaves. Traffic flies overhead, thickening the air with exhaust fumes and the sounds of brakes and engines blurring into car radios: *Tie a yellow ribbon Angie you're so ten-fifty* CHUM *rainy night in Georgia scorcher again today in the golden horseshoe war what is it good for absolutely nothing a thousand yellow ribbons round the old oak tree.*

Lily crouches next to her. She's wearing two different tennis shoes—one blue, one pink. Only the pink shoe has laces.

"Why are you digging up the dandelions?" Lily asks, picking a scab off one knee.

"I make an *insalata* for my husband to eat."

Ida stumbles over *huz*-BAND, the consonants grinding against each other like hard cheese on a rasp. Like many English words, she finds *husband* a little harsh. It could use a few more vowels. *Hus-a-band. Husa-banda. My husabanda, Marcello.*

She also stumbles over *husband* because it's a bald-faced lie—what Marcello calls "a smokescreen"—to cover up the fact that she has another husband—well, not *another*, she can only have one: Marcello's father, Senior. Unless the old man grants her an annulment or dies, Marcello can never be her *husabanda*, a mildly incestuous situation that is scandalous even by the slackening moral standards of 1974.

Inamorato is the correct word for what Marcello is to Ida, but it makes him sound like a dashing Renaissance prince rather than a melancholic muscle-bound ditch digger who spends most of his time down manholes. He reminds her of a line from a favourite old film, *Mezzogiorno di Fuoco*—in English, *High Noon*: *You're a good-looking boy: you've big, broad shoulders. But it takes more than big, broad shoulders to make a man.*

Per dire la veritá, thinks Ida, yanking dandelions out of the cracked, rain-starved earth, Marcello has the looks to play the romantic hero. Ida catches other women (and some men) gazing at him with a certain interest, almost a hunger, very unusual in this chilly country where nothing seems to ignite passion except hockey.

She's not sure whether they're more excited by the unlikely coupling of Marcello's angelic face with his workhorse of a body, or the air of tragic nobility that clings to him like cheap cologne.

Marcello is a Southern Ontario Orpheus, a lover of opera and mathematics, forced by shameful circumstances to grub around in Toronto's underworld of subway tunnels and sewers. He plays his part stoically because, after all, he's sacrificed his life to Ida. Just like that *inglese* King Such-and-Such from the 1930s giving up the throne for the woman he loves. Heart-breaking, is it not? No wonder women are drawn to Marcello despite his ditch digger status.

But Ida knows something about him that these women can't see. Marcello likes to suffer. Enjoys it. That's why he rubs himself raw with frustration and guilt over Ida being married to his father. They came back to Ontario so he could find a way to break the legal bonds of Ida's unconsummated proxy marriage to Senior and make Ida his own—in the eyes of the State, the Church, His Holiness Pope Paul, and all the Angels and Saints in Heaven, for all Ida knows. Sometimes, the *tragedia* gets on a girl's nerves.

"I can't believe you're feeding Dreamboat weeds," says Lily, frowning at the growing pile of dirty dandelions in Ida's bowl. "Aren't you afraid you'll poison him?"

Better than feeding him food from the supermarket, thinks Ida, still aghast at what passes for *insalata* in Canada. Dandelion leaves make a bitter salad, requiring plenty of olive oil and salt, but they're still much better than watery iceberg lettuce covered in bottled orange dressing. Ida gags slightly at the thought.

As she straightens up, the pedal pushers fall low on her hips, the crotch down between her knees. "*Oop-a-lah!*" she says, yanking up the waist. "Your *mamma*, she bigger than me."

"You look like a clown!" laughs Lily, dancing around Ida.

"You're the clown," answers Ida, grabbing her hand. She likes walking hand in hand with the girl, but Lily wrenches away from her.

"You're weird!" she yells. "Let's go to the office. It's time for Mamére's story."

"I meet you there. First, I put the *cicoria* in the tub to soak."

"Blecch!" says Lily, sticking her tongue out. "Just don't make me eat any!"

As Lily runs to join her mother, Ida goes to her cabin and places the bowl of weeds in the bathtub, fills it with cold water, and collects her rubber gloves, rags, and pail. She'll need them to clean cabins Eight and Eleven after the story is over.

To finish her work at the Seahorse before check-in, she has to rise at six—noon, Italian time. Back home, her brother Rico will be fixing lunch while Zara coaxes hung-over guests out of their rooms so she can make the beds.

The dusty ceiling in the cabin Ida shares with Marcello is the same grubby eggshell colour as her bedroom at Ca'Rosa. True, there are no *putti* in the corners, no dusty oil painting of the Grand Canal on the wall, no Zara pounding on the door shouting, *Ida! Muoviti! Vieni subito qui, pigrona!* But a chambermaid is a chambermaid, no matter where she's scrubbing toilets.

In the office of the Seahorse Motor Court and Housekeeping Cabins, the television goes on at 3:55 p.m. sharp every weekday, right on time for *General Hospital*. When Ida walks in with her cleaning things, Jeanie is already on the high stool behind the registration desk, tapping the ash off her Chesterfield into a seahorse-shaped glass ashtray, watching one of her favourite commercials. A manicurist places another woman's fingertips in a bowl of green water.

Dishwashing liquid?

You're soaking in it!

Jeanie snorts. "*Mon Dieu,* that Madge, she's got a mouth on her!"

Ida settles on the orange vinyl love seat, the oversized pedal pushers puddling around her like deflated balloons. "What happens with Nurse Jessie?" she asks about her favourite character, the show's long-suffering head nurse with an unrequited passion for the hospital's chief surgeon.

Jeanie takes another drag on her Chesterfield and shakes her head, a pitying smile on her candy pink lips. "That nurse is a loser. So good, so perfect! What does she get for it? *Pfff!* That bastard, Phil."

Lily sprawls on the floor with a box of fashion dolls, religious statues, and superheroes. She likes to act out *General Hospital* with Barbies and Skippers for the nurses, a plaster Saint Anthony as Nurse Jessie's awful husband Phil, and a Superman doll as the chief surgeon, Dr. Steve Hardy. "Kiss me you fool!" croaks the girl, pressing the dolls' faces together. "Smooch, smooch! Why can't Nurse Jessie just marry Dr. Steve and live happily ever after?"

"This is a good question," agrees Ida, looking at Jeanie. The stories in these shows are as crazy as opera *libretti*, if not worse.

Jeanie takes another drag on her Chesterfield. "If everybody was happy, it'd be a pretty boring story."

Ida would love to be bored and happy. That morning, exasperated with the watery excuse for coffee that Marcello made from boiled water and Nescafé, she had said: "I will never get used to Canadian food. Never."

Marcello slammed his cup on the counter. "*Basta*. Enough. You know I'm working hard to make you happy."

Ida looked at his face, sad and handsome, so tragically in love with her. No matter how much she provokes him, he absorbs her criticisms like a boxer taking punches. Why, for once, can he not simply let himself get angry? Had he become too Canadian even for that?

"Some things cannot be fixed, Cello," she told him. "Not even by you."

For a moment, Marcello looked as if, finally, she had found a way into his anger, to the blank knot of regret that they never talk about but which squats in the corner of every room with them, crawls into bed between them at night, eats meals at the table with them: the one time Marcello spectacularly failed Ida. They never talk about it, so the two of them continue to live as three: Marcello, Ida, and The Past.

"Don't talk like that," said Marcello, trying to pull Ida into his arms. A foot shorter than him, she ducked out of his embrace and threw open the screen door, letting it slam behind her as she headed to the edge of the lake. She dropped into one of the splintery deck chairs to watch ducks peck garbage out of the waves. With her back straight and chin up, she forced herself not to turn around to see if Marcello was standing outside the cabin.

He finally came up behind her and mumbled: "*Mi dispiace.* I'm sorry, Ida." Then he kissed her hand and left for work.

After he was out of sight, she bent over and wailed loudly enough to frighten the ducks. Fortunately, no one was around that morning to see her blowing her runny nose into the tail of an old work shirt Jeanie had given her. She sat for an hour, snuffling and staring at the lake, more like a sea really, vast and often stormy. Wild, like the landscapes she had become accustomed to in other parts of Canada they've passed through: Thunder Bay, Winnipeg, Prince George, Nanaimo. It's when she turned her back to the water that she wasn't sure where she was anymore, disoriented by the ugliness of the elevated expressway, the ridiculously-named Buena Vista Motor Hotel on the other side of Lakeshore Road, and the industrial smoke-stacks and billboards north of the Seahorse. She used to think that "north" meant clear skies and forests full of animals, but here it means factories and cramped red brick row houses, greasy diners and sagging storefronts full of drab goods. Ida is never quite sure where Toronto starts, exactly, even though she's told she's living in it.

No matter how much her restless eye looks for beauty, she fails to find it in the stern skyline. The only spot of colour for miles is on a billboard advertising SunQuest Travel: beneath the words *Fly Away to La Dolce Vita!* a canary yellow sailboat floats on a blue ocean. In her shapeless hand-me-down clothes, she stares at the billboard and wonders what exactly she has flown away to, and why.

Rubbing her eyes to push back the tears, Ida forces herself to stop thinking about her fight with Marcello and pay attention to the show. Today's episode opens with Nurse Jessie at home in a bathrobe, worrying that she's pregnant by her ex-husband, Phil. Just when it seems that Jessie and Dr. Steve Hardy might get together —this! Phil is delighted; anything he can do to weasel his way back into Nurse Jessie's life and make her as miserable as possible is fine by him. Jessie puts one hand on her stomach and closes her eyes.

Quella povera, povera donna! thinks Ida. The poor, poor woman. She knows exactly how Nurse Jessie feels. Confused, frightened, violated. Ida rests a hand on her belly.

The show moves excruciatingly slowly; the only time anything new happens is on Fridays, the day when someone inevitably turns up with amnesia or finds out they're not who they thought they were, cases of mistaken identity being extraordinarily common in the city where the story takes place.

Ida knows something about mistaken identities, she and Marcello having changed theirs several times. In Prince George, they became Mike and Irene, so as not to stand out; Marcello was anxious that someone might be looking for them. Now that five years have passed and they've moved to Toronto, they have taken back half their identities, Italian first names being as common as dirt in Ontario and held in about as much regard. Out of an abundance of caution, they used a new surname, Umbriaco, which Marcello had pulled out of the air somewhere in Northern Ontario.

Out of the frying pan, into the fire, as the Canadians like to say.

After *General Hospital*, Lily goes outside to play on the rusty swing while the two women launder towels and bed linens. "If you don't mind me asking, are you and Dreamboat thinking about having kids?" Jeanie asks as they fold sheets.

Ida doesn't answer right away. The unexpected question has put her in a bad position. She tries not to lie to Jeanie because she claims to have something called a *bullshit detector*, a supernatural sixth sense that allows her to tell instantly when a guest will try to skip out overnight without payment, or a lover will never call her again. Jeanie's instincts for truth and deception are unerring, almost supernatural.

"This is not a good time for children," says Ida carefully.

"So what are you doing to prevent it? If you don't want to end up like Nurse Jessie, it better be more than the rhythm method."

Ida keeps her eyes on the linen. "My Marcello he, you know, removes himself. He uses self-control."

Jeanie snorts. "*Ah oui,* self-control! That's exactly how I ended up with Lily at the tender age of eighteen, sweetie. You should go to the doctor, be measured for a diaphragm. Better yet, go on the Pill. I'll write down how to get to the Free Clinic on College Street. They'll fix you up."

"I don't know what Marcello will think—"

"Dreamboat doesn't have to have the babies," points out Jeanie, lifting her shirt. "Want to see my c-section scar?"

Ida holds up her hands in surrender. "I go tomorrow while Marcello is at work."

"Smart girl," nods Jeanie, unsteadily lighting a fresh cigarette off the tip of the old one. Jeanie's hand is trembling. Ida has noticed this slight tremor before. Jeanie occasionally even drops things—dishware, laundry baskets—yet she's robust, a tall woman with fiery red hair and green eyes, the embodiment of an Amazon warrior. The tremors seem odd in someone so young. Ida almost suggests that Jeanie come to the clinic with her, get checked out herself, then decides: *No.* She has to start dealing with this city on her own. Maybe she'll even find a decent *mercato.* Somewhere in this city, someone must sell arugula and rapini, maybe even *parmigiano* that doesn't come out of a cardboard box.

The next day, after Marcello drives into town to stand on a street corner with a bunch of other men, waiting for a job—there being a big demand in Toronto for young guys with strong backs who don't mind dirty, dangerous work—Ida takes the Queen streetcar east to Bathurst, then catches the bus up to College Street, following Jeanie's directions scribbled inside a matchbook. The women's clinic is inside a building with the ridiculously unimaginative name of Doctors Hospital. Who else's hospital would it be? wonders Ida.

She wears some of her nice clothes from Italy: the first time she's been able to dress up in a long time, although she knows the outfits she brought to Canada in 1969 are out of fashion. These days, hems are longer and colours earth-toned—harvest gold, avocado, mud brown, forest green. In her pink miniskirt and paisley print blouse, Ida looks like she is stuck in the swinging sixties rather than living in these sombre, nervous times.

Twisting and twisting the dull gold band on her finger, she tries not to make eye contact with a vacant-looking blonde girl on one side of her, her pregnancy a protuberance on her slender body, like a root growing out of a potato. The girl thumbs slowly through a magazine, humming to herself. On the other side of Ida sits a toothless man, his long hair a ratted tangle, aged anywhere from eighteen to eighty. He could use a bath.

When the girl drops the magazine on the table with a sigh, Ida picks it up. The pages are as shiny and colourful as candy, full of photographs of healthy American girls in blue jeans and smock tops. It's called *Seventeen*. Ida starts reading; the articles all seem to be about boys and dating and dieting. She finds herself absorbed in a quiz called "Is This Boy 'The One'?", mentally ticking off boxes with Marcello in mind, when the nurse at the front desk sings out, "*Mrs. Oom-bree-yako?*"

The nurse leads her to a windowless beige room, decorated with posters reading VD DOESN'T HAVE TO BE A LIFE SENTENCE! and PREGNANT? SINGLE? YOU'RE NOT ALONE, BABY!

The nurse tells Ida to remove everything from the waist down, pull on a dingy cotton gown, and lie on an examination table in the middle of the room. A pair of ominous-looking steel clamps at the bottom of the table remind Ida of torture devices. She stares at them distrustfully.

"Once you've got the gown on, put your feet in the stirrups and wait for Dr. Stevenson," the nurse tells her, then leaves.

Ida carefully folds and piles her clothes on a chair, ties on the gown, and climbs on to the high table. Carefully she rests her heels in the steel stirrups; her knees automatically fall open, as if she's astride an invisible horse. Legs trembling, she stares at the tiny ventilation holes in the ceiling. Even though it's warm outside, the room is very cold.

The door opens suddenly and a man in a white coat strides in, smelling of tobacco and fried onions. He gives off a whiff of impatience, not smiling or saying hello, not even looking at her, just glancing over the sheet she filled out in the waiting room. "Mrs. ... Umbilical?" he mutters uncertainly, peering at the sheet.

Ida sighs; why does everyone have so much trouble with this simple name? The doctor sits on a wheeled metal stool, which he propels to the end of the examining table. "When did you finish your last period?" he asks.

Ida counts backwards in her head to that last time she bought a box of Kotex. "Fourteen days," she tells him. She can hear the clink of metal against metal.

"A little pinch," the doctor mutters.

Ida feels a hard object, stingingly cold, pushed inside her, and hears the sounds of screws being ratcheted open. She holds her breath.

"Relax, love," mutters the man, scraping away.

Ida starts to tremble uncontrollably. She cries out and tries to press her legs together; the doctor pushes them apart again, his hand cold against the insides of her thighs.

"Be a good girl," he mumbles.

Looking toward the end of the table, she can see the man's head framed by her flexed knees as he peers between her legs, the light glaring off a mirror strapped to his forehead.

"How long since you gave birth?"

Ida feels a bubble of tears and shame rising in her throat, mixed with something else. Anger. No, not anger: what would be the correct word?

Rage.

"I am not a mother."

The doctor snorts. "You do remember having a baby?"

Ida remains silent. Closes her eyes. She hums a song in her

head, that insipid tune she hears drifting down from the car radios on the elevated expressway: *Tie a yellow ribbon...*

The doctor makes a small noise that comes out like a grunt of surprise. "Somebody did a slapdash job on your episiotomy. You have it here or in the old country?"

Ida stares up at the tiny ventilation holes. She notices how much they look like tiny black mouths gaping at her from the beige ceiling. She closes her eyes to make them go away and sees Margarethe's wind-burned face, an explosion of veins bulging from her nose like *la befana,* the witch, even though she turned out to be kind. She even refused Ida's money. "Nothing I can do for you, dear, you're too far along. It could kill you. Better go home and pretend it's your husband's kid."

I think it probably is, Ida wanted to say, then thought of Kowalchuk's face leering at her, her wrists crushed under the weight of his hands. Marcello burst in too late to prevent the worst of it, but managed to send Kowalchuk to hell. Still, he could never burn away the fact of Ida's violation. That's why Ida couldn't be sure whose child she was carrying, Kowalchuk's or Marcello's. In Margarethe's back room, she had started to cry, twisting the old woman's hand in hers. She must be sniffling in this room, too, under the little black gaping mouths, because the doctor says, "Get a grip on yourself, Mrs. Oom-Bree-yak-oh."

"It happen in Prince George," she whispers. "How you say it? A birth without life."

"A stillbirth. Uh huh, that explains it," mumbles the doctor. "Should've been on your chart."

He unratchets the device. Ida breathes again. The tiny mouths above her turn back into black dots. She thinks about hitting the doctor over the head with the instrument of torture he's using on her. Or, if she could get her hands around his skinny neck, she might be able to strangle him, maybe use his tie as a makeshift garrote. She imagines this with some satisfaction.

"According to this form, you came here for the birth control pill. I'll be honest with you, Mrs. Oom-bree-yak-o, I don't think you need it."

Ida wipes her eyes with the back of her hand. "Why you say this?"

"Because I can see you've been damaged," says the doctor. "I doubt you'll conceive again, dear. I've been delivering babies for over thirty years so I know my business. Whatever backwoods MD attended to you, he botched things up. I'd like you to see a specialist, a man over at Women's College."

Ida shakes her head. "No."

"What?"

She finally turns to face the doctor. He's a pink-faced man with thinning blond hair, his surprised blue eyes swimming behind thick glasses.

"No special man at the College of Women Hospital," says Ida. "No further examination. Just the Pill, please."

The doctor clears his throat. "You should go home and discuss this with your husband."

Ida imagines the tragic look Marcello would give her if she tells him that she probably can't have any more children but wants to be very careful not to get pregnant anyway.

"All right, I go to see this other doctor," she agrees.

"Good. You can get dressed now," says the doctor, propelling the stool over to a desk and pulling out a white paper pad. "You take one pill every day at the same time for three weeks. Understand? You stop for seven days. That's when you get your period. Then you start all over again. The days are all marked on the pack so you can't make a mistake. Unless you want to, of course. I see a lot of gals like you who secretly want to get pregnant. Otherwise, you'll need some other form of contraception until you finish one full cycle. Condoms and spermicidal foam. Not that I think you'll need it, but just to be on the safe side."

Ida walks out of the exam room holding her prescription for the Pill and the referral to the specialist. Out in the hallway, she finds a ladies' room where she tears the referral slip into tiny pieces, empties her bladder over them, and flushes them down the toilet.

Standing in the sunshine on College Street, Ida is surprised to see that life outside the clinic has continued as if nothing at all unusual was happening. The street musicians and young, vacant-eyed vagrants have carried on with their busking and begging; a flock of monks in saffron robes flutter at the corner of Spadina, handing out flowers and trying to strike up conversations with potential converts. When a young man with a shaved head approaches her, she says a few impenetrable words in Croatian, a language hardly anyone understands, causing him to step out of her path.

Ida finds a Rexall and goes in to fill the prescription. A pimply-necked pharmacist, his collar too tight for his Adam's apple, hands her a disc-shaped package while casually glancing at her left hand to check her marital status. When she asks for the foam and condoms the doctor mentioned, he nods briskly and leads her to an aisle full of white and pink packages.

"The family planning aisle," he tells Ida with a sweep of his hand. "Any questions at all, just ask the girl to get me."

A rack of condoms presents her with a variety of words she doesn't recognize. Ribbed, lubricated, latex. As Ida examines a box of Sheiks—a name she likes—she overhears two women coming up the aisle.

"After all this hassle, Jim'll better not be stuck with wifey tonight," says one. The other giggles.

Ida looks up to see two women in crisp blue-and-red uniforms. Flight attendants. Both of them are Mia Farrow look-alikes, their blonde hair smoothed back from perfectly made-up faces. Ida watches them out of the corner of her eye. One woman picks up a clamshell-shaped package with red-tipped fingers.

"I should get a new diaphragm but I can never remember my size."

The other woman shakes her head. "Why don't you just go on the Pill?"

The first woman snorts. "I tried it but I bloated up like a pig." She sighs and shakes her head. "I'll just get Trojans and foam for now."

The woman with the bloating problem is even slimmer than Ida, although the tautness of her A-line skirt suggests she's wearing a panty girdle under the uniform. Ida doesn't realize that she's staring at the flight attendants until one of them looks back at her and smiles.

"Excuse us for all the sex talk; we're jet lagged. Just got in from Paris," she tells Ida with more than a hint of condescension.

Ida nods briskly, as she grabs one of the packages of spermicide off the shelf. "Excuse me," she says, pushing past the stewardesses in the narrow aisle. She catches a whiff of a familiar scent on one of them. Jean Patou.

As she hands her money to the cashier, she can hear one stewardess say something to her friend in a low, amused voice. The two of them break out into giggles. Ida's face warms. She suspects they're laughing at her.

I could be you, she thinks bitterly. I'm the perfect height and weight, I speak four languages, and I've been trained by Alitalia. The only thing I don't have is respectability.

Feeling like a dowdy old *nonna*, she pushes through the exit and finds herself back on the street, breathing exhaust fumes.

With her family planning devices in her purse, Ida decides to walk to Bathurst to catch the southbound bus to Lakeshore. As she heads west, she sees a movie marquee up ahead, its neon letters calling to her: FRIDAY MATINEE 99¢ WESTERN TRIPLE FEATURE!!!! MAGNIFICENT 7 * ONCE UPON A TIME WEST * FISTFUL $$$$

Ida checks her watch. It's almost high noon. At the outdoor ticket booth, a bored-looking teenage girl takes Ida's dollar without lifting her eyes off her magazine.

Inside, the theatre seats are mostly empty except for a few furtively huddled couples. Ida slides into a middle row. She tries not to notice the mingled smells of piss, weed, popcorn, and stale cigarettes.

She hears quiet moans from behind her. Turning, she sees a man a few rows back, with his head resting on the top of his seat, another man's head bobbing over his lap. Ida quickly turns to face the screen again.

Ida remembers her first movie, Rico taking her by the hand to a schoolroom where a young priest with a love of cinema had set up a projector and managed to obtain a copy of *High Noon* dubbed into Italian. Ida was only six, far too young for such a violent and morally questionable film. She loved it. Back at Ca'Rosa, she stole Rico's toy pistols, strapping the holster and six-guns over her dress to play at being Grace Kelly shooting the bad guy. Out on the street, the outfit made Ida an object of ridicule. No matter. None of the children would be caught dead playing with her, no matter how she dressed.

Even after the Pope closed down Italy's licensed bordellos, the neighbours always called Ca'Rosa "the whorehouse," and Ida, "the Dalmatian's girl"—not even a real Italian, a half-blood, the daughter of a woman from the Croatian city of Zara, occupied by Italy during the War. As for her father—the part of Ida that was truly Italian—well, *that* half was the most shameful thing about her of all.

The theme music finally swells up, carrying Ida away from the past. A pizzicato of strings like a glacier-fed stream falling over a cliff builds to a crescendo of French horns, bassoons, and kettledrums stampeding like wild horses. All the epic flourishes of Italian grand opera, but confidently, aggressively American.

Ida slumps deep into the cracked leather seat so that she's hidden from view. Not that she needs to worry about anyone seeing her in the middle of the afternoon. Not Marcello, hard at work digging a subway trench. Certainly not Jeanie, who must think Ida is still at the clinic with the doctor winching her open to look inside and predict her future. For a few precious hours, Ida can escape into a world of cowboys and horses and gunfights and vendettas. Good versus evil. Her favourite kind of story.

She sits through *The Magnificent Seven* in a comfortable trance. She's seen this movie several times, but never in English before. The second film, a spaghetti western called *Once Upon a Time in the West*, is new to her, even though it was made in Italy when Ida was still living there. This film is tougher than the first. Angrier. A woman named Jill, played by Claudia Cardinale—who bears more than a passing resemblance to Zara in her prime, not to mention Ida herself—is threatened with death by a man looking for information. But Jill is not fooled. As she boils water in a kettle on the stove, she turns to him defiantly and dares him to have his way with her. She tells him that no woman ever died from that, and that afterward all she'll need is a tub of hot water and she'll be exactly as she was before.

Ida's heart pounds. Why doesn't Jill throw the boiling water in the man's face? What *testadura* wrote her lines? A man, for sure. Even as a child at Ca'Rosa, Ida knew that women could die from sex. A drunk or violent customer who was too rough with a girl. A difficult birth when the doctor refused to come. Untreated social disease.

Can a filthy memory also kill a woman? Ida thinks yes. Hers repeats itself in a dream of that rapist Kowalchuk rising from the dead before her, again and again. Senior gave him the right to have Ida first, in return for money to pay for the marriage broker, the proxy wedding, and Ida's trip from Italy. Marcello had tried to rescue her: again and again, she dreams of him bursting in too late, the room in flames, Ida's thighs sticky with shame. In the dream, Kowalchuk laughs while he burns. *You can't kill me,* he sneers as his face melts away. When she wakes screaming, Marcello always asks what her nightmare is about and she sobs *I don't remember*.

Ida leaves her seat so quickly that she forgets the Rexall bag. Finding herself empty handed outside the ticket booth, she runs back inside for her things, staining the sleeve of her blouse with furious tears.

When she finally gets home in the late afternoon, it's almost time for Jeanie's story. She goes to the cabin to change; as she does, she examines the neat round plastic dispenser she got from the Rexall. She takes out the pill from the slot marked FRI, pours a glass of water, and swallows it, then sits quietly on the bed for a few minutes to see if she bloats up like a pig. She doesn't. She slips the package back into the Rexall bag with the other things the doctor told her to get, stuffs it under the bed, then goes to join Jeanie and Lily for *General Hospital*.

Ida is surprised to see a car with Illinois plates parked in front of the office. She walks in quietly, not wanting to disturb the story, but sees Jeanie standing at the desk, speaking with a man in a cowboy hat, a guitar case in one hand.

Jeanie looks up from where she's taking his particulars. "Here's our chambermaid. She'll prepare your cabin for you, sir." The man turns and looks at Ida, raises his eyebrows, and gives her a wide, dimpled smile; he's a young man, but with the weather beaten skin of someone who spends a great deal of time outdoors. He reminds Ida of a character from her favourite film, *Il Buono, Il Brutto, Il Cattivo*. Or in English, *The Good, The Bad and the Ugly. What was that handsome actor's name, again? Clint Eastwood*.

Ida goes into the linen room off the office and gathers up towels and bedding. When she comes back out the man is waiting for her, key in hand.

"Number Ten, Ida," Jeanie says, getting ready to turn the TV back up. It's a Friday, the worst possible day to interrupt

General Hospital. "If you give us about ten minutes we'll have you all fixed up."

"I'd appreciate that," says the man, removing his hat. His eyes haven't left Ida.

In Number Ten, Ida stretches the washed-to-death sheets over the mattress, folding them neatly at the corners the way Jeanie showed her. When she turns, she sees the man standing at the door, grinning at her. "That looks comfortable. Want to help me test it out?" he asks.

The man is probably in his late twenties, not as tall as Marcello but just as thickly muscled, a working man, his skin sunburned, the lines around his mouth furrowing every time he smiles. Which he does a lot. Ignoring his question, Ida hands him the thin stack of towels. "If you need anything, go to the front desk."

He smiles again. "I like your accent. Spanish?"

"Italian," says Ida. "You have one too. You are from America?"

"Chicago. My name's Jeff but everyone calls me Cowboy. You?"

"Ida."

"I've been in a lot of fleabag motels on my way up here, Ida. You are definitely the best looking chambermaid for five hundred miles." He sits on the bed and pats the space beside him. "Sure you don't want to join me?"

Ida opens her mouth to offer a put-down—she's had lots of practice putting male guests in their place, Jeanie having explained the concept of *all talk, no action* to her—but she doesn't have a chance to say anything before a loud voice says: "*Ida!* Go OUTSIDE."

Marcello, home early from work in a grease-stained coverall, fills the doorway. He reeks strongly of sweat and sewer water. Fine dust from whatever dirty job he was up to today has turned his black hair grey.

Ida, open-mouthed, turns to look at him, then back at Cowboy, who is staring at Marcello in surprise.

"Marcello, I..."

"Just. Go. OUTSIDE," he repeats.

"This was a joke, just this man makes," she says, forgetting her English; she tries switching to Italian, but even then, words fail her. *"Marcello, no..."*

"Who's this guy?" interrupts Cowboy.

"He is my *huza-banda*, Marcello," she stutters.

"I don't want to have to say this again, Ida," says Marcello, who seems somehow to have increased in size since he appeared in the doorway. "Go OUTSIDE, goddamnit!"

Cowboy gets up from the bed, slowly, holding his empty hands in front of him like an unarmed gunfighter. "Simmer down, man. The girl was just making the bed. I had no idea she was married to you or anyone else. We didn't get that far."

"You didn't get that far?" Marcello echoes, looking back and forth between Cowboy and Ida.

Ida realizes that she has finally discovered the key that picks open the lock of Marcello's anger: sexual jealousy. She can see that he is about to move on Cowboy when a shadow appears behind him in the doorway. It takes a moment for her to register that it's Lily, carrying her box of Barbies and saints. "Ida, did you feed the weeds to Dreamboat yet?" she chirps.

Marcello swings around, fists clenched. When the child sees his enraged face, she steps back in fear. Ida runs to put herself between Lily and Marcello. Crouching, she wraps her arms around the girl. That's when Jeanie appears, nine iron in hand.

"I don't want to have to call the cops," she says, pulling Lily away from Ida, but keeping her eyes on Marcello. "What's going on?"

"Nothing, ma'am," Cowboy says. He hasn't moved from beside the bed.

"Nothing *yet*," says Marcello. He seizes Ida's hand and heads for the cabin, Ida stumbling along in his wake.

Jeanie shouts: "Dreamboat!"

Marcello stops dead, still crushing Ida's hand in his.

"The cabin walls are thin. If I hear anyone being hurt, I won't call the cops. I'll deal with you myself. *Compris?*" She brandishes the club at him.

Marcello lets go of Ida's hand. "I would never hurt Ida."

"Just like you're not hurting her now?" says Jeanie. "Yelling at her, grabbing her—you think that doesn't hurt?"

Jeanie leads Lily away by the hand; the little girl's eyes are huge, watching this big, stinking, dirty, grey-headed man. With the hours he works, she rarely sees Marcello but when she does, he's funny, or friendly, or tired, or all three at once. From time to time, he sits next to her to look at what she's reading or to help with her arithmetic. He always seems like such a nice, patient man. This angry, shouting Marcello is new to Lily, to all of them.

Once inside the cabin, Marcello slams the door and picks up a water glass from beside the bed—the one Ida used to take her first Pill—and hurls it at the wall. Shards explode across the floor, the violence of the sound taking some of the fury out of him. He slumps slightly.

Ida stands at his back, not afraid anymore. She touches his arm, lightly, but he doesn't respond. She has the feeling that he hardly realizes she's there. "This is a big overreaction," she says, quietly. "Nothing happens with this man. I mean: nothing happened. It's just the way men talk sometimes. Stupid talk."

Marcello turns to look at her, the grey dust on his hair and face making him look years older than twenty-four. "I don't want you working for Jeanie anymore."

"The money is, how you say—handy. And Jeanie gives us the broken rent."

"A break on the rent," Marcello corrects her. He turns to face her and for the first time, Ida notices a thin gash along his hairline, caked with dried blood.

"What happen to you? There's a wound on your forehead."

Marcello reaches up to touch it, checks his fingers for blood. "Accident at work today. Two guys died. They were right off the boat."

Ida reaches up to turn his head, examining the gash. It's full of dirt. "How?"

Marcello takes her hand from his cheek and grips it tightly. "Buried alive in the mud, in the sewer we were digging. The tunnel collapsed. We kept digging and digging but it just kept filling back in, crap falling all over us."

Ida eases her fingers out of his grip and puts her arms around him; the stink coming off his coveralls is horrible. She pulls down the zipper and eases the filthy material away from his shoulders and chest. It's so hot, he has nothing on underneath but his briefs. She guides him into a chair, helps him undress, unties the laces of his work boots hardened with mud and cement. She pushes the reeking pile of clothing out the door, followed by the boots. He stands before her naked, welts visible now on his face and neck, a large purple contusion flowering across one side of his chest.

Ida places one hand against the contusion; she's not sure what to do about this type of wound. Ice? "Maybe it's you who needs the new job."

He places his battered face on top of her head.

"Or to do the thing you really want to do. Study at the university," she suggests.

"Yeah. Maybe."

Marcello washes. Ida sweeps up glass. She wads together a handful of toilet paper and soaks it with peroxide. As Marcello holds the pulpy mess against his head, she puts out dinner: a *zuppa* with a half-decent Calabrese bread and some *prosciutto* and *melone* she was able to find on College Street on the way home from the clinic.

The salad of dandelions leaves a bitter taste in her mouth.

Definitely, it is too late in the season for cicoria, she tells herself. She watches Marcello wolf down the greens, unconcerned by the taste. To him, food is food, senses Ida. He takes what he can get. What he is *offered,* whether it's a job, a meal, or the comfort of a woman. This thought makes her feel cold inside, as if the speculum has touched a sensitive spot. Is it Ida he loves? Or simply the idea of being the noble lover? And how long will that feeling last, given that his passion for her is the only thing tying him to her? What if he meets another women who excites him more than she does? As Zara always said, men are led by their passions, as if implying that women were different. Ida saw little evidence of that in Zara's case, who took her to the confessional every Saturday so that she could have a few words with her father. What would possess Zara to stay loyal to a priest, if not passion?

Marcello glances at her plate. "You not finishing that?"

Ida shakes her head. Marcello shrugs and dumps the bitter greens onto his plate.

They eat in silence. No anger between them now, just a great weariness radiating from Marcello, like heat waves off a carburetor. He doesn't talk further about the men.

Just as they finish, they hear a knock at the door and trade looks. Jeanie perhaps, coming to double-check on them?

Marcello opens the door to Cowboy, holding his hat. "Think I owe you and your lady an apology. Sometimes I can be kind of an asshole."

"Yeah, well. Me too," concedes Marcello, shaking Cowboy's hand. "Sorry I overreacted."

"If I had a chick who looked like Ida, I probably would've done the same. That your Chevy out back of the cabins? Hell of a paint job."

"You should see what's under the hood."

"Wouldn't mind having a look."

The two of them wander over to where the car is parked, between the cabins and the lakeshore. Ida can see their bodies relaxing as they walk together. She closes the door and starts clearing the table. From the window over the bathtub, where Ida washes dishes, she sees Marcello and Cowboy looking at the car, the hood propped open.

By the time she goes outside, Marcello and Cowboy are sitting on the hood of the Chevy, a case of beer between them. The two of them gesture at Ida, waving her over, holding up bottles of Canadian. *Come join us!*

Ida nods and laughs. Who needs language when you have your hands, and beer?

By nightfall, the two men are deeply in conversation about cars and work and music and Vietnam; Marcello keeps cycling back to Rino and Giorgio, the men who were killed—*Why them and not me, man?* Cowboy keeps shaking his head and telling him he can't think like that.

Ida sits listening to the rhythms of their deep voices, laughing at jokes she doesn't get, hearing vocabulary she doesn't understand (*overhead cams, funny cars, four on the floor, souped up*), sipping her warm beer, happy that peace has settled on the Seahorse. Finally, Jeanie comes out carrying a case of Brador.

"You boys like to try some real beer from *la belle province*?"

"Hey! You must be one of those French-Canadian girls I've heard so much about," says Cowboy. "You as much fun as everyone says?"

"*Bien sur*," answers Jeanie.

That's when it turns into a party. With Lily asleep in Cabin One, behind the office, Jeanie starts to relax. Cowboy gets his guitar and the four of them sing—or three of them, Ida not knowing the words.

"Four Strong Winds." "This Land Is My Land." "Has Anyone Here Seen My Old Friend John?" "If I Had A Hammer." "Blowing in the Wind."

Finally, Jeanie takes the guitar from Cowboy and accompanies herself on a haunting song in French. "*Un Canadien errant.*"

"That was great, Jeanie," says Cowboy. "What's it about?"

"A French-Canadian, wandering far from home," she says, taking a sip of Cowboy's Canadian. "Something I know something about."

"I guess I'm an American *errant*," says Cowboy. "Thanks to the war."

"You're a draft dodger?" asks Jeanie.

"War resister. It comes down to the same thing."

Eventually, the beer is gone. Jeanie is curled up against Cowboy, the guitar in front of them both. She's playing with his fingers, he's nuzzling her ear.

"Think it's time for bed, Ida?" whispers Marcello in Italian.

"*Si*," she yawns.

Back in Number Fourteen, Marcello pulls Ida to him, gently. They sit on the narrow bed and he brushes her lips, softly tugging off her blouse and shorts and panties, then placing his lips against the nipple of one breast, then the other. Ida leans back; her breasts are small and sometimes when Marcello does this to her, they begin to ache and swell. It's a nice feeling.

He reaches down and touches her. Ida catches her breath. She's starting to feel something happening that she hasn't felt before, like a fluttering of butterflies.

"I'll make you forget that draft dodger," he whispers. "You like this?"

"*Ah, si*," she breathes. "Is good."

Then, unbidden, Dr. Stevenson slips back into her mind, speculum in hand. *You have to take a full cycle before it's effective. Until then...*

The spermicidal foam and condoms are still in the Rexall bag under the bed, next to the package of pills. Ida doesn't want to stop what Marcello is doing to retrieve them. She's starting to feel a pent-up storm inside her is about to break into thunder and rain, the way it does over the lake sometimes. But before this explosion happens, Marcello stops touching her, pulls her on top of him and enters her quickly. "Oh Ida," he moans.

Why did he have to stop touching, she wonders. Although it doesn't hurt anymore, this prodding and pushing does nothing for her. She keeps thinking about stopping him, reaching down to get the Rexall bag, but she keeps not doing it; the thought of the sterile collection of products, the smooth condom packets like vinegar and ketchup in a diner, the clinical-looking bottle of foam, sold by the pharmacist with the chafed, pimply neck. The instructions on the bottle read: *Fill the dispenser with foam and empty it into the vagina no more than twenty minutes before intercourse.*

Marcello gasps, rocks back and forth, back and forth. Ida looks down on his face in alarm. He's losing his self-control. Wetness covers her thighs.

"Oh dammit, I'm sorry, Ida. I just couldn't help it this time."

"Is all right," she murmurs, not at all sure it really is, wondering if she reached down and inserted the foam right now, whether it would go in and stop the baby. Then remembers again: the doctor claimed there will never be another baby to stop.

Marcello gathers Ida up, handling her like a tender little package. "You're so beautiful. I love you so much."

She thinks back to the pop quiz in the waiting room of the Free Clinic. Question: *Is he sincere?* Answer: *Yes.* Five points. Sincerity counts for a lot in *Seventeen.*

Pressed up against his body, his arms thrown around her like iron bars, Ida tries to sleep, but her mouth is burning. *The cicoria,* she thinks, the bitter taste still clinging to her teeth. She gets up to pour a glass of water at the bathroom sink and catches sight of her face in the mirror. Her eyes look startled under the fluorescent light, her lips pulled tight as if in disgust.

A salad of weeds. An ox of a husband. For this, I come to Canada.

She remembers herself five years ago in her Alitalia uniform, her short skirt and tight jacket, the elegant pumps and gloves.

A lacy little girdle underneath, even though she didn't need it. If the doctor is right and she can never have children, what would prevent her from going back to the planes? Even Marcello couldn't stop her.

Back in bed, she stares up at the cobwebby ceiling, lit by moonlight, and thinks about that ugly word the doctor used to describe her insides. Damaged. Another hard-edged English word with too many consonants crashing against one another.

She rolls the word over in her head for a while until it breaks down into harmless syllables. Like *husabanda*. Ida pushes the word into the knot of things in the back of her mind she chooses not to think about, for now.

She places her hand where Marcello put his and imagines Cowboy above her with his dimpled American smile. She comforts and comforts and comforts herself, until the tension inside her snaps like an elastic band, and she drifts off.

Ida wakes to bright sun and a blistering headache. All that beer. Marcello is still sleeping, his body sprawled across the bed, the sheet on the floor. Ida stands and finds his robe, pulling it on; so huge and smelling like Cello, she finds it comforting. Looking down at him, she can see the bruises, dull purples and yellows, and caked blood from the gash on his head. His poor body, so battered and bruised, like a work horse. That's what he is really, like all the other men he works with, most of them just off the boat, hanging around on street corners, waiting to be handed a job, no questions asked. A collection of muscles to be used again and again until they break or give out. The thought brings on a cold ripple of fear: what if something happens to him? What would happen to her?

She leaves the cabin to search for coffee. Jeanie keeps small packets of Nescafé at the front desk; it's awful but Ida is desperate. Rubbing her forehead, she lets herself into the office.

Jeanie and Cowboy are already there, sipping from chipped mugs, Cowboy's arm around her waist.

"*Bonjour,* Ida. You're up early," Jeanie greets her.

"I need *une café,*" answers Ida.

"*Ah, oui. Dreamboat dorme?*"

"He'll sleep for a long time yet, I think," says Ida.

"Best thing for him," says Jeanie.

At the back of the office, as Ida pours hot water into a cup and tears open packets of Nescafé and sugar, she hears the sound of a car engine outside. A guest, this early on a Saturday? Peering through a window she sees two men getting out of a white Impala. It takes Ida a moment to recognize Niagara Glen Kowalchuk's right-hand man, Stan, hoisting his threatening bulk out from behind the steering wheel. Pressed into black leathers, he hasn't changed at all in five years. From the passenger side, an old man grips the top of the door, pulling himself to his feet. Grey hair, grey skin, a paunch like a pregnant horse: Ida's husband, Senior.

Her first instinct is to hide. But where? She presses herself up against the shelves of linen, trying to make herself invisible. There's no time to warn Jeanie and Cowboy not to give her away. Panicking, she looks around the room for a cubby hole or escape route; could she possibly fit under the cupboard that holds the towels? (No.) Or maybe she could pull herself through the window, sprint through the motor court to Number Fourteen, wake Marcello, and jump in the Chevy.

It's impossible. All she can do is hide in the back room. It's like waiting for an animal to sniff her out and pounce. Unbidden, an image pops into her mind of Stan and Senior going to Number Fourteen, finding Marcello asleep, and putting a bullet in his head. Or hitting him with a baseball bat. Or pressing down on his face with a pillow. As she knows from *The Good, The Bad, and The Ugly*, there are a lot of ways to kill a man in bed.

She was never yours. That's what Senior will say, just before Marcello dies. Ida is terrified. She feels a warm trickle of urine down her leg.

"Can I help you?" Jeanie's voice comes briskly through the door of the back room. Stan's voice drifts back to her; Senior must have brought him along to do the talking, among other things.

"Hope so. We're looking for someone. Two someones. Girl and guy. Guy's tall with black, curly hair, looks older than he really is, girl's a cute little blonde with an accent. There's money in it if you have information."

"You two cops?" It's Cowboy's voice now, using his Clint Eastwood voice. Not quite friendly. Giving nothing away.

There's a pause. "You might say I'm a private investigator. This gentleman is the blonde's husband."

Ida does something she hasn't done in years. She starts to pray.

There's a long pause from the front of the office.

"We don't have anyone like that," Jeanie finally says again.

Perhaps sensing something, Stan persists: "Names are Trovato. Marcello and Ida."

Another pause. "You'd kind of remember a name like that. Spick name?" asks Cowboy.

"Italian," says Stan. "Might be going under assumed names. I'll leave my number, just in case. If you meet them, be careful. The guy's dangerous. He kidnapped my client's wife. He might even be involved in an old murder case in Niagara. Might be driving a Chevy with a racing stripe and decals. 1959. Cherry red."

"I'd remember if I'd seen that!" laughs Jeanie.

Ida thinks of the car, parked behind their cabin. Impossible to see it from the office, but what if Stan and Senior stroll around the property?

They don't. From her vantage point, Ida watches the Impala pull out of the Seahorse parking lot and into the Buena Vista on the other side of Lakeshore.

When she comes out of the back room, Jeanie and Cowboy look at her, faces serious. Ida expects questions. *What was that all about? Who are you two, really? Were you kidnapped?*

Did you kill someone? Instead, Jeanie enfolds Ida in her arms. "Don't be scared."

"Get your man up right now," Cowboy tells her. "Him and me got work to do."

"I thought the B.C. plates would be enough to throw them off," says Marcello, yawning as he pulls on his pants.

Cowboy snorts. "Think again brother. But repainting a '59 Chevy ain't easy. Not like your later models. Even if you don't mind doing a shit job, it's a bitch. All that chrome, that's the problem."

Marcello grunts as he tugs his tee shirt over his head. "No kidding. I painted her myself in the first place. We'll need a few things from Canadian Tire, and a clean, dry, well-ventilated place."

"How long?" asks Ida.

"Two days. Minimum," answers Marcello.

Cowboy and Marcello drive their cars to the barn of a friend of Jeanie's, out in Oakville. Over the two days that they paint, let dry, and repaint the Chevy, Jeanie helps Ida get organized. The two of them scan the classifieds in the *Star* for apartments to let and Help Wanted ads.

Lily takes Ida's departure hard. "Do you and Dreamboat really have to go?"

"There are bad guys looking for us. We need to hide among more people."

"Why are they looking for you? Did you do something wrong?"

"No. We just fell in love."

"You mean like Nurse Jessie and Dr. Hardy?"

"Yes. Just like that."

Lily takes out her box of dolls and saints. "Would you rather be St. Therese or Beach Party Skipper?"

"Beach Party Skipper."

"Okay. And from now on, this one will be Dreamboat." Lily

shakes St. Sebastian in Ida's face, a handsome, dark-haired young martyr shot through with arrows.

Cowboy and Marcello paint the Chevy navy blue, as dark a tone as they can manage to cover the glossy red and racing stripe and decals, breaking Marcello's heart.

The morning they leave, Jeanie comes to their cabin with a camera. "For my scrapbook."

She takes one of Marcello and Ida in front of the car.

One of the two of them, against the lake.

One of Lily, hoisted on Marcello's shoulders, Ida's arm around his waist.

One of Cowboy standing between them, an arm around both of their shoulders.

"Thanks for all your help, brother," says Marcello, kissing Cowboy, who pulls back in surprise.

Ida kisses Cowboy, too. "Are you staying?"

"For a spell. I'm still trying to talk Jeanie into moving to Montreal with me. She could be out of a job soon. The owner of this dump is talking about putting up an apartment house."

When they drive out of the parking lot of the Seahorse, heading toward the on-ramp of the elevated expressway, Ida turns to look through the back window of the Chevy. She sees Jeanie, Lily, and Cowboy waving her and Marcello into the invisibility of the inner city.

3. ESCAPE FROM LOVE CANAL

BRAMBOROUGH TOWNSHIP, 1975

BUM BUM'S KNEECAP SINGS a high note as the tips of his crutches dig into gravel. A bag of cake, soft and brown as manure, swings from his wrist, slapping the crutch at every grinding step. He'd like to toss the fucking thing in the ditch, but it's the only food he's got.

The sound of barking, sharp as shotgun blasts, carries on the warm night air. The dogs could be miles away but Bum Bum is afraid they're already on the alert, their super-senses telling them that a skinny, heartbroken seventeen-year-old is limping along the verge of the concession road alone.

He imagines a pack of Shepherd-Lab crosses running at him down the driveway of some farmhouse where everyone is plopped on the sofa in front of *All in the Family*. They'd never hear the sound of his screams for help over the laugh track. He can almost feel the canine teeth ripping into the tight ball of muscle on the back of his thigh, confusing it with the pain of his real wound, now that the rheumatism pills he stole from Prima have worn off.

"Dogs smell your fear. You're making them think they're *supposed* to bite you," Rocco told him, that time the two of them biked past the chicken farm.

With a pair of snarling mixed breeds closing in from behind, Bum Bum's legs spun out of control on a hand-me-down one-speed while Rocco clicked smoothly into tenth gear and disappeared into the distance to his shouts of "Wait up!"

At the sound of a whistle, the mongrels padded grudgingly home, but Bum Bum's adrenalin kept pumping and pumping until he caught up with Rocco, who seemed to be on the dogs' side. "It's their *job* to run after you, for Chrissake. Just stop being scared and they'll leave you alone."

Bum Bum pictured himself bitten to death a million times that day. Now his imagination is slaughtering him all over again. He'd happily sacrifice the cake to save himself but he doubts even a hungry Labrador would go for the Duncan Hines double chocolate fudge layer cake with Dream Whip icing, so sweet it made his teeth ache.

"*Mangia, mangia,* Pasquale!" urged Prima, sitting across from him at the kitchen table, watching him choke down a slice.

"Isn't Rocco coming over?" he asked through a full mouth.

Prima pressed her lips into a weathered line the colour of boiled beets. She usually liked nothing better than talking about twenty-year-old Rocco, also known as "God's Gift." He was the only one of Prima's many grandchildren, living in the ornate bungalows clustered around her farmhouse, to make friends with Bum Bum. Rocco's friendship with him hinted at some previously unsuspected capacity for kindness. The others treated him like a stray cat.

Don't touch him; he'll make you sick! You don't know where he's been!

Prima fingered the crucifix hanging between her sweatered breasts, a sign she was begging God's forgiveness for her lie. "Rocco, he busy working on his motorcycle. He no come today."

That was when Bum Bum knew he was screwed. Once the other Andolini boys suspected that Cousin Rocco had abandoned him, they would start following him with baseball bats and mumbled threats of what-he-had-coming.

Marcello used to say: Measure twice, cut once. By which he meant, think ahead.

So, Bum Bum thought ahead. What would he need to run away from his so-called home? Money and food.

Money was easy, Prima being a big believer in cash trans-actions. As soon as she was zonked out on little white pills and in bed, her charge, her burden, her sacrifice, her unofficial foster child Bum Bum (ungrateful little rat shit bastard that he was) stuck his hand in her underwear drawer and pulled out a sheaf of freshly-ironed tens and twenties from among the tangle of elastic stockings, slipping them inside the cover of his favourite book, *I, Robot*. Marcello's favourite, too, his name still scrawled on the inside cover. He'd given the paperback to Bum Bum, who read it so many times that the spine was held together with black electrician's tape.

Sneaking through the dark kitchen, Bum Bum could hear Marcello's practical voice in his head, advising him: *Take some food along. You never know when you'll have a chance to eat again.*

He grabbed the biggest Tupperware container in the fridge, dumping the contents into a plastic bag without checking them first. Food is food when you're on the run. But what did he take? The leftover cake. He wishes he had found some cheese, maybe a hunk of salami. By the time he realized his mistake, he had already painfully crutched through the yard where the family's Buicks, Mercs, and trucks with ANDOLINI BROS. on the doors were ringed like circled wagons.

He worried that the old lady might wake up and catch him—not that she could stop him, but she might lay a guilt trip on him: *Marcello, he say you stay here with me till you grown.*

Yeah right. Like Marcello really gives a shit anymore.

In the two hours since he left Prima's house, Bum Bum has managed to cover a mile, maybe. Inching along in the sweaty darkness feels like squeezing through the asshole of a pig.

Fuck his smashed-up knee. Fuck Rocco. But most of all, fuck Marcello for dumping him with the old lady instead of taking him along when he ran away with Holy Mother Ida, the only person Bum Bum ever truly loved.

Ida's proxy husband, a *paesan* of the Andolinis known as Senior, liked to drop by the farm to get drunk and bitch about the treachery of wives and sons, his having run away together. When he was younger, Bum Bum would feel the brunt of Senior's rage, a kick or a slap, because he'd been friends with Marcello—had helped him put one over on Senior, in fact. Now that Bum Bum was bigger than he was, Senior would just glower at him over the grappa bottle in the middle of the table.

Prima would always shrug and say, *so what you want us to do about it*, as if Senior should resign himself to his fate. Senior would answer that he'd like to filet the face of that daughter of a bohunk whore, so that no man would ever be tricked by her beauty again. As for his so-called son, Marcello — Senior would make a slashing motion across his throat, causing Prima to cross herself.

Over the years, Bum Bum himself had developed a mild resentment toward Marcello for turning out to be less than perfect. Marcello was too passionate, letting his heart and dick lead him around by the nose, causing him to make mistakes like leaving Senior alive to seek revenge. Mr. Spock from *Star Trek* was a better role model, all cold logic, except for a little bit of his human side peeking through during mating season on his home planet of Vulcan. Bum Bum had come to think of Marcello as a failed Spock, intelligent and noble, yet fallible in a way that the Vulcan science officer was not. He should never have left Bum Bum behind in the care of the Andolinis.

Prima would say Bum Bum was being ungrateful. That he should thank Marcello for saving him from his awful life, and thank God for his second chance, living on the farm with saintly Prima. She spent years trying to convince him that "God is Everywhere," that Bum Bum could carry the Almighty in his pocket like a penny or a smooth stone—or even like the condom in its scuffed and wrinkled pouch that Rocco shoplifted from Big V Drugs. "I keep it in my jeans, just in case," Rocco explained, his bulgy arm crooked behind his head, he and Bum

Bum on their backs staring up at the clouds from the middle of the peach orchard, Rocco pointing out the one that looked like two horses doing it.

Prima used to get Bum Bum down on his knees to yawn pre-dawn rosaries and Saturday evening folk masses with teenagers in unisex hot-rollered flips playing *Kumbaya* on acoustic guitars and the groovy priest raising his hands in blessing like Bruce Lee getting ready to deliver double Judo chops. Despite all that, Bum Bum doesn't believe God is everywhere. He sure isn't out here on the concession road, unless He drives a 1969 Chevrolet Corvair Monza soft-top sedan with New York plates.

The car's high beams catch him full in the face, blinding him for a second. Bum Bum is limping north-north-west (isn't that where Marcello and Ida are, the closest things to Our Lady and An Avenging Angel he's ever met?). God's Corvair, however, is cruising north by northeast.

He's so surprised he doesn't have time to consider: should he stay hidden in the darkness or try to hitch a ride? His plan was to walk out of Bramborough Township, but his knee is killing him.

He steps closer to the pavement. Extends his arm. Jerks his thumb. To his amazement, the Corvair doesn't slow down but veers wildly onto the gravel verge, coming straight at him. Bum Bum stumbles backwards, crutches flailing, knee wailing *no no no no no* as he tries not to fall into the weed-choked drainage ditch. The car screams to a stop.

Engine idling, the passenger-side window lowers on its own. Motown music and cool air trickle out.

Bum Bum is afraid to look at the driver. The power windows and air conditioning trigger a memory of being picked up in a similarly equipped car, a Caddy, years before he came to live with Prima. Some guy drove him up Hamilton Mountain to look at the flaring steel mill stacks and pass a bottle of sweet booze back and forth. "Tia Maria," he called it. "You kids love it." Then he lifted a big white box out of the back seat and put it in Bum Bum's lap. Inside was a chocolate cake with pink writing on top.

"See what it says?"

Bum Bum shook his head. Ten years old and he still couldn't read. (This was before Marcello taught him, in those shadowy years he tries hard not to remember.)

"What are you, retarded or something? It says 'Happy Birthday Patty.' She's my little girl. I'm giving you her cake. Because I'm a nice guy."

He insisted Bum Bum eat the whole thing in front of him. The boy choked down the soft shitlike cake with frosting as metallically sweet as buttered steel. On his final mouthful the man unzipped his pants and shoved Bum Bum's head between his thighs and held him there, making him gag. He's hated cakes ever since.

Don't let it be the Tia Maria guy, Bum Bum prays to the empty sky. He peers into the car. In the gold lamé light of the dashboard, he sees a girl's face curtained by straight blonde hair, her hands balled up in front of her mouth as if she's getting ready to throw a punch. She's sitting on a pile of crushed velvet couch cushions, brocaded and tasseled. Skinny arms, skinny legs, stomach as big and round as a beach ball, like one of the starving kids on the cover of Prima's magazines from the missions.

"Jesus Christ, you almost made me hit you!" Despite her anger, her voice sounds high and light and harmless.

Leaning on his crutches, he lifts his hands the way soldiers do in the movies when they're giving up: look, no weapons.

"I'm just a kid like you," he tells her, stating the obvious.

"Yeah, and you were almost a dead kid just now. What the hell you doing in the road?"

"Hitchhiking."

"On crutches? In the pitch dark? That's nuts. Where you going?"

"B.C. I got friends there," answers Bum Bum.

"I'm heading to Toronto. You want me to let you out on the ramp where you can hitch a ride west?"

Bum Bum stares at the front seat beside her. The smooth leather looks soft and comfortable. She has a Buffalo radio station on. The Jackson Five is singing *A-B-C*. *As easy as one, two, three...*

"I could go to Toronto, I guess," answers Bum Bum.

"Get a move on and get in," she says.

Tossing the crutches into the back seat, he slides in among crumpled chip bags, empty soda bottles, and Oh Henry wrappers. He hasn't even closed the door before she floors it, peeling off the shoulder like Steve McQueen in *Bullitt*.

He steadies himself against the glove. Even sitting on the pile of pillows, she's barely able to peer over the steering wheel.

She nods at his lap. "What's in the bag?"

He'd forgotten he was still holding it. "Chocolate cake. My birthday's today. Or yesterday, by now, I guess."

"Cool. Reach in back and grab my purse, you'll find some weed in there. Roll us a doobie and we'll celebrate."

Bum Bum removes the baggie and clumsily rolls a joint against his thigh, nice and tight, the way Rocco taught him. The girl tells him her name is Claire. "What's yours?"

Bum Bum considers his answer. It's hard to know whether to give her his real name (the only one who ever called him "Pasquale" was Prima—and Marcello and Ida of course) or his nickname which, although disgusting, has stuck to him for as long as he can remember, signaling that his ass is available to be kicked by anyone, any time.

"I could use a new name. Any ideas?"

The girl laughs. "Only one I ever named was our dog, Benny. He got hit by a car chasing some kids on the road. You want his name?"

He rolls the dead dog's name around in his head. Benny. He likes it. But the coincidence worries him. "I got chased by dogs on a farm road, once. You don't think Benny was one of them, do you?"

"Course not, I live in a subdivision in Niagara Falls, American side. Love Canal. Too far away for Benny to have chased you. Besides, all dogs give chase to show they're the boss of you. Same as when they hump one another."

Bum Bum thinks this over. If he takes a dog's name, maybe it'll mean he's finally the boss of somebody else. The humper rather than humpee. "Benny sounds good. Thanks."

The girl fiddles with the radio when the Buffalo station fades into static. CHUM Toronto comes in so loudly that it almost makes Bum Bum drop the half-rolled joint. He slides the doobie in and out of his mouth to spit-seal it, strikes a match, and takes a couple of puffs to get it started.

"Nice car," he offers, handing her the joint.

Claire takes a long, greedy toke. "My stepfather's. He locked me up so I took his 'baby.' That's what he calls it."

"Why'd he lock you up?"

She exhales, giving him a you-must-be-kidding look. "I started showing."

Bum Bum is getting a nice little buzz on. Even his knee doesn't hurt so bad. "If he was mad enough to lock you up, why didn't he just force the guy to marry you?"

Claire goes alarmingly silent. Like she's trying not to cry. Why'd he open his big mouth? But when she answers, she just sounds pissed. "There was no guy."

Bum Bum scratches his balls; the money-laden paperback in his underwear is starting to chafe. "But you must have done it with someone," he says.

"Nope. I woke up one morning, looked down, and saw the bump under the sheet. My mom got the Bible out and prayed over me but it didn't do any good. It's been growing ever since."

Bum Bum knows he shouldn't argue with her but the pot is making him honest and open and curious. "Come on. There had to be a guy."

"Not to my knowledge," says Claire, sounding like someone on the witness stand in an old *Perry Mason*.

Bum Bum can't let this go. "The only one that ever happened to was the Virgin Mary. It's like something out of science fiction. *Star Trek*, or *Dune*, or something. You'd have to be a hermaphrodite. Like worms."

"Maybe I am," says Claire quietly.

"Are what?"

"One of those things you just said. A hermaf... whatever. Where I'm from, a lot of kids are special." Claire takes another long drag and passes the doobie back to Bum Bum. "I knew kids with big heads, or one regular eye and one screwed up one. Some retarded. Others get fits. There's a girl went to school with me who had an extra set of teeth. It just goes to show. They say it's 'cause of the black ooze. Big ponds of oil, coming right up through the schoolyard. We got a pool of ooze in our basement too. You touch it, it burns your skin." She looks over at Bum Bum. "If the black ooze can give kids a giant head, why can't it make a baby without a man?"

"I guess," says Bum Bum, unconvinced. "How long you been locked up?"

"About three months. I missed junior prom, even though I was head of the decorating committee. They were going to keep me in my room till the baby came."

"What were they gonna do with it?"

Claire shrugs. "Give it away, I guess. There's ladies on my street who can't have kids. Even some whose babies died."

Something about this story seems horribly familiar to Bum Bum. Older people can be really scary, even when they read the Bible and are supposed to be looking after you. His own dimly remembered parents were terrifying. "That sucks," he finally says.

"Sucks the big one," agrees Claire. "My brother scored me the car keys so I could get away. We live ten minutes from the Peace Bridge, practically like we're in Canada anyway. I just jumped in the car and went over the river. If my brother gets drafted, he's coming up here, too. Not that I think the army'll send him to Vietnam, with all his conditions. What about you, Benny? What's your life story?"

Bum Bum takes a long pull on the joint and lets time fly backward like a flip card animation in reverse. Life as he knows it started the day he woke up behind the bars of a giant crib in a hospital room in Shipman's Corners, the crucifix of Prima's rosary swinging over his head.

"Marcello say I take care of you now, just like I take care of him when he was little," she explained.

"Where is Marcello?" Bum Bum had mumbled in his delirium.

"He run off with that *puttana*!" stated Prima.

Bum Bum closed his eyes. Prima meant Ida, the most holy and beautiful and perfect woman he had ever met in his life. Ida was the opposite of the whore Prima said she was. But he was too tired to argue. And besides, he was only eleven. Both too old and too young to argue with elderly Italian ladies.

A few days later Prima returned in the Merc and took Bum Bum home to the farm in Bramborough Township. For the first time he slept in a bed every night, went to school every day, picked fruit in summer, went to church, ate three meals a day, every day. He didn't miss the going-hungry part of his old life. He missed the freedom, though. On warm nights he'd sneak out of Prima's house to sleep in the grass. Sometimes Rocco would come out, too, lie down next to him and stare up at the stars.

Curious about Bum Bum's old life, Rocco prodded him for details: "What was it like, Bum?"

"Can't remember," Bum Bum would say at first, then go on to pick out jagged bits of memory, working their way to the surface.

Helping Kowalchuk rip people off. Hanging out with the craps players. Guys taking him into back alleys, stuffing a couple bucks into Bum Bum's pocket then unzipping their flies. His mother mostly ignored him, his father hurt him sometimes, or worse, let other guys hurt him.

None of it seemed to shock Rocco or bother him much. "Did Marcello and you ever, you know, do it?"

"Whadya mean?"

Rocco shrugged. "I always figured Marcello for a fairy. All them books and opera records and shit. Real fag stuff."

"He isn't like that," said Bum Bum. He considered adding, *And I'm not either.* But he was fairly sure that he was—a fact that Bum Bum accepted about himself without much thought, so long as it didn't get his teeth knocked out.

Then, a couple of weeks ago, Rocco said he wanted to teach Bum Bum how to fight, the way he did in Golden Gloves. The two went into the tool shed. "Take your shirt off," commanded Rocco.

Before Bum Bum could even get his shirt over his head, Rocco balled his fists and smashed him in the face. It wasn't that hard a punch—didn't even break his nose—but the pain drilled into Bum Bum, blood spattering on the tool shed floor. Rocco dabbed his fingers in it and smeared it across his cheeks like war paint.

"Okay, so I've bloodied you, big deal. Had to be done. Put 'em up."

Bum Bum took a swing, and Rocco stepped away, then stepped back in, and punched him in the bread basket. Bum Bum ended up whimpering and winded on the dirt floor.

Rocco stood over him, one sneakered foot on either side of his chest. "On your feet, Bum," he ordered. "Stop fooling around and I'll teach you something so you don't have to be scared all the time. You'll thank me for it one day."

He showed Bum Bum how to punch. Block. Dance like Muhammad Ali. They sparred. Got into a clinch, Bum Bum clinging to Rocco's waist. Suddenly they'd switched from boxing to wrestling. Rocco put him in a headlock, rock hard bicep against soft windpipe. As Bum Bum struggled for breath,

Rocco twisted his head and pressed his mouth down hard on his. For a second Bum Bum thought it was an accident or a joke or something but then he felt Rocco's tongue thrusting between his lips, tasting his blood. Bum Bum's hard-on was as big as his whole body, as big as the inside of the tool shed, as big as the whole world. Bum Bum could feel Rocco's boner, too, pressing into his hip.

Enter Frank—son of Prima, father of Rocco, layer of concrete—looking for a posthole-digger. He saw Rocco's arm around Bum Bum's neck, Bum Bum's lips on Rocco's mouth. Next thing Bum Bum knew, he was on his back again, arms covering his head, as Frank stomped on his knee: "You little rat shit fag bastard. I warned Ma not to take you in." Rocco stood by, head down, and did nothing.

Prima told the doctor Bum Bum was kicked by a horse.

He hasn't seen Rocco since.

"Who hurt you?" Claire asks, her casual question sneaking up on him.

"Nobody. I got kicked by a horse." It's a good story—why tinker?

Claire snorts. "I wasn't talking about your knee."

Bum Bum senses an invisible dog in the back seat, or a sucker punch about to plough into the side of his head through the window. Claire's face glows in the light of the dashboard like one of Prima's Mass card virgins. She pats his crushed knee, her warmth penetrating the thick bandage.

"You were in love with someone who didn't love you back, weren't you?"

"Sort of," he grunts.

Claire fiddles with the radio again. "I can spot a broken heart a mile away. I'm psychic. Don't worry, you're so good-looking, someone'll fall in love with you in Toronto for sure. Hey, I got the munchies, Benny, how about some cake?"

Holding open the bag, he watches her scoop out a mess of

chocolate fudge and lick it off her fingers like a dirty angel. He tries a bit of frosting: it's not as bad as he remembered.

They have just tossed the end of the roach out the window, thank God (there He is again), when two white lights and a cherry red one appear, dead ahead.

"Shit fuck hell piss damn," sighs Claire, hitting a button to lower the windows.

Bum Bum pees himself, a little. Cops scare him almost as much as German Shepherd-Lab crosses.

"Maybe we should turn around," he suggests.

The girl shakes her head. "I'm not so good at three point turns. Besides they'll think we're trying to get away and that'll bring 'em right down on us. Wonder what they're doing out here anyway?"

"Looking for you?" suggests Bum Bum. "You just said the car was stolen."

The girl shakes her head. "My stepdad's probably still sleeping it off. Doesn't even know the car's gone yet, I bet. What about you? Anything you done that might deserve a road block?"

Bum Bum doesn't answer. Remembering the remaining weed in Claire's purse, he grabs the baggie and rolling papers and tosses them out the window in the direction of the ditch.

Then he reaches into his underwear and pulls out *I, Robot*. His hands shake as he holds it in front of him. It's damp and smells of pee. He sinks the paperback into the crushed black heart of his bag of birthday cake and tosses it on the floor under the glove.

Claire slows the car as they approach the roadblock. At first Bum Bum can only see one regional prowler, but then he notices a string of provincial police cars parked on the verge, six in a row, one half in, half out of the ditch. What the hell are they doing? Bum Bum wonders. In one of the fields bordering the road, a light illuminates an expanse of ground, as if they're getting ready to have a night game of touch football. A crowd of OPP officers is standing out there in the mud, hands on hips, watching another bunch of guys in hardhats. Some of them have shovels.

Bum Bum sees what they're doing now. Digging. A couple of dogs are running around, sniffing the ground. He feels his stomach flatten itself from a near empty pouch into a tight little pancake. Chunks of Prima's cake threaten to come back up in a hurry.

How deep will they go before they find what they're looking for? He's heard plenty of stories about disposals being done in the soft earth of Bramborough Township. None of the victims ever make the news.

At the roadblock, Claire is polite. Relaxed. Cool. "How can I help you officer?" she asks.

The cop, a big-bellied guy with a bullet-shaped head full of black stubble, says nothing. Shines a light in Bum Bum's face, then Claire's, then back to Bum Bum's. "What the hell you kids doing out here this time of night?"

"Just driving my friend home, sir," Claire says brightly.

"From where? You got New York state plates."

"Niagara Falls, sir, just on the other side of the bridge."

"Let's see your licence and ownership."

To Bum Bum's relief, Claire pulls the papers out of the top of the sun visor.

The cop shines a light on them, then turns it back on Bum Bum's face. "You a draft dodger or something? Where's home?"

No time to concoct a lie. "Concession Twelve near Orchard Road."

"That's ten miles in the other direction. Pop the trunk and get out of the car."

The cops search the Corvair, right there on the side of the road. They examine Claire's couch cushions, sniffing and shaking them. The big cop growls into his walkie-talkie: "We could use Fritzie here, over." A little cop comes out of the field with a Doberman on a choke-chain. Bum Bum is queasy with terror. Of all dogs, he fears Dobermans the most. Fritzie has docked ears and the black expressionless eyes of a shark.

The little cop takes off her chain. First thing she does is charge up to Bum Bum and stick her nose in his crotch. He prays, to no one in particular, for a quick death. Don't let it hurt, he begs.

The little cop laughs. "Hey, Fritzie likes you!"

After a few sniffs, the Doberman loses interest in Bum Bum and runs around the car excitedly. The cop opens the passenger side door and Fritzie sticks her nose into the bag of cake under the glove. Bum Bum is slick with sweat.

The little cop peers inside the bag. "What the hell's this? Looks like shit."

Bum Bum swallows hard. Last thing he wants is for them to find the cash. "There was no place else to go, and she didn't want to stop the car, so I, so I..."

The little cop grunts in disgust. He tosses the bag into a ditch. "You kids these days, you're like animals. You know that? I don't know where the hell the world is going. Sometimes I wish the Rooskis had dropped the bomb on your whole generation."

They don't have a reason to hold us, Bum Bum tells himself. Problem is, they don't need a reason. Maybe they're just bored. Maybe they're naturally suspicious. Maybe they don't like kids. Maybe Frank discovered the money missing from Prima's underwear drawer and alerted them. He sits silently beside Claire as the two of them ride in the back seat of the cop car. It's the big bullet-headed cop driving, with the little cop at the wheel of the Corvair, following behind. Claire folds her tiny hands over her tummy. She stares at the back of the cop's head like she's bored as hell.

"Sucks the big one," she says to Bum Bum.

At the cop shop, they talk to Claire alone, while Bum Bum waits in a small concrete room the colour of wet mud. They won't let him use his crutches. The pressure on his knee, as he limps into the room, is excruciating.

The little cop finally returns and motions to him. Bum Bum limps into the next room and takes a seat in a plastic chair next to Claire. The big cop from the roadblock has given her a cream soda. He doesn't offer one to Bum Bum.

"You look familiar, kid. You're an Andolini, right?" says the cop.

"I'm not an Andolini. I just live there."

"Oh yeah. I know you now, you're the vagrant Prima took in," says Bullethead, happy to get him pegged. In a town the size of Bramborough everyone is supposed to know everyone else. "Some people don't know when they got it good, I guess."

The guy picks up the phone, and sticks a thick index finger into the dial. Bum Bum realizes with a sinking heart that the cop knows the Andolinis' number off by heart.

Bum Bum bends over. He's pretty sure he's going to blow chunks on the cop's shoes. Head on his knees, he listens to the cop ask for Frank. It's clear he's being told that Frank's not there.

"Who's speaking? Oh—hey, Rocco. Your dad not there?"

Now Bum Bum is certain he's going to spew. He feels the cop's hand shaking his shoulder.

"He wants to talk to you," says the cop, offering the phone.

Rocco's voice sounds puzzled. "What the hell? What you think you're doing? Nonna Prima's going to kill you."

"Thought I'd better split," mumbles Bum Bum.

He hears the scratching sound of Rocco lighting a cigarette, something he always does when he's trying to think. Bum Bum can picture him exhaling, rubbing his dark eyes with one hand.

"We kind of crossed the line, eh? Look, I was just horsing around. Testing you. It didn't mean nothing, Bum. Locker room stuff. Anyways, sorry about Dad hurting you so bad. Guess it was my fault."

Bum Bum hears something he's never heard before in Rocco's voice. Fear. He feels something new toward Rocco, too. Anger. He wants to say: Fuck off you fucking fuck-head! You're too chicken-shit to admit you wanted it, you coward!

But he doesn't say any of this because he knows that Bullet-head will yank his arms behind his back and snap on the cuffs if he starts swearing at Rocco. Besides, Bum Bum now has what Prima would call "a mission": to get Claire out of here. Slumped in her plastic chair, sucking listlessly on her cream soda, she looks like a thin-shelled egg about to crack, the authorities (whoever they are) ready to swoop down like flying monkeys and carry her immaculately-conceived baby back to the land of black ooze. Like a hero from an Isaac Asimov novel, Bum Bum must get Claire to a safe haven on a star cluster far, far away—Alpha Centauri, if possible, Toronto, if not. As for Rocco, Bum Bum knows it's better to have something over him. Might come in handy later.

"S'okay. Not your fault, Roc," answers Bum Bum steadily, even though it was.

Silence. A sigh. "Maybe you're right. I'll figure out a way to explain things to Nonna Prima."

"Thanks," says Bum Bum.

Bullethead is watching him, head tipped back, eyes half closed, as if he's trying to decide whether Bum Bum's worth the trouble. Bum Bum knows that look well.

Rocco says, "That cop who brought you in? He's a volunteer Golden Gloves coach. He's a prime asshole but he won't want to piss me off. He's got no reason to keep you. Where you headed?"

Bum Bum pauses for a moment. Marcello would say, measure once, cut twice, think ahead. Mr. Spock would add that the logical thing to do in this situation would be to lie. He might not want the Andolinis to come looking for him.

"Out west."

A long sigh of relief reaches Bum Bum through the phone line.

"I should've figured. Say hi to Marcello, or whatever he's calling himself. Tell him, be careful. Senior's still on the warpath. Niagara Regional, too. Now, put the cop back on."

After a short discussion during which the cop does nothing but listen to Rocco and go *um hum um hum*, Bum Bum and Claire are free to go. She puts her arm around him, helping him limp out to her car.

"How come they let us go?"

"My family wants rid of me. They got a lot of pull," says Bum Bum, only realizing after the fact that he's referred to the Andolinis as "family." "Look, Claire, we have to drive out near the concession road and lay low till the cops leave so I can get that bag out of the ditch. I hid money in it."

"Whatever you say, boss," says Claire, opening the passenger side door and helping him in. "How much money?"

"Five hundred."

Claire shakes her head in amazement. "Wow. That'll keep us going for years in Toronto."

Bum Bum eases himself into the shotgun seat thinking: *Us. Yeah. Benny-and-Claire.* He likes the sound of that.

"Let's get the hell out of here," he says.

4. THE PEACH AND THE DITCH DIGGER

"A *BASIMENTO* DEEP ENOUGH for a tall man to stand up in?" says Marcello doubtfully. "What the hell for?"

Lou Agnelli sighs. Before hiring Marcello, he'd never had a labourer ask so many damn questions. Most of the guys just want to go to work, get their pay, go home. Marcello always wants to know *why*.

"Because *'cakes* like it that way," Lou explains patiently, the blueprints unfurled across his kitchen table. "Those new houses in the suburbs, they all got a finished rumpus room. People want the same in the old houses too so they can fix up the *basimento* and rent it out."

"Who'd want to live in a basement apartment?" asks Marcello, still skeptical.

"*Joosta-comes*," says Lou. "They take anything they can get."

When Marcello showed up at his door looking for a job, Lou hired him on the spot. You could see right away that he was the kind of guy who wasn't afraid to swing a sledgehammer. He's come in handy in other ways, too. If you need a quick square footage calculation, Marcello can figure it out in his head. And his English is so good, he sounds more like a *mangiacake*—a regular Canadian—than an Italian guy. Lou has even started taking Marcello with him to see customers. He thinks that they respect him more when he shows up with Marcello. And although Lou never says it out loud, a big guy like Marcello might make certain customers think twice about skipping out on their bills. "This customer we're seeing today, if he got any questions I don't answer right away, you say something," Lou instructs him on the ride over.

"Yeah, sure, okay, no problem." Marcello frowns at the increasingly ritzy facades as they drive north on Yonge.

"Nice homes, eh? I lay bricks on a few of these, years ago."

Marcello takes a drag on his Export A, pushing himself further back in his seat to find more legroom. "Too ostentatious." He rolls the words around in his mouth with his cigarette smoke.

Lou reaches over and grabs the boy's shoulder, giving him a shake—the way he would a son, if he had one. "Be nice. This customer we see today, he practically live in a castle."

Marcello lights a fresh cigarette off the butt of the last one. "I'm always nice."

The customer is a middle-aged guy—"Some hotshot lawyer," Lou says—living in a big Tudor rock pile in North Toronto. He also owns condemned houses on the Corso Italia that he wants Lou to fix up so he can make a bundle renting them out to *joosta-comes*. When Lou and Marcello drive up in the truck, he comes trotting down his flagstone path to greet them, in the kind of get-up the movie stars wear on Johnny Carson—*come si dice?*—a leisure suit. He shakes Lou's hand and slaps Marcello's back as if he were a workhorse. No introductions are offered.

The leisure-suited customer leads Lou and Marcello through an oak door with an iron knocker in the shape of a Gothic letter C. *So, he's Mr. C.*, thinks Marcello, trying to come up with a good name for the customer. *Christ. Crap. Crybaby.* Clunking the knocker as he walks in, he settles on *Cake.* Lou gives him a look: *Watch it.*

They walk through one room after another, Lou chatting with Mr. Cake about the crazy weather, the cancellation of the Apollo 18 Moon shot, and *that arsehole Trudeau,* in the customer's words. Marcello trails them, taking in the over-supply of furniture, paintings of horses and landscapes, and mounted animal heads. In a distant room, someone is plunking out scales on a piano. Marcello winces at every wrong note. They finally reach a high-ceilinged reception hall, brilliant with sunshine, where a teenage girl in riding breeches sits marooned at a baby grand, a finger exercise book propped in front of her like a death sentence.

Mr. Cake's daughter can't play worth a damn but Marcello shoots her a hey-baby-you're-cute smile. Eyes wide, her lips form a glossy O. A string of wrong notes echoes through the vast space.

Lou turns and frowns at Marcello: *What the hell you doing?*

Marcello grins and shrugs.

As they leave the room, he gives the girl a wave. She waves back timidly. Mr. Cake doesn't notice.

At last, they enter the room the customer calls his *study*, all dark hardwood and leather chairs. When Lou rolls out the plans on a wide oak desktop, the customer taps his finger on the proposed basement height and shakes his head. "Not deep enough, Lou. I want it high enough for someone like your big Luigi here to be able to walk around without cracking his head."

Lou takes out a stub of pencil. "How tall are you, Cello?"

Marcello glares at Mr. Cake. "Six-three," he answers, his voice thick with anger. "And a half. By the way, mister, my name's not Luigi."

The man laughs. "Hey Lou, I thought he was one of your *no-speaka-English* boys. Where'd you get this guy?"

Lou laughs nervously. He can sense that Marcello is starting to steam up. "Oh, Marcello here, he's a smart guy, he's in university. He works for me on the side."

"No shit! I thought all you Wop guys wanted to be grease monkeys."

"I'm going to teach high school math," says Marcello, through gritted teeth.

"Bully for you. I just hope you're good with a shovel."

"Marcello is very strong," Lou assures him. "He dig out your *basimento* in under a week, I bet."

Marcello says nothing until they get back in the truck. "I don't like him, Lou. He's an asshole."

"Yeah, maybe, but his money's good," answers Lou. "And you better watch yourself, making love to that young girl back there."

Marcello laughs. "*Make love?* Lou, I was flirting with her! *Make love* is something you say when you have sex."

"*Beh!* You kids today all have such dirty mouths. Don't think you're the only good-looking Italian in town, *paesano*! I used to have girls look at me like that when I was your age. Not that Canadian girls would give guys like me the time of day. That's why I marry Lina by proxy, bring her over from Sicily. Best way to get a wife in the fifties."

"Yeah, well. Times have changed," murmurs Marcello.

The two drive in silence for a few minutes. Glancing at his watch, Lou says, "Want Lina to set a place for you?"

"That'll be the third time this week, Lou. If Ida's not home, I can fend for myself."

Lou says nothing. *A dire la verità, Marcello may be smart as hell but when it came to picking a wife, he stopped thinking with his brains. Okay, Ida could be Miss Universe. But when does she ever put a hot meal on the table for Marcello? She's a working woman, an Air Canada stewardess. And she's a Venetian—not the warmest woman you've ever met. A woman should be soft and full of sweetness, like a ripe peach.* To Lou's way of thinking, Ida is more like one of those rock-hard lemons they overcharge you for at the IGA.

The guys at Esposito's social club refer to Ida as *Miss Coffee, Tea, or Burn My Bra.* They know better than say that to Marcello's face, of course.

And then there's that funny accent. Lou's never heard another Italian sound quite the way Ida does—not that he's met a lot of Venetians, but it almost sounds as if Italian isn't her mother tongue. *Which would be crazy, since she came from Italy, right?*

Sometimes Lou wonders what Marcello's parents think of Ida. He also wonders where his parents are. Marcello never mentions them, or any family members, or anything about their past. It's as if Marcello and Ida live on a little island of their own in the sea of extended families that make up the neighbourhood. Lou sometimes has the feeling that something about the couple isn't on the up-and-up, that there's some type of problem, but Marcello is such a good kid, he doesn't want to mention it. Trouble with the law, maybe. Lou has noticed that Marcello breaks out in a sweat any time a cop is around. Maybe, one day, he'll come to trust Lou enough to explain what's going on. Lou hopes so anyway.

Lou Agnelli isn't just Marcello's boss, he's his landlord. He and Lina own two semi-detached houses on Barrie Avenue, just north of St. Clair. Lou and Lina live on one side of the shared wall, Marcello and Ida on the other. The backyard of Marcello and Ida's half offers just enough room for a latticework *topia* wide enough to grow a few tough-skinned blue grapes, a long-fingered mulberry tree, and a plot of earth. When they first moved in, Marcello picked up a handful of the sandy soil, sniffed it, and rolled it in his hands.

"You look like an old *nonno* when you do that," Ida laughed.

"I was thinking of staking tomatoes, like all the other guys in the neighbourhood. You must have had a garden in the old country, Ida."

"In *Venezia*? Marcello, Venezia is all piazzas and canals and piers and buildings. We look to the sea, not the earth. My mamma grew herbs and flowers in the windows of our *pensione*, but that's it."

It was one of the rare times she mentioned home. There wouldn't be many others. Talking to Ida about her family almost always led to evasions, contradictions, or more often, a stubborn refusal to discuss them at all. "That is the past,

Cello. All in the past. We are young and we should only think about the future, yes?"

Marcello and Ida rent the main and second floors of the semi. A tiny attic flat is tenanted by a series of men who clatter up and down the fire escape at all hours. It usually takes about six months for a guy to save up enough to bring over his wife and kids from the old country, then move on to be replaced by another *joosta-come*. In the meantime, the men's loneliness seeps through Marcello and Ida's bedroom ceiling in the form of folk music and arias played on hi-fis. Marcello always wants to invite them downstairs to talk or share a meal but Ida will have none of it. "What if they start poking their noses in our business?" she demands.

In Ida's opinion, Marcello has already been too open about their business, especially with Lina Agnelli. When Marcello let it slip that Ida was a year older than him, and that he was only nineteen when he and Ida "got married," Lina had laughed and said, "Ida, you rob the cradle!"

Ida didn't think this was funny. She went to a neighbourhood beauty salon and got a pixie cut to make herself look younger. "And you, Cello, you have to watch what you say. And grow a mustache to make yourself look older. Please do this immediately!"

The mustache isn't much of a disguise but it doesn't hurt to look like every other guy in the neighbourhood, Marcello figures. Hiding behind the name *Umbriaco* was a good idea too, a legal name change requiring nothing more than some government paperwork and a little money. Easier than he imagined. At least he no longer carries the burden of "Trovato" for that *buffone* back at the candy store.

If Senior or Stan come nosing around the neighbourhood, asking for a heavy-set guy named Marcello with black, curly hair, they'll have a long line of candidates. As Lou likes to say, Toronto is home to more Italians than any city on earth save

Rome. The Corso Italia, as St. Clair is called, is an easy place for Marcello to disappear in plain sight.

Still, the neighbourhood took getting used to. His hometown of Shipman's Corners was a mix of many nationalities, mostly Poles, Ukrainians, and other Eastern Europeans. Not since leaving Italy as a baby had Marcello lived among so many Italians. He could recite in his head like a nursery rhyme the sing-songy Latin names fronting the businesses on St. Clair: Esposito (Café), Bertinelli (Groceteria), Di Marco (Shoes), Ricci (Music), Di Pietro (Monuments), Bagazolli (Heating and Air Conditioning), Ciccone (Ladies Wear), Marconi (Radio and TV), Ferrara (Religious Statues and Devotional Items). *Et cetera, et cetera, et cetera.* The storefronts marched confidently westward, interspersed with coffee bars and restaurants, the menus heavy on spaghetti with meatballs and veal *scallopini.*

Ida complained that the neighbourhood was a mish-mash of dialects and customs that were already dying out in Italy. To her way of thinking, the neighbours' notion of *home* was a lost dream of a country that they didn't want to admit no longer existed. Besides, she said, the Corso Italia was too old-fashioned and religious. Too uptight, compared to Italy. But unlike other parts of Toronto, there was plenty of street life, a little too much for the liking of the police who regularly cruised past the pizzerias, trattorias, and social clubs to make sure no one was drinking alcohol on the sidewalks, a grave sin as far as the authorities were concerned. The café owners shrugged, waited for the cruisers to disappear, and filled their customers' glasses in the bright sunshine as God intended.

Missing the homemade cabbage rolls and perogies he knew in Shipman's Corners, Marcello went hunting for the restaurants run by Poles, Ukrainians, and Lithuanians, and found a few further west in Roncesvalles and High Park. Eventually, he discovered the Jewish diners on Spadina, where he enjoyed blintzes and the occasional chess game with old men from Poland or Hungary.

Once, at the United Dairy Restaurant, a middle-aged waitress pushed up her sleeves to take Ida's order, exposing a numbered tattoo on the inside of her arm. When she left the table, Ida wiped tears from her eyes with a paper serviette. "I hope the monster who did that to her is dead, or worse. In Venezia, during the war, they took hundreds out of the Jewish Ghetto to the camps."

"At least you can feel proud that your father fought with the Partisans," pointed out Marcello.

Ida looked at Marcello with a puzzled expression; then, as if suddenly remembering a forgotten conversation, she said, "Oh, yes, of course. He did fight with the Partisans. But in the mountains, not Venezia."

Marcello notices that every time Ida talks about her father, he has a different profession. Over the past five years, she's called him a soldier, a sailor, a businessman, a horse trainer, and a lawyer. Of course, the man might have managed to be all these things, but Marcello suspects that Ida has many different fathers, one for every day of the week, each one freshly minted by her imagination. Marcello never voices his suspicions because he senses that doing so would cause Ida to stop talking about her past at all.

At least Ida mentions her father, if rarely. About her mother, she never says a word.

On weekends, they head to Yorkville or Yonge Street for movies and music, or simply to be part of what people liked to call *the scene*. One evening on Yonge Street, to celebrate his graduation from night school and acceptance at university, Marcello took Ida to *The Godfather*, amazed that anyone would bother to make a movie about Italian immigrants. "I've been to weddings just like this one, when I lived with the Andolinis. We even sang the same songs!" he whispered to her during the opening scenes.

When Michael Corleone's Sicilian bride, Apollonia, died in a booby-trapped car, Marcello seized Ida's hand. He felt his heart breaking: what will Michael do now? What would *he* do, if someone blew up his Chevy with Ida in it?

Ida sat through the movie silently, lips pressed together. As they left the theatre, she shook her head: "*Beh!* What a fairy tale! You think it is romantic, the Mafia? You think these men are *heroic*? They were *killers!*"

"I think the movie was trying to say more about families than the Mafia," suggested Marcello.

"Oh, yes? You want a family like *that* one?"

I was raised by a family a little like that one, thought Marcello, but he kept this to himself.

On these trips downtown, Marcello makes a point of giving spare change to panhandlers and hippies, especially young runaways playing battered acoustic guitars. Every once in a while he sees someone who reminds him of Bum Bum: skinny, dark-eyed, a little vacant, drunk or drugged-out, maybe. Once, Marcello surprised a kid sitting on a street corner by emptying all the money in his wallet into his hat. He often wonders how Bum Bum is doing at the Andolinis. Prima can be overbearing, but at least she'll make sure he gets three squares a day and finishes high school.

Ida mentions Bum Bum to him every once in a while, as if trying to weigh Marcello's remaining burden of guilt. She suspects that he now feels he should never have left the boy behind with Prima. But Marcello can't bring himself to talk to Ida about the boy, just as she doesn't want to talk to him about her childhood in Italy.

There's a lot they aren't talking about these days.

When Marcello gets back from seeing the customer with Lou, he walks into the semi and calls, "Ida?" No answer. She must be working a late flight. Once again it's up to Marcello to make himself a meal. Rooting around in a cupboard, he finds one of the cans of cream of mushroom soup he bought at a *mangiacake* supermarket, after seeing it advertised on TV as an ultra-modern ingredient that can be used to whip up any number of exciting dishes in minutes. There are even step-by-step recipes on the labels! "Space age food," Marcello told a skeptical Ida. As she predicted, the resulting meals all tasted like salty glue. Convinced that processed foods are the wave of the future, Marcello persists in experimenting with ways to make them tastier; usually, he only manages to make them mushier.

After dinner, he lies on the bed with *Advanced Calculus, Edition VI*. Despite his attempt to study, his eyes close and he drifts into a recurring dream of himself with his wrists in handcuffs, floating on his back in a limitless blue sea. The dream always ends with him sinking into the water and seeing someone or other from his past. Tonight, it's Niagara Glen Kowalchuk, his face as white and bloated as a dead fish, yellow hair waving like seaweed, his lidless guys staring at Marcello as he floats past. *I'll never die, you know that, don't you?*

Kowalchuk laughs as his body spasms, the way it did that night in 1969 with the candy store burning down around him. An accidental fire and electrocution, not a murder. A defensible act, but one Marcello has never answered for.

When Marcello breaks through the surface of the dream, he feels as though a rock is resting on his chest speaking in a strange tongue that sounds like gravel clattering through a metal funnel. He reaches down: the rock is Ida's head. Gently, he tries to move her head onto a pillow but knocks the textbook to the floor, waking her.

"*Che?*" Ida asks vaguely, groping with her hand to see where Marcello is. He catches her fingers and kisses them.

"*Shhhh,* go back to sleep," he whispers, but can't resist asking, "Did you eat the dinner I made?"

"*Un poco,*" she yawns. "Cream of mush again."

"I got the recipe off the can. You should show me how to cook properly, like an Italian."

"You are the man! It's not your job to cook," murmurs Ida, her eyes still closed.

"Whether it's my job or not, I'm doing it," points out Marcello, reaching over to scoop Ida's body close to his. He presses his face into the back of her neck, where the short blonde hairs are musky with sweat and stale perfume and cigarette smoke from her shift on the plane. She curves her back, the birdlike bones along her spine pressing into his stomach and chest. He feels himself hardening, but Ida has already fallen back to sleep.

Marcello sighs, then pulls himself up to sit on the edge of the bed and smooths Ida's hair off her face. Maybe he'll go back to the kitchen to dig up something to eat. He can always heat cream of mush in a saucepan and disguise the taste with grated parmesan from a box. When he finally returns to bed, he falls into a dreamless sleep, muscles preparing for a day digging in the dirt for Lou Agnelli.

"Jesus, this is a real shithole, Lou. I can't even straighten up."

"That's why the customer wants the *basimento* dug out," answers Lou, his plans spread out on the bumpy concrete of the basement floor. Someone did a half-assed renovation down here, which makes the process even worse; they have to undo the work of the previous owner before they can start digging. A rusty gas-line, capped off, sticks out of the middle of the floor. At the back of the basement, in front of the door of a root cellar, a wooden pillar has been jammed into place. The pillar has slipped a little to one side, bowing under pressure from the floor above.

"You think they stuck this in here because they knocked down the load-bearing walls?" asks Marcello. His height makes it impossible to work in the basement without stooping.

Lou runs his hand along a horizontal crack in the foundation. "Yeah, could be. This don't look good. We're gonna have to be real careful with this one. Four feet at a time, then we reinforce the foundation. Let's dig around this spot before we take down the pillar."

"Am I going to be working down here alone?" Marcello doesn't want to admit to Lou how uncomfortable he feels in this tight space. The low ceilings and lack of light make him feel as though he's inside a coffin.

"I hired a couple other guys to help, too."

The two other labourers, Vincenzo and Leo, turn out to be the latest *joosta-come* guys living in the attic flat over Ida and Marcello's house. Marcello has heard their music from above, but with the hours they keep, no one has ever met face to face before.

Lou assigns Vincenzo, also known as Enzo, to help Marcello shovel dirt onto a conveyer belt that runs from the basement floor to the outside through a tiny window. Enzo turns out to be a talker who explains that he's saving to bring over his wife and kids from Puglia. When he hears Marcello's name, he laughs and says, in Italian: "When I first come to Canada, I stay with my wife's cousin in that little town on the other side of the lake. Shipman's Corners. I hear this crazy story from her, about this kid named Marcello who kidnap his father's wife."

Marcello tries to get his heart to stop racing. *Kidnapping?* After six years, they're still saying this about him back home? That he took Ida by *force*?

"Craziest damn story! Like something out of an opera!" Enzo goes on. "They said the wife was a real dish, know what I mean? The son, he tie her up one night and throw her in the trunk of his car and disappear. So the father, the *real* husband, he talk to a tough guy, some big Polack, I think, who's, you know…" Here Enzo touches the side of his nose as if to indicate someone not entirely on the up-and-up. "Anyway, the son, he kill the tough guy and burn down the father's store. The police no catch him. The father still wants to get he wife back and teach the son a lesson."

"Yeah?" says Marcello through gritted teeth, staring at the pile of dirt appearing at his feet. "Where they looking for them?"

"Detroit, Buffalo, Fort Erie, Hamilton, here in Toronto down around College Street ... that's all I know, I left when the search was still going on."

Marcello drives the shovel into the earth with such force that he almost twists his arm out of its socket.

Around noon, Leo sticks his head through the window. "Someone up here to see you, Cello. A real looker."

"That's probably my wife," says Marcello, throwing down his shovel.

"She's in some sort of uniform, what does she do, work on the planes?"

Marcello doesn't answer but climbs out of the basement on a ladder reaching to a door that now hangs in space, four feet off the ground. Up top, Ida is talking to Mr. Cake who's dropped by to see how things are going. He's in a baby blue leisure suit, his grey hair carefully blow-dried so that it floats over his scalp like a bird's nest. Marcello notices that Mr. Cake is looking at Ida with interest, while Ida is smiling and chatting with him in a lively sort of way. She's acting—what's the right word?—*vivaciously*.

When Ida notices him, she smiles. "Cello, *ecco!* I bring your lunch before I go to work."

"Thank you, *cara*," he says, leaning down but before he can kiss her, Ida steps away: "*Uffa*, no, Cello, you are too dirty! You look like a beast!"

Mr. Cake gives a little chuckle. "How's the excavation going?"

"We're about four feet down. But there's a pillar holding up the basement ceiling, doesn't look stable. Lou wants to reinforce the foundation before we go any further."

"What! Why? Just knock down the pillar and dig like hell!"

"If it's holding up the house, the whole thing could come down on us," answers Marcello, strongly suspecting that this guy doesn't give a good goddamn.

Mr. Cake snorts. "You guys are ditch diggers, not structural engineers. The house'll just sag a bit! I would've thought you had more balls. You tell Lou to call me before there are any more delays."

Marcello is having a hard time convincing himself not to shove the guy, maybe muss up his hairdo, bloody his nice leisure suit. But he knows what will come of that: a visit from the police. As much as he doubts they'll connect him with the Marcello Trovato wanted for questioning by Niagara Regional Police, he'd rather avoid having to deal with cops altogether. He takes one deep, slow breath, trying to calm himself.

As the customer climbs into his car, Ida touches Marcello's hand. "You won't be a working man forever, *caro*." Dirt or no dirt, she puts her arms around him. As Marcello embraces her, he whispers, "I'm sorry to have to scare you, *cara*, but there's a guy down in the basement with me who told me a story he heard in Shipman's Corners. *Our* story. He said I kidnapped you and Pop's got some guy searching Little Italy to bring you back and teach me a lesson."

Ida takes a step back and looks around, as if expecting to see Kowalchuk beside them. "Make sure he does not find out who we are. I will not go back, Cello."

"Look, the best thing we can do is get your marriage to Pop annulled and get married. Once that happens, you belong to me."

Ida looks up at Marcello's face, a smudge of dirt across one pale cheek. "I am no one's property, Cello. Not even yours."

"I know, I know," he says quickly. "It's the way they think. Not the way I think."

Ida reaches up to touch his face. "I will be back from Ottawa tomorrow. We talk then, *caro*."

That afternoon, with Marcello at the library, Ida invites two flight attendants, Diane and Georgia, to the house for a drink after work. It's a beautiful early fall day—one of only a few nice days, Ida suspects, that they will see in this city of grey stone. She has discovered that Toronto has three short seasons of pallid sunlight and intense humidity, followed by a long, stingingly-cold, slushy winter. She figures they might as well enjoy a nice day while they've got one.

At the local liquor control board outlet, Ida fills out a slip of paper and hands it to a man whose neck is strangled in a tight collar and tie. He takes the slip suspiciously, as if wondering what this woman is up to, buying rye whisky in the afternoon. Finally he comes back with the bottle, tightly wrapped in a brown paper bag. "Can I see some ID, please?"

Ida shows him her birth certificate. She stands impassively, watching him examine the birth date, then peer at her face. She raises her eyebrows as if to say, *Che?* Then he raises his. Finally, he sighs and gives her the bottle. She goes through this every time she buys something at the liquor control outlet from this very same man. No matter how many times she shows him her birth certificate, he wants to see it again. *What a strange country, that buying a bottle of whisky is controlled!* thinks Ida.

In the backyard, the three women take off their high heels and sip their rye-and-gingers on ice. Georgia pulls off her panty hose, right there in the yard. "Anyone looking?" she giggles. Mrs. Agnelli casts a look at Georgia, over the fence, from where she's hanging her laundry. Ida tries not to make eye contact with her.

A few minutes later, Marcello comes home from the library, carrying a Mac's Milk bag: he has the ingredients for that night's awful dinner. Something with cream of mushroom soup again, Ida suspects.

When Marcello appears, Ida notices Georgia and Diane's eyes widening. Ida is used to seeing women react to Marcello this way. At first, she liked it, was proud to be with someone who seemed to excite, if not exactly *passion*—very rare, in this city—then at least interest.

"Mind if I join you, ladies?" he asks, eyeing the whiskies in their hands.

"Oh, please do!" says Georgia. She thrusts out her chest and sits up a little straighter.

Marcello goes inside to put his textbooks away. At least, thinks Ida with satisfaction, they know that Marcello is a student, not just some ditch digger. This always seems to be the assumption when people hear his name.

"How long have you been with loverboy?" asks Diane.

"Six years," says Ida.

"He looks like that actor who just played Zorro," says Georgia. "What's his name? Frank Langella. Gorgeous! Where did you meet him?"

"A long, long story," says Ida—then adds, not untruthfully: "Marcello's father introduced us."

On Sunday morning, after a few hours of digging alone, Marcello hands his shovel to Vincenzo, then heads for the public library. Sitting at a study table, he notices a young man, about his age, his head in a book. He has a narrow face with an impressive nose and a high, worried forehead. The man looks up while Marcello is staring into the distance, wrestling with an equation, one just troublesome enough to make it interesting. When their eyes meet, the man smiles. "Writs and Torts," he says, grimacing. "I'm at Osgoode Hall, the law school at York."

"I'm at York, too," says Marcello. "Mathematics and Education."

The man offers his hand across the table: "Ed Ceci."

"Marcello Trov ... I mean, Umbriaco."

They agree to reward themselves for studying on a beautiful day with espressos at a local café. Like Marcello, Ed was born in Italy and came to Canada as a child.

Since then, he has always lived on Corso Italia. He tells Marcello stories about the history of the area, how the many fruit stores and restaurants got started, the characters who live there, the love affairs, the criminal activity, who's rumoured to be in the Mafia, the bad blood between some of the neighbours.

"So, you're a lawyer?" Marcello says casually, sipping his espresso.

"Almost. I still have to find a firm to article with."

"But you have the knowledge. Of the law, I mean."

Ed lifts his eyebrows at Marcello. "Are you in trouble?"

"Yes and no," says Marcello.

He confides in Ed, telling him the story of Ida, his father, the proxy wedding. Ed sits listening raptly. He tells Marcello that for Ida to get an annulment, she would need to appeal to the Archdiocese of Toronto.

"They'll want a signed affidavit from both Ida and your father swearing that the marriage was never consummated," explains Ed.

Marcello shakes his head. "I don't think Pop would ever do anything to make life easier for us. Is there some other way?"

"Let me look into it a bit," says Ed. "One thing I know, Ida's situation is not unique. I've heard of many proxy marriages in Little Italy and not all work out well. There have been more than a few runaway brides."

"I didn't know that," says Marcello, suddenly uneasy.

"Funny, Ida doesn't sound like the proxy wife type," Ed continues. "Usually, they're young girls from little villages, or sometimes women from towns where all the men have left. I've never heard of a Venetian proxy bride, let alone one who became a stewardess. I wonder what Ida was thinking, coming over here like that?"

"It's a long, long story," says Marcello, wishing he knew it himself.

A week later, Ed calls Marcello at home. "A buddy of mine is a priest at St. Lucy's. I used to play hockey with him at St. Mike's. He gave me the name of someone to talk to at the Archdiocese. And I've got an idea about how to get the affidavit signed by your father."

Ed would write a letter to Marcello Senior care of the Andolinis, using lots of intimidating legal language: *"Please find enclosed for your immediate attention and signature..."* He would enclose an affidavit from the Archdiocese.

"I won't tell her about this until we get Pop's signature," says Marcello. "If we ever do. One problem though—I don't want Pop to know where we're living."

"The return address will be the Archdiocese. Once they get a signed copy, they'll forward his response to you. He'll know you're somewhere in the region, though."

"Chance I'll have to take," shrugs Marcello.

The following week, as they're flying back from Ottawa, Georgia says to Ida, "Diane and I are going to a women's consciousness-raising workshop tonight in High Park. Not far from your neighbourhood. Want to come?"

Ida asks, "Raising consciousness?"

"Yeah, you know. Women's Lib! It's a workshop about getting in touch with your true self. Come along with us, Ida! It'll be good for you."

Ida shrugs. Why not? For all she knows, women in Venice are burning their bras by now—maybe even Zara.

When they arrive at the house where the workshop is taking place, Ida feels ridiculously formally dressed. Everyone is in jeans or flowing batik dresses, their hair long and loose, sandals on their feet, bangles on their wrists. A marijuana cigarette is making the rounds and Carole King's *Tapestry* is on the stereo. Some of the women sit cross-legged on the floor, paging through a book called *Our Bodies, Our Selves*.

"I think this not my scene," she whispers to Georgia.

"Give it a chance. The workshop leader is pretty cool. Jasmine's been to parties at The Factory."

"She make cars?"

"No, no. The Factory is a place in New York City. Like ... an artistic salon. Andy Warhol. Viva. Bohemians!"

Ida thinks she understands now. "Okay, Bohemians. *La Bohème*. I know this opera."

Georgia sighs and pats Ida's hand.

Jasmine is a woman in her forties, wearing a long saffron dress with strands of coloured beads, grey hair falling to her waist. When she sees Ida in her skirt, pantyhose, and heels, her eyes flick up and down her quickly. Ida lifts her chin, giving Jasmine what Marcello calls her *Il Duce* look.

"Welcome, powerful women of Toronto," Jasmine says, sweeping her hands around the packed living room. "I'm delighted you could come to our 'Sisters Doing It For Themselves' workshop. We're going to start with a few minutes of self-examination." Jasmine hands out small hand mirrors. "Many of us have never actually *looked* at ourselves. We think we know what's down there, and yet we've never taken the time to truly examine our bodies."

She explains that everyone will take a moment—whether in the presence of their sisters in the living room (which would be a positive step and in the spirit of feminist solidarity) or if they're too up-tight (*and that's cool!*), in the privacy of one of the bedrooms or bathrooms—to use the mirrors to reveal themselves to themselves.

Ida takes a mirror and locks herself in a powder room. She feels ridiculous, but also curious. She pulls down her pantyhose and panties and angles the mirror. There it is, a fuzz of blonde hair. Big deal. She separates the labia, sees the pinkness within, then pulls up her pantyhose and goes back into the living room, where women are now sitting or lying on the floor. All eyes are on Jasmine.

"This exercise is called 'Eating a Peach,'" Jasmine explains. "I'll demonstrate."

She holds up a large peach, sliced in half. Gently, Jasmine picks out the pit, then holds the peach up, towards the group, so that they can see the neat hole. "What does this look like to you?" she asks.

Half a peach, thinks Ida, stifling a yawn.

"It's very much like your own vagina, isn't it?"

Ida trades looks with Diane.

"The vulva looks just like a ripe, juicy peach," Jasmine continues. "That's why it's one of the best ways to demonstrate the technique of a woman receiving oral pleasure. Pretend the clitoris—your 'pleasure centre'—is right *here*." Jasmine points to a spot on the peach. "This is where your partner should be kissing, licking, tongue thrusting. Man or woman, whatever your scene is. I'm not here to judge you."

Jasmine demonstrates by delicately sliding the edge of the peach between her lips and nibbling on it.

Ida stares at Jasmine. She tries to keep her face perfectly still, not showing any emotion. She crosses her ankles and places her hands in her lap. But inside her head, a storm is raging as she imagines Marcello's mouth on the peach-coloured fuzz she saw in the mirror. *Yes, right there,* she'd say to him, and he'd kiss that spot. His mustache might tickle.

She feels her pantyhose getting damp. Turning to Georgia, Ida whispers fiercely: "I go home now, Georgia. I need to get the evening meal. Italian men, they expect hot food on the table."

Georgia reaches over and pats Ida's hand, but she's watching Jasmine. "Okay, honey, you just do what you need to do."

When Ida is out the door, hurrying toward the streetcar stop, Georgia tells the others what she said, and they burst into laughter. "Barbaric," someone says. "Wife beater, I bet."

"Catholics," says Jasmine. "Believe me, it will take another thousand years for one of them to have the big O."

"Actually, I think her husband is very sweet," says Diane. "He looks like that actor from *Zorro*."

Everyone in the room groans in derision.

When Ida gets home, she finds Marcello with an apron knotted over his jeans, trying to cook a risotto Milanese with Uncle Ben's rice. "I've always wanted to try this. I went next door and got the recipe from Mrs. Agnelli." He has a handwritten index card propped on the counter in front of him.

"You need special rice for *risotto alla milanese*," explains Ida, examining the mess inside the saucepan. "Arborio rice."

"Can I find that at Mac's Milk?"

"Forget about this," says Ida, untying the apron from around his waist, flinging it onto the floor. "Cooking is not what you are for."

"No?"

"We are going to make love, now," says Ida. "*Andiamo!*"

Marcello follows Ida into the bedroom. Nothing remotely like this has ever happened before. She tells him to stand in the middle of the bedroom so that she can undress him. "I want to have a good look at you, Cello."

"Oh yeah? You look at me every day."

"Not specifically," answers Ida.

She unbuttons and pulls off his shirt, then unzips and pulls down his jeans and boxers. Then she runs her hands over the muscles of his chest and arms, his buttocks and thighs, hard from all the physical labour, then down his stomach to his cock, already springing to attention. She holds it for a moment, examining the tip and the shaft then slips her hand around his testicles. Marcello gives a sharp gasp.

"Your turn now. You look at *me*.

Marcello obliges, gently easing Ida out of her blouse and skirt and bra. When he gets to the pantyhose, a garment he hates because it reminds him of the casing of a sausage, Ida sits on the edge of the bed so he can yank them off.

"Now *look* at me, Cello," she whispers, spreading her legs slightly. Marcello kneels before Ida and puts his hands on her breasts, which are about the size and shape of teacups, then brings his mouth to her nipples.

"No, you already know that part," says Ida impatiently, pushing his head away from her breasts. "Look *down there*."

Marcello eases her legs apart. She's right. He hasn't taken the time to really look at the light fuzz of hair or the pinkness inside her. He touches his finger to a spot he can see is moist.

Ida shudders. "Now," she says. "Imagine you are eating a peach. Gently, with your lips, your tongue. *Capito*?"

Marcello nods. He leans forward and brushes Ida with his lips. Then he licks her. She cries out and thrusts her hips violently forward, her knee hitting a glancing blow to the side of Marcello's head. He falls back on the floor. "Are you all right?" Marcello asks, rubbing his head.

"Your mustache tickles. Try again, *caro*."

Marcello does. Ida cries out, raising her hips to Marcello's lips. When he finally climbs onto the bed to thrust into her, he can feel her climax coming in waves, like a series of crescendos. *Wagner*, he thinks, gazing down at Ida's face.

He gets out the old record player, puts on *Madama Butterfly*, and they make love to it. Then, they try Verdi. When Marcello gets tired of stopping to change records, he turns on the radio: 10:50 CHUM. Rock and roll. When Marcello brings Ida to a noisy climax during "Nights in White Satin," the Agnellis next door start banging on the shared wall.

"Shhh!" giggles Ida and clamps a hand over Marcello's mouth.

When she removes it, he asks, "Where did you learn how to make love like this?"

"You haven't heard of this before?"

"Well, of course," says Marcello. "I just didn't think you would like…"

"Women," she says quickly. "It's knowledge women pass from one to another. To teach their men, when the time is right. In Italy, is very traditional. Like cooking. "

Marcello grins. "Traditional women's knowledge, eh? Okay, let's just go with that." Pulling Ida to him, he says, "Teach me something else Italian men are supposed to learn."

Daylight starts filtering through the curtains as Ida and Marcello begin to drift into sleep. "Do you have to work?" Marcello asks, yawning.

"Day off. You?"

"Not until this afternoon. Vincenzo is working the morning shift."

"Cello?" says Ida. "You want to know something?"

"Mm-hmm," he answers, on the verge of sleep.

"Every morning, my mamma would send me to go get the mail. I had to walk a long way to the post office. My brother Riccardo came with me."

Marcello lays his hand on Ida's breast and closes his eyes, but knows he won't sleep now. "You never told me you had a brother. Tell me something else."

"The other children would not play with me. Only Riccardo. The other children, they would make a big path around me. Not wanting to walk near me. Sometimes, some of them would even throw things at me and call cruel names."

Marcello waits to see if she will say anything else. When she doesn't, he says, "I'm sorry, *cara*. That must have hurt you."

They lie quietly. Marcello cups her face in his hand, feeling a rush of tenderness for her.

"Did you ever love any other girls, Cello?" Ida asks, out of nowhere.

"You are the only one, Ida," answers Marcello immediately.

Ida rolls toward Marcello, pressing her head into the centre of his chest like a mountain goat. He can feel her drifting away, into sleep. "Why did the children throw things, Ida?" he whispers into her ear.

She sighs. "My mother was not popular with our neighbours. A very strong woman who always did just what she wanted, no matter what anyone thinks. A businesswoman, running the *pensione* on her own. And she was an outsider—not from Venice. The other mothers did not like her, so their children did not like me."

Marcello holds Ida closer. "Where did your mother come from?"

Ida hesitates. "A city on the Adriatic called Zara."

"Why did she go to Venice?"

Ida yawns. "It was all to do with the war, of course. I tell you, one day. For now, we sleep." Then she opens her eyes again and looks into Marcello's eyes. "*Ti amo*, Cello."

"I love you, too," Marcello says, his hand still cupping her face.

The two of them doze. At about noon, Marcello rises and goes downstairs to put the coffee on. He has a raging hunger; the burnt rice in the saucepan reminds him that they missed their evening meal. Maybe now that Ida has shown him how to make love like an Italian, she'll teach him how to cook like one too. When he goes onto the front porch to pick up their newspaper and the mail, Mrs. Agnelli, out watering the driveway, glares at him. She lifts her hand dismissively at him, palm up, and shouts: "Hey, Romeo!"

He smiles and shrugs in resignation. "*Scusi*, Signora Agnelli. We were trying to make…" And then he mimes the universal symbol for someone cradling a baby in their arms.

Mrs. Agnelli smiles back at him. "*Ah, si? Buona fortuna!*" and blows him a kiss.

When he opens the mailbox, he sees a large, legal envelope, addressed to Ida. The return address is the Archdiocese of Toronto. Marcello rips it open. It is a note informing Ida of the receipt of the affidavit. For a moment, his heart lifts, eyes scanning the document for Senior's scrawled signature. Instead, he sees the words: "Declined to affirm the statement of non-consummation of marriage."

And something else. An "addendum," the diocesan letter calls it. A document Senior mailed back to the bishop's office along with his refusal to sign the affidavit. An invoice, listing the costs of Ida's travel from Italy and upkeep. Senior's message is clear: *She belongs to me. Your debt is not forgiven.*

Marcello crumples the message in his fist.

The law has failed them. So has the Church. Time to take matters into his own hands.

5. THE OLD GODS ARE DYING

BENNY STANDS AT ONE of the open-air stores in Kensington Market, digging through a huge cardboard box of black rubber boots. The hand-lettered sign reads "99 cents." Cheap, but he's tempted to shoplift and save the buck. It won't be easy. The storeowner, a dark-haired, dark-eyed guy about Rocco's age, keeps glancing over at him as he uses a long pole to hang nylon Toronto Maple Leafs jerseys on hooks along the roof gutter. The thin blue-and-white shirts flap in the breeze like flags.

"You needs some helps?" the guy asks in a slushy Portuguese accent.

"I'm okay, man, " says Benny, pulling a pair of size tens out of the rubbery pile. He gives a crumpled dollar bill to the guy, who drops a penny in Benny's hand without a smile. Like he knew all along what he was planning.

Anyway, it's better not to be caught stealing in his own neighbourhood. Living a few minutes away on Robert Street, he's a regular visitor at the open-air fruit and vegetable stores, the bakery, Global Cheese, and the butcher with the blunt name MEAT, whenever he's scraped together enough money for protein. The cheapest place he's found to buy eggs is from a Portuguese kid who stands on the curb with stacks of unmarked cartons yelling *eggs eggs eggs*. Benny could survive on Wonderbread and Nutella but Claire needs good food. The baby inside her seems to be eating her alive.

With twenty-five hard earned bucks going each month to rent a basement apartment (if you can call a windowless cockroach-infested cellar reeking of damp earth and mildew an "apartment"), he's worried about cutting too far into the cash he stole from Prima's underwear drawer. The stack hidden inside *I, Robot* is growing thinner and thinner.

The Corvair got them a lot less than they hoped. A mechanic on Spadina took it off their hands for fifty bucks, no questions asked, saying he'd sell it for parts. "GM don't make Corvairs no more," he told them.

Luckily, jobs are plentiful in Toronto, if you don't mind getting your feet wet. Benny signed on with Gentlemen's Executive Hand Touch AutoWash 2000 near Baldwin Street. He's on a crew of six guys who run out to the curb and rinse soap off freshly washed cars with buckets of water, then dry them with a shammy. They have to pay for their buckets and shammies out of their own pockets. The boots aren't strictly necessary but Benny's already had two pairs of cheap basketball shoes rot off his feet. He stands at the curb six days a week, taking his turn holding up a sheet of cardboard reading TODAY ONLY! CARE-FULL "STEAM AND MANPOWER" CAR WASH 55 CENTS. They are paid by the car, not by the hour.

The others are mostly Spanish-speaking guys from Chile and Guatemala, and Benny recognizes a few as DPs, tall, thin, poorly shaved, heavily accented. The DPs have seen a few things. There's also a black guy from the States, a draft dodger (he claims), a deserter according to the DPs, an ex-Marine who ran away rather than fight the North Vietnamese. The DPs call him a Commie lover and treat him with vicious derision. Benny doesn't think he'll last long.

Don, a charmer with a prison record and a leering grin full of chipped teeth, has been at Gentlemen's Hand Touch the longest. Don watches Benny, hungrily. When he's invited into an alley for a smoke, Benny knows exactly what's coming. He's starting to be aware of his physical power: he's still thin and wiry, but tall. The knee has heeled and despite a noticeable limp, his leg has regained strength. When Don pats Benny's ass, Benny backs him up against a wall and puts him in a headlock, exactly the way Rocco showed him in the tool shed.

"I'm not like that, so just fuck off," said Benny through gritted teeth.

"Hey, hey, hey, I didn't know you were George Chuvalo." Don held up his hands in mock surrender.

Not that Benny would turn down cash for sex—with Claire to worry about, he'd do just about anything for money at this point—but he knows Don couldn't pay enough to make it worthwhile. It would just be one poor guy fucking another poor guy. What's the percentage in that? Right now he has to be practical. No wasted effort. No something-for-nothing. He has to focus on making money for his new life in the spongy-carpeted basement flat with Claire. The last thing he wants is for the two of them to end up on the street, like the hollow-eyed, runny-nosed junkies he sees outside the mission on Yonge Street or playing broken guitars for spare change in Yorkville. As awful as it is, the basement is shelter. An address. He's even kind of proud of renting. He's never had a place of his own before.

Claire doesn't much like living underground. "This certainly sucks. I feel like a giant mushroom," she says. Not that she's saying much these days, stuck in the dark flat, growing bigger and bigger.

Claire hates going outside. Benny hates being inside. The ceiling is so low he has to stoop just to use the rusty shower. They hardly ever turn out the lights, even at night, because when they do, the other residents, the roaches, swarm out in numbers big enough to fill a football stadium (or at least Benny imagines them that way, like the cartoon bugs in a Raid commercial, filling the grandstands with tiny flags waving).

At night, Benny and Clair curl up on a sheet spread over the spongy carpet, Benny's chest to Claire's back, his hand cradling her lump of a belly. He can feel the baby moving inside her, punching and pushing against the surface of Claire's skin, pale as an eggshell. He finds the baby's invisible energy fascinating, as if it were an alien being from one of his sci-fi novels, fighting its way into the world.

Claire likes being held but tells Benny that she doesn't want him to do anything else to her. Or as she puts it, "no funny business." Which is fine by him. Claire has never seemed particularly sexual to him. She's more like a child out of a fairy tale, who eats a magical seed and finds herself carrying a mysterious burden. Benny thinks of himself as the handsome peasant boy who must protect her from a witch, or maybe evil dwarves—something like that. He is even starting to sort-of believe Claire's claim that the baby was conceived by radioactive goo, without a man's assistance, although he knows Mr. Spock would pronounce it illogical.

The air is getting cooler. Now that he's got boots, Benny needs to think about heavy socks, long underwear, a parka maybe. That's what Marco upstairs told him, that to work outside all winter long at a Spadina car wash is colder even than farm work. You're always wet and standing around, not working up enough body heat to stay warm. Claire will need things too; he knows that. Both of them ran off in summer clothes, shorts and T-shirts. At least he has an excuse—the cake was all he could manage with those crutches—but Claire could have filled the Corvair with warm clothes if she'd been thinking ahead. Benny's starting to learn that Claire *never* thinks ahead.

"My mom says I have a short attention span," explained Claire.

Benny went to the St. Vincent de Paul that sells clothes by the pound and picked up some maternity dresses for Claire, faded and worn, in the smallest sizes they had, but they still fit her like a tent. She's skinny as hell, the baby growing out of her like the burl on a tree. She'll need a heavy coat soon, suspects Benny. Even though it's only September, he can feel an early-autumn chill coming on, an awareness brought on by a childhood sleeping in alleyways and three years on Prima's farm watching weather roll in over the lake. He's learned to read the signs. Across the street from the house where they live, the children at Lord Lansdowne Public School run screaming through the yard in jackets and long pants, their mothers taking care to keep them warm. Some of them, it's clear from their skin colour and mother tongues, have never seen a Canadian winter. Watching them in the playground, Benny feels a sense of loss. If he were at Prima's, he would be starting grade eleven. Although he got a late start, he was doing not-bad in school. He liked the library, in particular—a good place to read stories. They even had a selection of Isaac Asimovs and Robert Heinleins. Benny had been looking forward to reading *Stranger in a Strange Land*. He keeps an eye out for it in the second-hand bookstores on Queen.

On junk days Benny patrols the neighbourhood, up and down Robert, Major, and Borden Streets, looking for stuff. Canadian *mangiacakes* are starting to renovate the old Victorians, tossing all sorts of good shit to the curb: oak cupboards, floor tiles, porcelain sinks, rusting gas stoves, furniture of all kinds. Benny picks up a kitchen chair here and a couch cushion there. He even finds a portable TV with a single rabbit ear: it works well enough to pull in three channels, even in the basement.

One day Benny notices a guy wrestling a mattress out of the front of a house that has been stripped of the St. Francis of Assisi grillwork that fronts every other screen door on Robert Street. (At Claire and Benny's house, St. Francis' head has been snapped off, leaving a headless robed monk with birds perching on one hand, an attentive dog at his feet.)

The mattress looks unripped and unstained. Benny sees his chance. He runs up the front steps of the saint-free Victorian and helps the guy ease the mattress down.

"Thanks man," says the guy. When his eyes meet Benny's, Benny *knows*. He is neither young nor old—in his thirties, maybe. Very nice-looking, in pressed Levi's and a T-shirt that exposes veiny muscular arms. His teeth are as straight and white as a mouthful of money.

Benny feels a tell-tale tightening in the front of his jeans but reminds himself: *You can't afford to give nothing for nothing.* Shifting his weight onto his good leg, he rests his hands on his hips and smiles. The guy smiles back and runs his hand through his sandy hair, blue eyes crinkling. Eating Benny up.

That's when a woman comes out the front door carrying a box of copper plumbing, topped by a toilet seat. "Look at all this crap, will you? You'd think after what we paid for this dump those Wops would've had the decency to clean it up."

The guy wrinkles his forehead. "My wife," he states apologetically.

Benny hoists the mattress. He's looking forward to the expression on Claire's face when she learns that they won't have to sleep on the floor another night.

"See you around," Benny says to the man.

"I work at home. Stop by for coffee some time," the man tells Benny, and the very next day, he does, knocking at the dignified door on his way to the car wash.

No sooner does Benny walk into the house "for coffee" then the two of them get naked in the kitchen. It's as big as Prima's farm kitchen but so spotless it looks like no one ever cooks in it. Scott perches Benny on the table-size butcher's block in the middle of the room and sucks him off, then Benny does the same to him.

Next Scott leads him upstairs to a bedroom and surprise, surprise, he turns out to be a bottom. He spreads himself face-down on a fancy new bed drenched in the sunshine streaming through a skylight he tells Benny he's just installed.

Benny stands at the foot of the massive bed, his cock pointing at Scott as if he's True North. "You're the big dog. Show me who's boss," says Scott, and turns his face to the mattress.

Afterwards, Benny asks for a few bucks. Why not, that's the only reason you're here, he reminds himself. Scott counts ten out of his wallet, saying: "Look, Benny, I'd love to do this again. But we've gotta be careful. Monica teaches a block away at Lord Lansdowne and comes home spur of the moment sometimes. We're trying to conceive."

"What's that mean?" frowned Benny, tugging on his underpants.

"She wants me to get her pregnant. Women want a baby. We've been trying for a while now but no luck."

Benny notes this as he picks his jeans off the floor. He'd been trying not to think of what will happen when Claire's baby comes. He's pretty sure a roach-infested basement isn't a good place to keep it.

"You got a lot of space here," observes Benny. "You renting the whole place?"

"No, no. We own it. Or maybe I should say the bank does. Want to look around?"

"Yeah, sure, okay," says Benny, wondering what the fuck the guy is talking about. He *owns* the place?

Scott leads Benny from room to room. One has nothing in it but a recliner chair, a framed wedding portrait of Monica and Scott on the wall, a footstool, and a TV. Another room holds a dresser and a pristine bed with a pink coverlet on it—the guest room, Scott calls it. But the best one of all is a big room with a bay window looking directly out onto Robert Street. In front of the window is a giant block of a wood desk holding a typewriter and neat stacks of paper, typed side down. The walls are covered by bookshelves, as high as Benny's head, a thick forest of books. The only place he has ever seen this many books at one time was in the library at his high school in Bramborough. He's not sure there were any books in Prima's house, except the Bible.

"These are all yours?"

Scott laughs, corners of his eyes crinkling. "I didn't write all of them, if that's what you mean."

"But you've read them?" asks Benny.

The man nods. "Sure, most of them. Well, a few, no, some of Monica's Doris Lessings and Margaret Laurences—who knows, if I stay blocked, I might even get around to those."

Benny is so shocked by the room, he can't move. He wants to run his hands over the books, the way he's been running his hands over Scott's body. He wants to cocoon himself in all this paper. It's a hidden paradise that just opened itself to him, right here on the street where he and Claire live.

"I'm a writer," volunteers Scott.

Benny stares at him. "A what?"

"I used to be a reporter, but now I write novels. Five published to date. I'm trying to work on a sixth but it's not coming. Writer's block."

"What kind of books?"

Scott runs his hand through his hair. "Uh, well. You know. I guess you'd call them science fiction. But, literary. I was always kind of into that. Loved Asimov, George Herbert, I think that's why I..."

"Have you got *Stranger in a Strange Land*?"

Scott slides his finger along a shelf, slips out a book, and hands it to Benny who stares at it in disbelief. It's a hardcover. With a dust jacket. Benny fishes the money Scott gave him back out of his jeans pocket.

"No, come on, now, no, it's second-hand. Picked it up years ago at a used book store," says Scott, pushing the money back into Benny's hand. "Besides, Heinlein's not much to my taste. Take it."

"No, no," insists Benny, suddenly confused, feeling as if the transaction is now out of whack, that the power balance has shifted. Minutes earlier Benny was the big dog—now, he owes Scott something. Not a feeling he likes.

"Take it. I'm just delighted that you're a reader," repeats

Scott, and, turning his back on Benny, leads him downstairs.

Sitting on a bench by the front door, Benny ties up his sneakers.

"You look like a Greek god. Anyone ever tell you that?" asks Scott.

Benny shakes his head. "I'm Italian, not Greek."

"It's just a figure of speech," says Scott, searching Benny's face. "I just meant, you're classically beautiful. Like something out a myth. You're young too, aren't you? You don't look more than twenty."

"Give or take," shrugs Benny, wishing he could claim three extra years. He senses that if Scott knew he was only seventeen, he might think twice about seeing him again. "Hey, thanks for the book. "

"Any time," says Scott and kisses him, at first lightly, then passionately, his hand gripping the back of Benny's head. Finally he opens the unsaintly front door, and Benny steps back into the cool air of the real world.

Behind him, the inside lock clicks firmly.

After his shift at the car wash, Benny uses Scott's money to buy two pork chops at MEAT and shoplifts a Mickey Mouse Club night-light from a second-hand store. Stuck into a socket in the pressboard room where he and Claire sleep, the sickly yellow glow still doesn't do much to keep the bugs from skittering around on the walls all night.

Something has got to be done. He must get rid of the roaches before the baby comes. Opening *I, Robot*, he fishes a dollar out of his stash. No choice.

Benny goes to the hardware store on Spadina, run by an old guy with numbers on his arm, the store a tight jumble of valves, nails, and dusty canisters with names like KIL-M-DEAD. The storekeeper has tremors. Benny imagines it's from booze, but Marco who lives upstairs says the old guy has a disease that makes him shake like a leaf in the wind all the time. These days everybody has a disease, it seems to Benny. Anyway, Benny shoplifts a lock-pick set in a soft leather wallet while the old guy goes up a ladder and brings down a roach bomb. He tells Benny to set it off in the basement flat and leave the place for twelve hours, minimum.

When Benny gently explains this, Claire sighs and fusses but finally comes blinking into the sunshine. They spend the day on the front porch drinking Kool-Aid and rye with Vera and Marco, who share the second floor flat. Vera is Hungarian. Marco, a printer in his native Chile, is an expert forger.

"Visas, passports, drivers' licences, you name it. But no money," Marco explains. "Cops'll turn a blind eye to fake documents, but they treat counterfeiters like murderers. That's capitalism for you."

Vera is the oldest-looking woman Benny has ever met who was not really old—"old" being someone Prima's age, in Benny's mind. Her face looks like one of the watercolour paint boxes he remembers from school art classes, blue shadow, bright pink cheeks, red lipstick, her pink-and- blonde hair teased and sprayed into the texture of cotton candy. She wears terry cloth shorts and snug little T-shirts with life lessons on them. *Fuddle Duddle. Give Peace A Chance. Don't Trust Anyone Over 30*. Today she's wearing one with a yellow smiling face and the words *Have A Nice Day*. A heavy syrupy smell clings to her, which she volunteers to Benny is a perfume called My Sin.

"Very French," Vera explains. "I'm a European, you know. We don't go for that light-hearted fruity shit the Canadian girls love so much. When you're a European, you know that life is suffering."

Vera used to be an exotic dancer, but now waits tables at the Horseshoe Tavern at Spadina and Queen. The change in careers had something to do with the effect of gravity on her boobs after her one-and-only pregnancy, the resulting daughter, Darlene, vaguely and variously referred to as living with her father, her grandparents, a friend's family, a cousin in Etobicoke, an asshole of a prison guard boyfriend in Penatanguishene, and on her own in something called "city housing." "Darl and I, we don't get along so good," says Vera with a sigh.

She explains all this to Benny and Claire on the front porch of the house at 62 Robert Street over the twelve hours that the roach bomb does its killing work in the cave of a cellar. Benny should be at the car wash, but something tells him to stay close to Claire, who has become not only larger and larger but also more and more distant, as if some part of her is drifting away while the baby grows. Sometimes, all she wants is to sleep away the day in the darkness of the cellar, but Benny hears stories about what roaches do to unmoving humans. And the sun will do her good but she won't stay out here unless Benny watches her. He bums a cigarette off Vera and listens politely to her life story, which involves running away in the night with her family wearing all her clothes at once, crossing a border, then another border, getting on a train and jumping off a train. There are bribes and a brother shot dead by a border guard. Finally they hide out in a farmhouse before being smuggled into Italy (here she pats Benny's arm and tells him she's always liked what she calls "his people." At first Benny thinks she means the Andolinis, then realizes she means Italians in general).

"All the DPs live in Parkdale, so we went to Parkdale," she explains. "When I moved to this part of town, I advertised in the *Sun* for a roommate and Marco showed up. I was looking for a woman but oh well. So it's a good thing Marco became my boyfriend." She waggles her hand; she's wearing a tarnished band on her ring finger. "I wear this, to keep the holy rollers off our ass."

Marco joins them on the porch from time to time. He's busy inside, forging documents for illegal immigrants on a second-hand printing press and crushing the roaches scrambling upstairs from Benny and Claire's apartment due to the roach bomb.

"My young friend, you realize this is pointless, don't you?" he says, pointing a flyswatter at Benny. "You send the bugs upstairs to us for a while, they come back down to you eventually. Our capitalist creep of a landlord needs to fumigate the whole place."

Marco reminds Benny of Marcello. He seems to know something about everything. He's a Communist, which makes it surprising he's living with Vera, a DP. Marco sees the illogic in this, too, but as he says to Benny, "Communism. Socialism. Fascism. Catholicism. All the old gods are dying, don't you see that, Benny? Everyone here just wants to drink and fuck and dance and forget."

6. IMMIGRANT SONG

TORONTO INTERNATIONAL AIRPORT, MALTON, OCTOBER 1975

IDA LOVES THE SENSATION of being suspended between heaven and earth. Walking the aisles after the dinner service, looking at the sleeping souls under blankets, the young mothers whispering stories to children, even the businessmen hunched over their paperback thrillers like monks at prayer, haloed by reading lights. She feels tenderness toward these strangers under her care in this little flying world where time not only stands still, but sometimes spins backwards.

She keeps trying to get Cello to fly with her. His immigration to Canada with his mother had been his last big trip. He still remembers the rolling of the ship, his mother's seasickness, and a hobby horse up on deck that he rode back and forth, back and forth, across the ocean. He crossed a world while hardly moving at all.

Marcello is like some of the old men Ida remembers from the old country, hanging on to some familiar patch of land, some grafted vines that grew just-so on the side of a particular hill in a particular town. Cello wants his familiar things around him. He has never even stepped onto a plane, although he promises that as soon as the annulment is final, and they're married, they'll fly somewhere for a proper honeymoon.

Coming off the red-eye from Vancouver with Georgia, Ida looks forward to a quick cab ride home, a bite to eat, then bed. But when the two women walk out of ARRIVALS, Ida is surprised to see Ed Ceci, his suit and hair covered with dust, his face bloodied as though he's been in a fight. Even his car, idling at the curb, is coated with dirt.

"Please Ida, just get in the car. I'll explain as we drive. There's been an accident."

Looking at Georgia, Ed asks, "Are you a friend?"

Georgia nods, slipping her arm through Ida's.

Earlier that day...

Ed and Marcello are together in the rectory of St. Lucy's Church. The priest's office smells like Scotch, cigar smoke, and a lemon-scented air freshener that fails to cover both.

Ida's dossier is spread-eagled on the oak veneer desk, the facts as shamelessly exposed as a blonde in the porno magazines Marcello's father used to sell at the candy store. Father Dave Como fingers the pages, chin in hand, forehead furrowed, looking over the unsigned affidavit.

He glances at Ed, who thought this meeting important enough for a business suit. Ed used to play hockey with Father Dave at St. Mike's. Maybe the suit and tie is his way of indicating what team he's on now.

Marcello wears overalls and work boots. Father Dave is in his black cassock. Each man dressed according to his proper role. The problem is that Father Dave can't quite figure out what Marcello's "proper role" is.

"Let me get this straight," the priest says, slowly. "You're *not* the Marcello who was supposed to sign the affidavit?"

"No, Father. I'm his son."

"Which makes Mrs. Umbriaco ... your stepmother?"

"Technically," admits Marcello. He glances at Ed, not liking where this discussion is headed. They had hoped to soft-pedal this little detail.

Dave is a red-haired, dark-eyed Italian-Irish priest. ("One of the worst combinations," Ed warned before the meeting. "Bad tempered, likes a drink, and half the female parishioners are secretly in love with him.") He looks up with a frown, dark eyes flicking back and forth between Marcello and Ed like a linesman who knows something fishy is going on against the boards. "Boys, what the hell is up here?"

Ed shoots Marcello his *Let-me-handle-this* look. Smooths his tie. Crosses his legs. "How do you mean, Dave?"

"For starters, neither of the parties being annulled is in the room. Why isn't Mrs. Umbriaco here?"

"She's working, Father," says Marcello, uncomfortable calling the priest "Dave," the way Ed does. "She's a flight attendant for Air Canada. Ed and I are here as her...." Marcello looked at Ed to supply the correct words.

"Spokesmen?" suggests the priest, an edge of sarcasm in his voice.

"Advocates," says Ed decisively.

Father Dave leans back in the chair. Taps the dossier. Stares at Marcello in silence.

"And what is Ida to you, Marcello?" asks Dave, staring at him steadily.

Ed stickhandles his way back into the conversation. "Oh come on, Dave! Let the guy make an honest woman of her. Ten years from now, no one's going to care how these two got together!"

Father Dave shakes his head. "Tell that to the archbishop, Ed. He still wants to go back to the Latin Mass."

"The real husband brought her over under false circumstances," Ed continues. "He claimed to be a horse rancher, but turned out to be petty criminal. A pornography smuggler using his candy store as a front. Try telling the archbishop that."

Dave glares at Ed. "You think he's the first guy on this street to lie to a woman he's married, but never met? You're going to have to do better than that, counsellor."

As Ed and Father Dave skate around one another, elbows up, Marcello's mind drifts to Ida, who continues to ask what difference it makes if they get married? Marcello knows that it shouldn't matter in a world where they could be blown up a by a nuclear bomb at any second, where guys are drifting back from Vietnam, no legs, no hands, no nothing. Who worries about an old-fashioned idea like marriage?

Running away together had been the right thing to do, even if he was technically sleeping with his stepmother. But Marcello can't escape the feeling that, right or not, it is the type of sin that exacts a heavy toll. He's never stopped believing that the stillbirth in Prince George was a form of punishment. Never again. A proper annulment and a real marriage will wipe the slate clean. It's the only reason he persuaded Ida to come to Toronto—far enough from Shipman's Corners that they'd never have to see Senior. Close enough that Marcello could force the issue if he had to. Maybe even resolve the problem with the cops, if he and Ed can figure out a way.

"Marcello? What do you think?"

"Huh?" says Marcello. His mind snaps back to the rectory office. He's conscious again of the smell of scotch and cigars, the cloying lemon disinfectant, Ed Ceci, the priest, the crucified Christ over the desk with the *And good luck to you pal* expression painted on His face.

"I'll come back with Ida next time," says Marcello, hoping this is a reasonable answer to whatever question he was just asked. It's also a promise he's not sure he can keep, Ida being reluctant to have anything to do with priests. Before they leave, he and Ed bow their heads while Father Dave mumbles a blessing. Marcello half expects him to drop a puck at the end of it.

The two men walk to Ed's car in the church parking lot. "Can you give me a lift? The Chevy's in the shop again," says Marcello.

"You're going to have to replace that old clunker sooner or later, brother."

Marcello pops out the dashboard lighter and touches it to the tip of an Export A. "I just need her a little while longer. Till I've saved up."

When they pull up in front of the house, they can see the

conveyor belt moving dirt through the window; Vincenzo must be hard at work. Leo stands on top of a mountain of earth inside the bin, tamping it down with the back of a shovel.

"Seems like you've been on this job forever," says Ed.

Marcello sits for a moment, drawing on his cigarette, staring at the growing pile of dirt. "We finally took down the pillar holding up the ceiling a couple of days ago, reinforced another four feet of foundation yesterday. Just got to dig out the cold cellar and I'm outta here."

"Lousy job, eh?"

"Let's just say I prefer the days I'm up at York." Marcello opens the door. "Thanks for the ride, brother."

Hopping out of Ed's car, he crosses the front yard, cigarette hanging from his mouth, and picks up a shovel. Just before he lowers himself into the pit, he turns and gives Ed a quick wave, tosses his cigarette to the ground, and disappears into the underworld of the house basement.

Ed starts the engine and turns on the radio, searching for music. Finally, he finds Led Zeppelin's "Immigrant Song" on CHUM FM. Nodding in time to the pounding guitar chords, he taps out a cigarette and pushes in the dashboard lighter.

He feels it before he hears it: a loud, deep boom like cannon fire. At first Ed thinks it's from the radio. He looks up, hand still poised to light the cigarette. When a sulfurous stench of rotten eggs fills his nose, he realizes what is happening. Too late.

The blast blows a wall of dirt, dust, and debris through the passenger side window of Ed's Pontiac where Marcello had been sitting minutes before. A chunk of wood flies in, hitting him in the side of the head. He reaches up to touch his face and his fingers come away bloody. His ears are full of a dull buzzing and the distant thumping of the "Immigrant Song" as though he's hearing it through three floors of an apartment house.

He sees Leo staggering toward the car, a shovel still in his hand. His mouth is moving, forming words. He's yelling something that Ed can't understand. Ed manages to get his door open and pull himself out of the car, legs shaking, then forces himself to run toward the pile of debris that a few minutes ago was a two-storey clapboard house.

Leo catches up with him, grabbing him by the shoulders. He mouths words into Ed's face. Ed can only make out one word: *Help.*

Ed and Leo limp past splintered piles of wood and slabs of ripped linoleum, twisted window frames, crushed doors, chunks of concrete like rotten teeth wrenched from the mouth of a giant. Broken glass and cement dust are everywhere. A stove leans against a toilet, blanketed by a sheet of plaster and lath decorated with *Snow White and the Seven Dwarves* wallpaper. Blackened roof shingles are scattered over the ground like autumn leaves.

An arm is sticking out from under a door. Stumbling over the debris field, the men grip the door and heave it away, Ed thinking, *Thank God, he must have been blown off the ladder before he got down into the basement.*

The man isn't Marcello.

"Vincenzo!" cries Leo, pulling debris off him. "Don't move! We call the ambulance."

"Marcello's still down there!" gasps Vincenzo. His face is a mask of cement dust except where blood trickles from his nose and lips, and down his cheeks from both ears. "He push me against the ladder when we smell the gas. I thought he was just behind me!"

Ed rushes to the edge of the house, to the spot where he judges the basement doorway used to be. The rubble pile is higher than his head.

"Marcello! Can you hear me?"

The sound of his own voice in his ears is muffled. He falls to his knees and starts digging with his hands, bloodying them in the splinters and glass shards. Others are around him now, neighbours who have run out of their homes to see what the commotion is. Someone shouts that they've called an ambulance and the fire department. Leo kneels beside Ed, and the two men dig with their hands. They scoop up handfuls of splintered wood, plaster, and wiring. They keep at it until the ambulance arrives for Vincenzo and the Consumers Gas men start to evacuate the neighbourhood.

"You look like you're in rough shape yourself, pal," says one of the gas men to Ed. "I think you should get to a hospital, too."

Ed shakes his head; he can hear a little more, the ringing receding to a roar like the sound of rushing water. "I've got to find my friend's wife."

"*Calmati.*" *Calm yourself.* A whisper, only. A breath. A thought. *Calmati* hangs in the blackness.

His lips are sticky and dry, his mouth and throat full of blood and grit, as though he's been force-fed sawdust. *Why can't I see anything?* His lashes are heavy with dust. He touches his eyes; he can feel something grinding under the lids. *Don't touch.* Has he been blinded? He reaches up and the tips of his fingers brush against a smooth, flat surface, an arms-length above him. Stretching, he can flatten the palms of his hands against it.

He decides that he isn't blind. The blackness isn't inside him—it's outside and all around him. Blackness and dull silence. As if the darkness has absorbed everything, even sound. Except for that one word. *Calmati.* Someone is whispering to him, over and over and over again.

He tries to shout. The dust in his mouth won't let him. His *Help!* comes out as a ragged gasp.

He reaches out to touch what's on either side of him. There's ... *stuff* ... piles of it, shifting and rough, some of it coming away in his hands when he touches it. Some spots feel jagged and slivered, others soft and powdery. If he digs with his fingers, he doesn't get far until he hits something immovable. He's hemmed in. Like being in a coffin. That's what the smooth surface above him is: a coffin lid. They thought he was dead and so they've buried him, and now he's woken up.

That's when the panic sets in. He tries to scream and sit up. He smacks his forehead against the smooth surface and falls back to the ground. He reaches up, touches the solid roof above him. His fingertips tell him it's cold and smooth. A metal table, he thinks. The canning table at the end of the cellar.

Calmati, says the voice again. Marcello closes his eyes.

By the time Ed drives Ida to Atlas Avenue, the street has been barricaded. He slows the car as they drive past. They see fire trucks, police cars, Consumers Gas vans, a *Toronto Star* car, and an ambulance parked in front of the exploded house, the street and sidewalk littered with debris.

Now that the gas has been cut off, neighbours come drifting back: women in aprons who were in the middle of preparing the noonday meal when the gas men told them to *get out now!*; old men in undershirts and bedroom slippers carrying rolled copies of *Corriere Canadese*; kids who keep climbing on the barricade to be shooed away by cops. Photographers from the newspapers shoot off rolls of film while a man with a notebook talks to neighbours wandering along the barricade. They try to explain to the reporters what they heard, what they saw, in a mixture of Italian, English, and hand gestures. Many of the women are crying. Some stand just outside the barricade with rosaries. Word has spread that that nice young *abruzzese*, the big guy with the pretty wife, living just over the way next to the Agnellis, is trapped under the house.

Ed finally finds a parking spot, about three blocks away on St. Clair. "Now, Ida," he says, turning to hold her hand. "You stay here with Georgia and I'll go tell them you're Marcello's —"

Ida throws open the car door and runs.

"Could have predicted that," says Georgia, raising an eyebrow at Ed.

The two of them take off after Ida. Ed is impressed by how quickly she can run in heels. When she reaches the barricade at Atlas and St. Clair, a cop grabs her arm, motioning to get back.

Ed catches up as she pleads with the cop: "Please sir, my husband is trapped in the house, you must let me through."

"It's too dangerous, ma'am. You go home for now. Could take a while to get him out."

"I won't leave without my husband," says Ida, gripping the barricade.

The cop looks at the chaos around them, then to Ida in her Air Canada uniform. He motions over a fireman.

As Ed rushes up, panting, he hears the cop say, "…The guy's wife…" and the fireman, glancing at Ida, responds, "We're gonna need her, eventually. For identification. Has she got people with her?"

"Right here," says Ed, raising his hand and seizing Georgia's. "We'll look after Mrs. Umbriaco."

One of the neighbours, an elderly man, recognizing Ida, shuffles over with a lawn chair. "You sit, missus," he says, putting the lawn chair firmly on the ground next to her. "My wife and me go to church and pray for Marcello. He save his friend."

"*Grazie*," whispers Ida nodding her head at the old man, then takes his hand and kisses it.

Ida sits in the lawn chair, a tiny, blonde spectator in an Air Canada uniform watching from the sidelines, Ed and Georgia on either side of her. They wait.

As the work crew starts debating whether to use a backhoe to shift a piece of roof, Ed notices a grey-haired guy in a hacking jacket and riding boots, standing on the edge of the debris field to watch the rescue effort. The guy looks ridiculous, as if he was off on a Sunday morning steeplechase.

Ida stands up and strides towards the man and taps him on his shoulder. When he turns, she hauls back and slaps him full in the face. Although she's about half the guy's size, he staggers back, but it's not clear whether he's hurt or just surprised.

"*Faccia di stronzo!*" Ida yells at him. When she hauls back to slap him again, Lou Agnelli rushes up to lead her away. Ida tries to fight him off but he holds her by the arms.

A reporter from the *Star* clicks his camera shutter.

It's the Feast of St. Arturo, also known as the Weeping Saint. When Mass lets out at St. Lucy's, neighbours start to wander up to the barricade, dressed for a celebration. Father Dave Como is among them, his red head bobbing above the others as he muscles his way through the crowd. He's wearing jeans and a black clerical shirt and collar as if he was half in, half out of his cassock when he heard the news. He carries a small black case inside of which, Ed suspects, are bottles of holy water and olive oil, a prayer book, and a stole. The tools of last rites.

"Marcello's ... *wife* ... is here, Dave," says Ed, giving the priest a look and nodding at Ida.

Dave crouches down next to her. "Mrs. Umbriaco? I know Marcello. Do you want to pray with me?" he asks.

She shakes her head but clings to his hand. "You go ahead. I just wait for Marcello."

In the fifth hour, Marcello tries to move his legs and arms to keep the blood flowing, but his body is beginning to feel like a sack of lead sinking into the earth. The air smells like rosewater. Marcello feels peaceful. He could die like this, right now. He thinks he just might do that.

The rosewater fragrance is disappearing, replaced with the odours of earth and oil and dust. Marcello can hear a roaring sound. Some type of machine. Voices sink down to him from above, muffled and distant, as though he's underwater.

"I'm here!" he tries to shout. It comes out as a croak, but louder than he thought he could manage. He starts banging with both fists.

The metal slides to one side, then rises straight up. The light of the setting sun slices painfully through the edges of Marcello's vision. Like watching the end of an eclipse. He turns his face away from the light. There's another sound now; he hears it faintly. Drums or a flock of birds. No, it's clapping.

Marcello's rescue makes the national network TV news twice that day: at six p.m. (when the rescue is still underway), then again at eleven p.m. (by which time Marcello, against doctor's orders, has released himself from the hospital with antibiotics and eye drops; by news time, he's drinking beer with Lou and listening to the rescue on the Agnellis' TV set, since he and Ida don't have one of their own). Although Marcello can still scarcely see or hear, he enjoys it when Lou turns up the sound of the crowd clapping.

"It's like something out of a damn movie," laughs Marcello hoarsely.

The story goes out in time for the dinnertime news: "Today was supposed to be a happy day in the Corso Italia neighbour-hood at Oakwood and St. Clair West—the Feast of St. Arturo di Napoli, known as the Weeping Saint. But for the Umbriacos, Ida and Marcello, of Barrie Avenue, it turned out to be a day of heroism, near-tragedy, and triumph…. Our reporter speaks with the wife of Marcello Umbriaco, the brave Italian-Canadian workman trapped in the rubble, a young man working his way through university, trying to better his station in life when pressure by an impatient customer caused corners to be cut and a terrible tragedy to occur…."

And so it goes. The story has everything. The hard-working immigrant. The uncaring rich guy. The feisty wife who just happens to be a sexy stewardess. The tragedy. The rescue. The neighbours gathered at the barricade who say that Marcello's survival was as much a miracle as the real tears wept by the image of St. Arturo. Some of them swear that Marcello talked to the Saint Arturo the whole time he was buried, while others claim he was comforted by the Holy Ghost itself.

The news report is picked up by broadcast affiliates across eastern Canada and down through the Niagara Frontier of Western New York state, making Marcello a one-day hero in the Golden Horseshoe, Buffalo, Tonawanda, Cheektowaga, all the way down to Rochester.

Inside the house, Lina Agnelli posts herself on a chair under the kitchen phone with a note pad, taking messages from some callers, letting others speak with Ida immediately, like those nice people from the radio show *As It Happens*. Waiting for Marcello to return from the hospital, Ida sits at the kitchen table with Ed and Georgia, drinking homemade vodka dropped off by a Ukrainian family who moved in a few blocks west of the neighbourhood.

"Very good for the nerves," Lina assures Ida, refilling her glass.

No one on Barrie Avenue goes to bed that evening. After the late news, Marcello and Ida sit on the Agnellis' front porch with a crowd of neighbours who want to shake Marcello's hand and chew over the events of the day. Ida keeps trying to get Marcello, slouched in Mrs. Agnelli's chaise, his eyes wrapped in gauze, home and into bed. He keeps refusing.

"I just want to stay out here in the open, breathe the air, and talk," says Marcello hoarsely. "Could you get me another Carling, *cara?*"

By two a.m., most people have drifted home. *Best damn festa of Sant'Arturo we ever have* is the general opinion.

Ida finally manages to get Marcello—who is more than a little drunk—into their half of the semi. After guiding him to the bedroom, she places a hand on his forehead. "I'm frightened," she says.

Marcello yawns. "What for, frightened? It's all over."

"I let people take my picture and yours. I told everyone where we live. Men from the *Star*. And someone from—*come si dice?*—the CBC. I was so upset, I talk, talk, talk, telling everyone our business! Now everyone knows where we live. Maybe they recognize us, even with the new name."

"I don't give a damn," mumbles Marcello.

"But they know how to find us. Maybe we should move, go to another city..."

"Let them come," he answers, and drops into sleep.

7. ZOO STORY

TORONTO, COLLEGE AND SPADINA, 1975

OCTOBER BRINGS STEADY RAIN. A curtain of grey fog hangs across the Toronto skyline for days on end, obscuring the needle-like tower rising on the waterfront. Benny's crew stands at the curb empty-handed. No one wants their car washed in dirty weather.

With no money coming in, Benny's stash inside *I, Robot* grows thinner. Vera makes things worse by convincing Benny to take Claire to Doctor's Hospital for a checkup. A nurse takes blood from her arm, then shoos Benny away and sends Claire into a white-curtained cubicle. She shuffles back into the waiting room with a tear-stained face and a sheaf of papers, which she silently hands to Benny, who shows them to Vera when they return home.

"Mostly vitamins," says Vera, frowning. "Your little lady must be anemic."

"The nurse said something about sugar in her blood," says Benny, staring at the mysterious scribble on a prescription.

Vera gives him a serious look. "Diabetes? That ain't good for a pregnant girl."

Benny shrugs. He tries not to let on to Vera how worried he is about Claire. She's gone from being a skinny, smart-mouthed, knocked-up teenager to a bloated, lethargic lump of a woman who barely speaks or moves. Her ankles are so swollen, she can't lace up her shoes. Her face has taken on the taut, shiny texture of a boiled egg.

Claire says the doctor wants her to come back to the hospital for more tests, but she refuses. "That asshole stuck something cold up me, Benny," she whimpers.

He doesn't bother Claire about medical stuff again, until Vera urges him to get her prescription filled: "The baby could be born sick if your girlfriend don't look after herself. Better do what the doctor says."

Benny slowly walks Claire to the Shoppers Drug Mart at Bloor and Spadina to search the shelves for folic acid and iron. As they wait in line at the pharmacy counter to pay, Benny casually slips a bottle of aspirin in his pocket—might come in handy when Claire's labour pains start. Then they go to a health food store where an emaciated hippie charges them two bucks for a bitter-tasting energy tea—Vera's idea. Benny feels ripped off, but it's impossible to steal anything in the tiny shop.

"Fat as she is, she looks like a ghost," says Vera. "Anyone can see your girlfriend needs a boost."

Benny worries the next boost is going to be out into the street. *I, Robot* only contains a few more bills. If he can't earn money, he won't be able to make the rent, and he and Claire will be evicted.

He's down to his last ten bucks when a green Volkswagen bug pulls into Gentlemen's Hand Touch, the first customer they've seen in days. As the car rolls out of the spinning brushes and Benny rushes up to wipe down the chassis with his shammy, he recognizes Scott behind the wheel. He and the other men rub the hood and doors for everything they're worth. When Benny cleans the driver's side-view mirror, Scott cranks down the car's tiny window.

"I've got a job. There's a hundred bucks in it."

Benny hesitates. Since meeting Scott, he has spent many afternoons in his house—on the butcher block, the bed, even on his writing desk. Every time, ten dollars appeared without Benny even asking. If it weren't for Scott's ten-spots, Benny and Claire would have been flat broke weeks ago.

But a *hundred* bucks? What the hell more could he possibly do to Scott to jack up the going rate that much? Benny is almost afraid to find out.

"When?" asks Benny.

"Around three this afternoon," says Scott. "Is there somewhere I can pick you up?"

"MEAT," says Benny. "Right around the corner."

Scott nods, rolls down the window, and drives the bug away. But first he tips everyone on the crew two bucks apiece.

Don stuffs his two-dollar bill into his pocket, lights a cigarette, and blows the smoke at Benny. "Who's the fag?"

"Some writer," says Benny. "He's always getting me to haul junk out of his house."

"Guess he's too delicate to do the job himself," says Don, and snorts out a laugh.

Under the striped awning of MEAT, Benny shivers inside his plastic windbreaker. Nerves, he thinks. He wishes he had enough extra cash to buy a pack of smokes. He's thinking of bumming one off the dark-eyed guy with the slushy accent at the Portuguese clothing store when Scott pulls up in the bug, sending a wave of backed-up sewer water as high as the store's awning. As they drive off, Benny notices the butcher barrelling out the front door of MEAT to give Scott a piece of his mind, but they're already too far away. In the side-view, Benny can see the guy shaking his fist at their disappearing rear end.

First thing Scott does, thank God, is offer him a cigarette.

Benny lights up, inhales, and asks, "Where we headed?"

"North," says Scott. "Do you know what writer's block is?"

Benny shakes his head and grips the edge of the seat. The little car's underpowered engine sounds like Prima's old sewing machine as it grinds its way to top speed to merge with traffic on the parkway. Benny spots a sign reading DVP SCARBOROUGH, followed by another with the silhouette of an antlered animal—a moose, maybe, or a deer?—outlined in white against a green background. Where the hell are they going? He's never been north of Bloor Street before; the other guys on the crew always claim that everyone north of Bloor is richer than God. Good place for B&Es, confirms Don. But he doesn't think that Scott is taking him to a break and enter.

Having finally merged the bug into the slow lane, Scott says, "Writer's block is an unforgiving bitch. A cock tease. You ever wanted to do something in your life very badly and just couldn't find it within yourself to do it?"

Benny remembers that day in the shed with Rocco. His abandoned plan to go out west and find Marcello and Ida. His desire to take revenge one day on the guys who have hurt him, especially Frank Andolini, and that sadistic jerk from Hamilton with the cake and the air-conditioned Caddy. Of course, Benny doesn't really think of these as failures but rather delayed goals. There's still lots of time for revenge. He could try to make Scott feel good about himself by admitting his own disappointments, but Benny doesn't feel like making himself look weak. In fact, Scott likes it better when he's tough and hard, when he acts like what Scott calls "the big dog."

"If I really want to do something, I just do it," lies Benny. "So, no, I don't know what the fuck you're talking about Scott."

Scott makes a little sighing sound. Benny can tell he's getting excited. "That's what I like about you, Ben. You're always so sure about things. That's why I know you can help me. See, writer's block is stopping me from finishing my book. And if I don't finish my book, what am I? I can't write, can't get my wife pregnant—what am I good for, Benny?"

Benny lights a new smoke off the end of the old one. "Fucked if I know."

"Well, here's the thing. I figured out a way to get past the block. I went to see a psychotherapist."

"A shrink," says Benny, who has read the word somewhere, probably in Arthur C. Clarke. That guy's always writing about intellectual shit.

"Right. Know what he said? That I should find a way to act out the scene I'm trying to write. You're going to help me."

Benny scratches his head. He's getting a hundred bucks to play-act a scene from a science fiction book? "Sounds like fun," he mutters, but his stomach clenches. There's something about this that is beginning to remind him of some of the weirder stuff Niagara Glen Kowalchuk used to make him do.

"Oh, it'll be fun all right," nods Scott. "But a little dangerous too. Guy like you, though, you don't mind a little physical risk. Right?"

"Of course not," says Benny, alarmed.

"It's just you look so much like my hero," says Scott, sounding a little too excited. "That's one of the first things that struck me when I met you. How much you looked like Giro."

"Like who?"

"Giro. He's the hero in my books. It means 'I travel' in Italian."

"I know what the hell it means," Benny snaps back. "What does Giro do in this book of yours?"

Scott laughs and pats Benny's thigh again. "Hand-to-hand combat with wild animals. But don't worry. They will be well fed by now, so chances are all they'll do is burp in your face."

Scott swings the bug into a huge, empty lot with pictures of animals fastened to the light stands, reminding visitors where their cars are parked. They park beside a rhino. Rummaging in his jeans, he pulls out two twenties and a ten. "First half, up front. You'll get the rest after you've run with the dholes."

With a rush of relief, Benny stuffs the cash in the front of his jeans—enough to cover two months' rent. "What the hell's a dhole?"

Scott grins. Pats Benny's leg. "An Asian wild dog."

"Dog?" Benny's anxiety begins to ratchet up again, despite the money. "How big?"

"Thirty, forty pounds, maybe. They're like a cross between a fox and a jackal."

"Small, then," says Benny, trying to slow the wild thumping of his heart.

"On the small side," allows Scott. "But vicious. They surround their prey, run them down, and kill by disembowelling them. Sometimes they even chase prey into deep water to drown them, then fish them out and eat them. But don't worry, I checked the zoo's feeding times and their tummies will be full of horse meat and guinea pigs by the time we get there." He offers Benny another gleaming smile. "They'll give chase, because that's their instinct. But as long you don't show any fear, you should be fine. They usually only kill when they're hungry, not for sport."

At the front gate, Scott pays admission for the two of them, the ticket booth girl frowning. "You've only got about an hour. We close the gates early on Saturdays."

"We won't be long," says Scott, flashing his hundred-watt smile. "We're doing research for a book about wildlife. Just need to have a look at the Eurasian Domain. Could you give us directions?"

"Follow the purple paw prints. That'll take you straight to Eurasia," she says, pulling out a folded map. She traces the route for them with her finger.

As they walk the almost empty pathways, Scott lays out his plan: they'll find the dhole exhibit, scope it out, then hide until closing time. "There should be lots of places to squirrel ourselves away in a zoo," says Scott, grinning at his own joke.

Eventually, they reach a sign reading EURASIAN DOMAIN and an arrow cheerily pointing out the City of Dholes.

The dholes live, not in a cage, as Benny expected, but in a fenced enclosure, separated from visitors by a guardrail and a deep trench with a high concrete wall on one side and a grassy slope on the other. Small hills camouflaged by scrubby bushes and trees dot the field beyond the trench. Scott explains that the zoo created the habitat especially for the dholes, who are an endangered species. They burrow into the earth to build their dens, then tunnel between them to join them up. That way they are always ready to help one another.

"They're pack animals, like wolves, but more like jackals in the way they hunt," says Scott.

"What do they eat?" asks Benny.

"Meat, primarily. Ungulates when they're in the wild—yaks, wild boar, that type of thing. The zoo dumps a box of live guinea pigs into their enclosure once a day. That way they can hunt their prey, the way nature intended."

"How do you know all this?" asks Benny, trying to keep his voice from shaking.

"I used to be a reporter, remember? I'm good at digging up information. I only hope they're not all sacked out in their dens, hiding from the rain," frets Scott, training a pair of binoculars on the habitat. "Oh wait. There's one now. Have a look."

Scott hands Benny the binoculars. When he gets the animal in focus, he sees a dog-like animal with the pointed muzzle, bushy tail, and reddish fur of a fox. He remembers seeing foxes from time to time at the Andolini farm, hunting rabbits in the fields. This animal is much smaller than Fritzie the Doberman or any of the other terrifying hounds that continue to pursue Benny in his nightmares. In fact, the dhole is kind of cute. Puppyish, even. He feels mildly reassured, until the dhole yawns, exposing a mouth full of long, curved teeth. The kind designed for tearing your guts out.

Fuck, thinks Benny. He's starting to picture himself sprawled on the ground with the dhole feasting on his internal organs. He puts a hand on his stomach, then over his groin.

Meanwhile, Scott scans the area with the binoculars, looking for hiding places. He settles on a dark green utility shed, tucked unobtrusively behind a thatched hut, so as not to break the illusion that they are actually in Eurasia, rather than north Scarborough.

Finding the shed unlocked, the two crouch behind a wheelbarrow and large sacks of fertilizer and grass seed. The smell reminds Benny of the Andolinis' toolshed, where Rocco kissed him and Frank beat him up. He closes his eyes and rests his head on his bad knee. It still hurts sometimes when it's damp.

He considers leaving. Claire needs him, he'll say—that would probably be the truth. She looked pretty bad when he left the basement that morning. But Scott might ask for the money back. And without money for food and rent, he and Claire might as well be dead.

He's got to see it through. But at least if he could get the entire hundred dollars from Scott, up front, he'd still have the cash, even if he chickened out at the last second. Then he'd just have to figure out how to get back downtown from the wilderness of Scarborough. It's worth a try. If he has the money, he has options; if he doesn't, he has to run with the dholes. Otherwise, who knows what would happen to Claire and her baby?

At five p.m., a loudspeaker announces that it's closing time. All visitors are asked to leave. Benny hears Scott moving next to him.

"How long should we wait?" asks Benny.

"Not long. Dusk. They've usually finished their rounds by then."

Benny decides to make his pitch for the full fee up front. "Look Scott, what you're asking me to do, it's a little dangerous."

A pause. "Well, yeah. That's why I'm paying you so handsomely, Ben."

"Right, but—I think you should give me the whole hundred up front. It's only fair."

"Don't you trust me?"

"It's just the way I like to do business," says Benny.

Scott fishes in his pockets. Instead of money, he presses his car keys into Benny's hand. "I don't have the other fifty on me, but here's the car for collateral. That do it for you?"

Benny fingers the keys and slips them into his jeans pocket. "Yeah, that'll do it."

When they come out of the shed at dusk, the rain has turned to a fine mist. The two walk side by side to the edge of the trench that fronts the dhole habitat. The dholes themselves are nowhere to be seen. Benny glances down at the deep trench. He figures he can hop the guardrail and drop over the wall, cross the trench, and scramble up the dirt slope on other side.

"Don't be nervous, Giro," advises Scott. "They'll smell your fear."

Benny looks at him. "Why are you calling me that?"

"Role playing helps get me into the creative headspace of my hero." Scott pats Benny on the shoulder. "Off you go."

Benny swings one leg over the guardrail, then the other, takes a deep breath, and lets himself drop into the trench. It's a surprisingly long way down, but the ground is soft from the rain and, luckily, he's wearing construction boots, a new rule the car wash reluctantly put in place after the government got on their asses. Once at the bottom of the trench, it's an easy scramble up the dirt slope on the far side.

As Benny slowly pulls himself to standing at the top edge of the trench, he's hit by a powerful odour. A wild animal smell of feces and rotting meat. Urine too. Dholes must mark their territory to warn off intruders, the way dogs do. Benny is acutely aware that he *is* an intruder.

When a dhole finally appears, it freezes and stares at Benny. At first, Benny thinks the animal is more frightened of him than he is of it. Then the first dhole is joined by a second. And a third. And a fourth.

The first dhole—the leader, Benny thinks—sniffs the air and takes a few cautious steps toward him. The other three crouch behind him. All the dholes are staring at him, fixedly. Their eyes are colder and wilder than a dog's, more alien. Shark-like. Benny starts to wonder whether he and the dhole pack will stay locked in a staring contest all night—until he hears a low, steady, malevolent chorus of growls.

Stay calm, stay calm, he reminds himself. They smell your

fear. Despite that, his heart picks up speed. He breaks into a sweat. Every hair on his body stands at attention. His knees began to shake and his teeth chatter. The pack leader stares him in the eye, opens his mouth, and makes a sound exactly like a human scream.

On instinct, Benny screams too.

The dholes charge at him as a pack, long legs flying through the air, jaws open, eyes fixed. Their hunting screams fill the air.

Benny turns to run, but forgets about the trench behind him. His foot comes down on nothing but air, and he goes over on his ankle. As he falls forward onto the muddy slope and starts to roll, he hears the screams of the pack surrounding him, and feels the pressure of powerful jaws clamping down on his foot. He's still rolling, but now he's dragging a dhole by his foot. He forces himself to look, expecting to see a bloody stump at the end of his leg, but the animal can't pierce his safety boot. It gives Benny's foot a frustrated shake, loosens its jaws, and tries to clamp down on his calf. Benny rolls out of reach.

He and the dhole are both at the bottom of the trench now, the other three circling. While he's trying to deke out dhole number one, the teeth of dhole number two penetrates the flesh at the back of his leg. Benny screams to Scott for help and kicks at the top of the dhole's skull with his boot. The animal retreats, but dhole number three snaps at Benny's hand, catching a finger—not solidly enough to sever it, but the pain is so sharp it triggers a burst of adrenalin. Benny hurls himself up, leaping for the guardrail, not quite making it—but his fingertips find the edge of the concrete wall. He hangs helplessly, barely able to maintain his grip. Meanwhile, the dholes scream as they spring at him from below, jaws snapping.

The pain in his wounded hand is beyond excruciating but he's more afraid of the animals eating him alive than he is of the pain. He sees Scott gazing down at him, slack-jawed, from the guardrail. His fly is open and he's jerking off as he watches Benny fight for his life.

"Give me your hand! Pull me up!" Benny screams, but Scott doesn't react. A white arc of semen hits Benny's face. The message is clear: save yourself, or be disembowelled. Benny is not sure which outcome would be better for Scott's book. He either wants to fuck his hero, or kill him. As he dangles by his fingertips, twin rivulets of blood trace down his arm and splash onto his face.

As Benny's feet scrabble against the wall, trying desperately to gain purchase, Claire's face flashes into his mind. Will she have enough strength to call for help from Vera or Marco if the baby is coming? He honestly doesn't think so. If he dies, she dies, and the baby from the black ooze dies. This thought gives him the strength to pull himself onto the wall and over the guardrail, collapsing at Scott's feet.

Scott stares at him, glassy-eyed. "Oh, Giro Giro Giro, my love," he breathes. "Look at you, you're injured, let me help you."

Benny kicks out at Scott. "Stay away from me, you sick fuck!"

"No, no, no. Let me bind your wounds, sweet Giro," he coos, like some sort of fairy queen from a fantasy novel. Scott tears off his wet shirt and wraps it around Benny's leg as a tourniquet, still cooing at him, when they hear the police sirens. The sound yanks Scott back to reality.

"Run!" yells Scott, abandoning Benny on the ground.

Benny sits up and watches Scott run for the utility shed. *What a stupid move. Doesn't he realize that's the first place they'll check?*

Slowly, Benny staggers to his feet and limps into the shadows, leaving a blood trail behind him. Once he's off the paved walkway, in the darkness of the trees and bushes and earth, his blood will be invisible to all but the dholes themselves. He can still hear them growling and screaming at the bottom of the trench.

Quietly and steadily, he keeps moving, ignoring the agony of his mangled finger and punctured leg. In the distance, he can hear voices and footsteps. Flashlights ripple along the pathways. Benny doesn't move faster or slower, just keeps heading for his goal: the parking lot.

When he reaches the front entrance, he sees a zookeeper and a cluster of cops gathered under a light stand just outside the ticket booth. Hands on their hips, laughing among themselves, the cops seem surprisingly relaxed.

"What is it this time? Someone taking tea with the tigers?" asks a cop in a voice that makes it sound as if he's there every night. "Or did some pervert expose himself in the giraffe cage?"

The zookeeper clears his throat. "This is a modern zoo, officer. No cages of any kind. In answer to your question, we believe an intruder breached the dhole enclosure."

"What the hell's a dhole?"

"Asian wild dogs. Quite dangerous when provoked."

"Maybe they took care of the intruder on their own," suggests one of the other cops.

"If so, we'll need a coroner," answers the zookeeper. "They're fierce, merciless predators. I just hope the pack hasn't been liberated by this individual or we could have a civil emergency on our hands."

The cops settle down when they hear that.

"Okay, let's take a look," says the lead cop. As they walk past Benny's hiding place, he unholsters his sidearm.

Benny listens to their voices disappear into the distance. He's worried that they've already impounded the VW but when he looks out into the parking lot, there it is, quietly waiting beside the picture of the rhino.

Leg screaming, Benny limps to the car, his bleeding hand clamped under one armpit. When Scott's key slides smoothly into the door lock, he almost drops to his knees in relief.

Once in the driver's seat, he considers waiting a few minutes to see if Scott shows up, but rejects that idea. When you run with wild dogs, you better be ready to leave the stragglers behind. Especially a straggler willing to sacrifice his friend for the sake of a good story. Benny slips the key in the ignition and peels out of the lot as quickly as the sewing machine engine will allow.

8. NOBODY'S BABY

TORONTO, DON VALLEY PARKWAY, OCTOBER 1975

BENNY ONCE SAW a headless chicken run itself to death on severed nerves. That's why he resists the urge to floor the gas pedal, forcing himself to stay under the speed limit all the way home from the zoo. He doesn't want to lose his head and attract attention from cops or anyone else.

To calm the tango in his heart, he tunes in to an Easy Listening station. Dionne Warwick is singing about guys who give her pneumonia every time they kiss, then never bother to phone her. *Sounds like Scott,* thinks Benny. *I'll never fall in love again again, either.*

Benny navigates the tangle of Toronto's outer suburbs by instinct. If you're lost, aim for the giant prick they're building, Scott once told him. He's relieved to finally see the almost-completed tower rising from the edge of Lake Ontario.

At a stoplight, he examines the leg wound through the rip in his jeans. He's still oozing blood but the bite is not as bad as he imagined—the dhole's teeth didn't go deep. The fucker did more damage to his hand, ripping open the flesh of his middle finger above the knuckle.

He rewraps his T-shirt around his left hand, grips the steering wheel with his right, and fixes his eyes on the horizon. No matter what's ahead of him, nothing could be as bad as what he's just left behind.

He cuts the engine in front of Scott's house. All the windows are dark. Even the security light at the front door is off. Benny toys with the idea that Scott's wife might have left him, once she heard from the cops. *You fucking asshole*, Monica would yell when Scott called her to bail him out. She'd pack her bags and go, leaving a void in Scott's life that Benny would have been more than happy to fill, before Scott tried to feed him to the wild dogs. There are worse things than living in a big house with a good-looking bottom who has money and lots of books, even if he is a homicidal maniac.

Benny locks up the VW, leaving the keys in Scott and Monica's mailbox so no one can claim he stole the car. With his bloodied shirt back on, he limps for home, grateful not to meet anyone on the dark street.

Letting himself in to his basement flat, he hears a sound, sharp and high and feral, so alarmingly similar to the cry of the dholes that he wonders if one of the pack tracked him home. Claire is curled on the mattress, knees to chest, hugging herself. The wild animal sounds are coming from her.

"Claire?"

She lets out a ragged sob. "Benny, where you been? It hurts so bad. I thought you'd never come back. I think I'm gonna die."

Crouching beside the mattress, he rests his hand on Claire's cheek. In the weak glow of the crookneck lamp, she looks as puffy and washed-out as the pillow she's lying on. Her skin feels chilled and damp. That can't be good.

"I'm taking you to the hospital," he says firmly, picking up his jacket from the floor. "Can you walk?"

He expects Claire to put up an argument—she hates anything to do with doctors and nurses—but she struggles to her feet, offering no resistance as Benny gently tugs a baggy sweatshirt over her head. Trailing from his hand like a leaky balloon, she shuffles and sighs and weeps as they make their way down Robert Street to College, stopping now and then to catch her breath, bending over with her hands on her knees while Benny rubs her back. The five-minute walk to the hospital takes them almost half an hour.

The Emergency Room at Doctors' Hospital is packed. Not one of the blue plastic chairs is empty. Benny stares down a kid holding his arm against his chest at a funny angle, who eventually stands up and mumbles something about giving his seat to Claire. She lowers herself into it with a sigh, then looks up at Benny, eyes wide. "I feel funny."

"Funny how?"

"Funny wet."

Benny looks down and sees a puddle spreading beneath the plastic chair. An elderly woman sitting next to Claire moves her bag away and says something to Benny in a language he doesn't understand. He is trying to knit together her meaning, when another woman takes his arm. "Your wife's water just broke. Better tell the nurse or she's gonna have the baby on the floor in front of us."

At the front desk, the nurse gives Claire a disinterested glance, then focuses on Benny's injured hand: "You look like you could use medical attention yourself."

Benny shrugs. "I got bit by a dog. I'm okay though."

The nurse lifts her eyebrows. "Let's have a doctor look at you while Mum gets squared away in Obstetrics."

As her wheelchair disappears through a set of double doors, pushed by an orderly in blue scrubs, Claire turns her head to look back imploringly at Benny. He feels uneasy about being separated from her, but the nurse makes it clear that he is not allowed to be with Claire during the birth, the delivery room being no place for a man unless he's a doctor. Besides, there's always a long wait for a first baby. The nurse points out that he'll have plenty of time to get his dog bites treated in Emerg, before he needs to go to the waiting room for expectant fathers.

Benny senses he shouldn't tell the nurse he's not the father. If he's not, who is?

Nobody, Claire would claim. At least, nothing human.

Benny sits on an examination table in his underwear, listening to cries of distress in every possible language through the privacy curtain. He feels a powerful urge to put his jeans back on and walk away. Who'd stop him? He won't announce to the nurse that he's leaving, just casually stroll through the hospital doors and back to the flat, where he'd collect *I, Robot* and a few other things. With fifty bucks in his pocket he could go almost anywhere. He has to get away from Scott, from the car wash—even from Claire, to be honest. With the baby coming, it's time to move on. Maybe he'll fall back on his original plan and go out west to find Ida and Marcello.

But as he stands with his wounded leg half-in, half-out of his jeans, he remembers that look on Claire's face as they pushed her through the double doors. Her backward glance of fear and trust. If she comes out of the delivery room and he's disappeared, he's not sure what would happen to her.

Well, they'll send her home where she belongs, he reassures himself, and starts putting his jeans on again.

What about the baby?

Well, what about it? Not my baby.

So, whose is it? The black ooze? Or the sleazy stepfather?

Either way, do you want to send Claire and her kid back to that?

If the stepfather is hurting her, he'll hurt the baby, too, when she's bigger. He likes little girls. Look what he did to Claire. Sure, she'll cry the first few times, but pretty soon, being some grown-up's special friend will start to seem normal. At least, until the ante gets upped and the grown-up starts bringing her to parties where he passes her around like candy.

And you know what that's *like, don't you, Bum Bum?*

Benny slowly removes his jeans again. Sits back down on the exam table. Puts his head in his hands. He's suddenly aware of just how exhausted he is. How much pain he's in. Oh fuck. Now he's crying, as if he's a baby himself.

When the privacy curtain whips open with a ring of metal on metal, Benny sits up fast and wipes the back of his hand across his eyes. He's ashamed of being found in tears but the doctor is looking at a clipboard, not him.

"Mr. Pesce? I'm Doctor Ferguson. What seems to be the problem?"

"Nothing much. Couple of dog bites."

The doctor has already taken Benny's hand, turning it back to front.

"Do you know who owns the dog?"

Benny shakes his head.

"We'd better contact Public Health. They'll want to talk to you and see if they can locate the animal. Might attack someone else. They'll need to isolate it and see if it shows rabies symptoms. Speaking of which, we should start you on the shots. But for now, let's just get you stitched up so you can join the other guys in the waiting room. I see by your chart that you came in with a woman in labour—your wife, I assume?"

"Claire's just a friend," clarifies Benny.

The doctor is scribbling something on his clipboard. "Well, if you're taking responsibility, you might as well know you could be here for a while. First babies are almost always a long labour."

After stitches, a Tetanus shot, a dose of painkillers, and a prescription for more if he needs them, Benny is escorted to the delivery ward by a nurse. At the front desk, a sheet of paper is presented to him. Fill it out with your wife's information, then sign here, here, and here, she tells him.

Benny stands with his pen poised over the form, wondering what to do. He doesn't even know Claire's birthdate. He makes it up, along with everything else on the form.

When he gets to "name of father," he hesitates. Will the nurse notice if his name doesn't match the one on Dr. Ferguson's clipboard? He thinks he can feel the nurse's suspicious eyes on him.

Benny identifies the father as Scott Chrysler.

Address: 45 Robert Street.

He leaves the space for a phone number blank. Benny and Claire have never been able to afford a phone. If the hospital wants to call Scott, they can get the number from directory assistance.

As Benny fills out the forms, a plan starts to take root. He can't look after this baby. Neither can Claire, living in a windowless, airless basement flat. Scott and Monica, on the other hand, have all that room—a nice big house with a yard where a kid could play. Not to mention, Monica wants a baby. Now, she can have one without Scott needing to get her pregnant. From what Benny's witnessed, there's no percentage in carrying a baby. It's misery, start to finish. He'd be doing Monica a big favour by handing her a perfectly good baby without her having to do any of the work.

Once the forms are completed, he follows the nurse to the fathers' waiting room. It's full of men Rocco and Marcello's age. Most of them look like shit. Five o'clock shadows, sprawled on vinyl couches in front of ashtrays overflowing with half-smoked cigarettes, half drunk bottles of Coke, and dirty coffee cups. One man is stretched out across several chairs, snoring, a battered copy of *Maclean's* shielding his eyes. A TV bolted to the wall with the sound turned down silently broadcasts news from the world outside the waiting room. Benny sees a house reduced to rubble, fire trucks and police cars all over the place. Must be a disaster, or maybe a war zone —some place in Israel or Ireland, maybe. When the camera focuses on a blonde woman in a stewardess' uniform, sitting in a lawn chair, Benny has a sudden sense of *dejá-vu*. Is that Ida? It couldn't be. She's out west with Marcello. But she sure looks like Ida. Benny rubs his eyes. He's got to be imagining things. Must be the painkillers.

"We got a young one here," announces the nurse brightly and the men look at him as if he's a newly caught animal dragged in by hunters.

"Welcome to purgatory, kid," says one of the men.

Benny nods hello to the men, then looks back at the TV. Ida has vanished, the disaster scene replaced by a weather report.

Most of the fathers-to-be are first-timers, but one, a brick-layer named Angelo, is waiting for his third child; an older Italian, Vince, his sixth. "Three in the old country, three here," he says, holding up his fingers in front of his face and pulling them down like ducks in a shooting gallery. "Maria, Giuseppe, Gianna, Carlo, Bruce, and now this one." He shrugs. "Gets to be old hat."

"Zat what your wife says?" jokes one of the men, and the rest of them laugh.

Angelo raises one eyebrow. "Bruce?"

Vince shrugs. "My wife, she thinks that guy on Batman's good-looking."

"Bruce Wayne," supplies Benny. "Batman's secret identity."

Vince frowns at Benny. "Look at you. You're a baby yourself. How old're you?"

"Eighteen," lies Benny, figuring it wouldn't hurt to give himself an extra year.

"Jesus," says Angelo, making a ramming motion with his fist. "Big man on campus."

Benny shrugs. "Shit happens."

The crowd grunts in agreement as if one man.

"At least you done the right thing and owned up to it," approves Vince.

Some of the guys have already been here for a day and a night. The longest is in his thirtieth hour. The nurse comes in and out, calling men's names—Mister Franco you have a beautiful boy. Mister Perreira, it's a girl. Mister Di Michaele, it's twins!

Waiting his turn, Benny drowses in the fug of cigarette smoke. He bums a few off the guys. As the room empties, he finds himself drifting off on the couch. When he wakes up, his cheek is stuck to the vinyl cushion. He's alone in the room. The clock reads four a.m. He can hear the distant ping of an intercom, female voices gently calling code blue, code yellow, code red,

Doctor McDonald, Doctor Blainey, Doctor Lee.

He wonders if the baby has been born and the nurse has forgotten to tell him. Maybe Claire had them call her mom. Maybe he, Benny, is off the hook. As quickly as the thought occurs to him, he rejects it. Claire would never take her baby back to her house on Love Canal, no matter how pretty it sounds. There's love, and there's love, thinks Benny. One kind breaks your heart. The other kind—the dirty kind of love—destroys your body and soul. Love Canal must have been named for the second kind of love.

He ponders, for a moment, which kind of love he and Scott had. Because even though Scott turned out to be completely bat-shit crazy and almost got Benny eaten alive by wild dogs, there were good times too. Love isn't simple. Benny thinks again about how great it would be to be like Mr. Spock on *Star Trek*. All logic. No love.

Late Late Movies silently flickers across the TV screen. A pretty brunette—a girl—is in bed with a young blond man. His shirt is off, his chest smooth and hairless, like Scott's. Benny turns up the sound.

A hundred dollars. I must say, she's very generous, says the brunette.

The blond man's temper flares. He starts to pull back the sheet to get out of the bed so he can throw the woman out, then realizes he's naked and hesitates. Benny snorts in disbelief. This chick just called the guy a whore. Is he really going to care if she sees his dick?

The brunette flops on the bed and tells the guy to simmer down. That she understands far too well.

So does Benny. He watches, fascinated. The movie takes place in New York City, a long, long time ago. Benny can sort-of remember people dressing like the brunette and the blond guy back when he himself was a very little kid. Yet there's something about this story that's reassuring. A girl from a grubby little town in the middle of nowhere runs away to the big city and makes money off men. Every time she goes to the powder room, she asks a guy for fifty dollars. Turns out, the blond guy is doing the same thing, more or less. Only, he's actually a writer. Like Scott.

Watching the brunette and the blond takes Benny's mind off the dull throb in his hand and leg. The painkillers have worn off. In a haze of pain and exhaustion, he starts to think that the writer in the movie is really Scott, and that the woman, Holly Golightly, is really ... well, is really Benny.

Because isn't Holly's story Benny's story too?

Holly has a wild party and plays loud cha-cha music, not rock and roll. A whole squad of cops show up to arrest everybody—for a noise complaint? New York isn't like that anymore. It's dangerous these days, full of muggings and rapes and riots, but it's also a place where a smart hustler can get rich. Especially a young, good-looking one, like the smooth blond writer. Even Benny knows that.

Oh, how I love New York, sighs Holly. She's smoking a cigarette outdoors, looking up at the skyscrapers before she flies off to Brazil with her super-rat boyfriend. The writer sits next to her in a jacket and tie. He's not a whore anymore (what do they call it when men do it—a gigolo). He's got a real job now, writing for a magazine. Outside of being in love with a woman, he seems very much like Scott.

Benny wants to know what will happen to Holly, whether she'll end up with her super-rat Brazilian boyfriend José or the formerly slutty writer, Paul. Will Paul try to feed Holly to the dogs, the way Scott did to Benny? He tries to keep his eyes open but falls asleep before the ending.

He wakes to someone shaking him and calling him sir. On the silent TV screen, a pair of hands are slicing open a tin can with a knife. "Sir, sir ... the doctor would like to speak with you about your wife."

"Friend," mutters Benny groggily.

"Come with me, please," says the nurse.

As Benny follows her down the windowless hallway, he can tell that it's early morning. Rattling racks of metal trays rumble past, pushed by men in blue uniforms. Benny can smell soggy eggs, oatmeal, buttered toast, and coffee. He's suddenly ravenous. When was the last time he ate?

"I never knew it took so long to have a baby," yawns Benny.

The nurse's mouth hardly moves. "Mum gave birth to a girl forty-five minutes ago."

She isn't smiling. There's none of the joy in her voice that he heard yesterday from the nurses announcing the birth of the other men's babies.

"Is she okay?" asks Benny.

The nurse opens and closes her mouth. Benny can see she's not sure whether he's asking about Claire or the baby. "Would you like to see her?"

Now it's Benny's turn to be confused. He nods.

The nurse leads him further down the hall and points at a window into an adjoining room. "Third bassinette from the left, front row."

A tiny head covered in thick black hair pokes out of a swaddling cloth. Claire's baby. Benny stares at her through the window. Somehow, he could never imagine the baby being so … real. He's amazed. To his own surprise and dismay, he feels a flutter of protectiveness. He reminds himself: *she's not yours*.

The nurse is gently moving him along now. "How's Claire?" Benny remembers to ask again.

The nurse doesn't look at him. "In here, please. The doctor's waiting for you."

Later, he'll remember that the room had pale green walls and that the dingy yellow privacy curtain was closed. A doctor was standing outside the curtain, his hands limp at his sides. Doctors never stand like that. They're always doing something. This one is absolutely still, as if he has nothing better to do than talk to Benny. As if time has stopped. When he sees Benny, the doctor says: "I'm afraid I have some bad news."

The doctor explains, step by step, how the birth presented. That's the word he uses—*presented*—as if childbirth were a presentation, like a movie or a carnival sideshow. Or like a TV commercial selling a knife that can slice a tin can in half. He says that Claire had something called gestational diabetes—did Benny not know that? There's a record of Claire having been given a prescription and being told to follow up at the hospital, but she never came back.

The baby was born healthy enough, all things considered. Unfortunately, and despite everything medical science could offer, Claire didn't make it.

Benny feels a wave of dizziness and leans against the wall to steady himself. The doctor puts his hand on his arm. Benny shoves him away. "I want to see her."

When the doctor pulls open the privacy curtain, the metal rings making a zipping sound. Someone is lying in the bed— Benny can see the outline of a body—with a sheet over its face. The doctor carefully folds it back. The lips are slightly open. The eyes are closed.

"I'm so sorry for your loss. We did everything we could," says the doctor.

Benny is startled by the realization that the doctor thinks that the body in the bed is Claire. It doesn't look like Claire. Not at all. The body's cheeks are slack and mottled, probably from whatever drugs they were giving her, but mostly it's as if Claire has simply vanished, leaving behind this sack of bruised flesh. She looks deflated. A dead balloon. The real Claire must have hitched a ride home to Love Canal, leaving this body in the bed to fool the nurses.

"You'll probably want to make some calls," suggests the doctor.

Benny can tell that the doctor is nervous—probably thinks that Benny thinks that it's his fault Claire died. He'll ask to see the baby. Then he decides, no, don't ask. Act like Rocco. Demand it.

"I want to see my baby now."

"Of course," says the doctor and pulls a cord to summon the nurse. Benny can tell he's relieved to escape any more talk about the dead body he's mistaken for Claire.

The nurse leads him into a place they call the Mum's Room, invites him to take a seat in a rocking chair, and places the baby in his arms, telling him to be careful to support her head. She softly closes the door behind her as she leaves.

Benny stares down at the blue-black eyes, which look up at him. The baby's gaze is intent. As if she's trying to figure out who he is.

Don't I know you from somewhere?

Benny realizes with startling certainty that the baby already recognizes him. As he does, her. They know each other well. Well, yeah; didn't he lie beside Claire all those months, this baby growing under his hand as he rubbed Claire's belly?

He wasn't sure, at first, how to hold her, but it turns out to be easy enough. She feels warm through her swaddling blanket. Like a loaf of bread fresh out of the oven.

Be Mr. Spock, Benny tells himself. Be Rocco. Be like stone. Feel nothing.

It's not working. The warm little muscle in his arms, the little person, clearly belongs to Benny. He can't not feel something for her.

Benny starts rocking, humming, the way he can distantly remember his *nonna* humming to him. The baby yawns, making a soft chirping noise. Her lips form an O. Benny offers her his pinkie. She sucks on it intently, her eyes stuck on Benny.

He knows that eventually the hospital will figure things out. Maybe they already know something is not on the up-and-up. Maybe they'll figure out that Claire is the missing girl from Love Canal. They'll make a few calls, and someone in her family will come and take the baby away. Benny doesn't even want to think about what's going to happen after that. *Be Rocco,* he decides. *Do what has to be done. Just do it.*

Benny opens his jacket and slips the baby inside—a soft, sweet-smelling bundle against his chest. The baby chirps again, as if happy to be snuggled between Benny's bloody T-shirt and a second-hand jacket stinking of cigarette smoke. He keeps his arm under the lump in his abdomen. Supporting her head.

He slips out the door and looks up and down the hallway. He can hear women's voices, but sees no one. He heads for the stairway, descends to the first floor, and opens the door marked EXIT. He finds himself at the back of the hospital next to a loading dock. Walks up the alleyway next to the hospital to College Street. They should be calling the police in, what, ten, fifteen minutes? Plenty of time to get home. But the cops won't go to Benny and Claire's basement flat. Oh no.

They'll go to the address on Claire's intake form: 45 Robert Street.

Scott's house.

As they round the corner of Robert and College, the front of a *Toronto Star* newspaper box catches his eye. A photo of a disaster scene. A blonde stewardess standing at the edge of a debris field, one hand on her face.

Benny hesitates. He looks up and down the street, then reaches in and steals a copy. Tucking it under his arm, he continues on his way.

9. RIDE INTO DARKNESS

IT'S HARD TO CONCEAL secrets in a blast of sunlight. In the weeks following the explosion, the neighbourhood shifts on its foundations like one of Mr. Cake's rooming houses. Not enough to bring down the roof on everyone's heads. Just enough to show some cracks in the walls. With her and Marcello's whereabouts known to anyone with a TV or radio, Ida wonders how long before her remaining secrets tumble into the open like dice thrown from a fist.

Despite her fears, Ida's life sweetens. The neighbours warm to her. Everyone enjoys the memory of her sitting in the lawn chair outside the barricade, nobly erect in her militaristic flight attendant uniform. Not to mention the way she flew off the handle at Mr. Cake. *Did you see her sock that guy? She's tougher than Muhammad Ali!*

There is a certain pride to be taken in a feisty neighbourhood woman standing up for herself and her man. Ida is *sfacciata*. Nervy. Gutsy, even. *She's okay, that Ida*, they're saying. She has even picked up a nickname: *La Contessa*. The Countess. Sure, it's a backhanded compliment, a good-natured jab at Ida's stiff-necked Northern Italian arrogance, but Ida doesn't mind that the neighbours accept her enough to mock her. She likes being liked, for a change.

Marcello remains simply "Cello" to the neighbours, but now buffed to the shine of a Queen's Park statue, as heroic as one of those big shots on horseback. For weeks, the neighbourhood wives have kept bringing over home-cooked meals under tea towels. The regulars at Esposito's ply him with espressos and cigars, driving him to the café while his eyes are bandaged.

Finally, on the third week after the accident, with a cold front licking at the women's red-painted toes and the men's open shirt collars, Ida drops by Esposito's. Time to put her foot down about the cigars.

"Cello is getting a cough from all this smoking. Maybe you could give him some pastries instead," suggests Ida to the proprietor.

Mike Esposito shoots an amused look at the regulars, huddled around tables with their coffees and cards, trying to pretend they're not listening. "Of course, *Contessa*! Does Cello like *cannoli*?"

"*Certo*," says Ida. "The kind with lemon custard inside."

"Are they for you? Or for your husband?" asks one card player.

"Don't make her mad! She has a wicked right hook!" warns another.

Ida tosses a smile to the laughing men as she leaves with the box of *cannoli* —compliments of the house, of course. As she walks across St. Clair Avenue toward home, she can tell the men's eyes are following her. But even after she's out of sight of Esposito's, she still feels as if she's being watched. The fine hairs at the nape of her neck tingle and lift—her personal danger signal, like the Distant Early Warning Line that is supposed to alert everyone to a nuclear attack. Ida has learned to trust this sensation, ever since Senior and Stan showed up the Seahorse looking for her and Marcello.

Someone is watching her. Possibly even following her. She's certain of it.

Using a parked car as a shield, she takes in the street from all directions but sees nothing unusual, just a few older ladies carrying their groceries in string bags, and children playing in the parkette across the street. A mother stands by a swing set, jiggling the handle of a baby buggy; she's tall and slender, a colourful granny gown billowing around her hips. Oddly, she seems to be wearing construction boots under her long floral skirt.

Ida tries to reassure herself. The coast is clear. No one is following her. Yet the uneasy tingling sensation lingers. Ever since Cello's accident, her imagination keeps working overtime, inventing disasters. Ida takes a deep, cleansing breath—the way she's been taught in Jasmine's yoga class—and heads for home with the box of cannoli, shoulders squared, chin high. She is the *Contessa*, after all.

As she nears the house, she sees a motorcycle parked in the driveway behind Marcello's battered Chevy. She admires the shine of the chrome, the thick leather saddle, the black and red insignia reading *Harley-Davidson*. A horse on wheels, she thinks, her head suddenly full of the strings and horns of the theme from *The Big Country*. She touches a handle grip, still warm from the rider's hand.

Lina Agnelli trots out to the porch in her apron, a letter in her hand. She jerks her chin at the Harley as if pointing out someone who has failed to curb a dog. "I was watching my story on TV and hear the racket on the street. I see the man go inside your house. He looks like one of those Hell's Devils. I almost call the police! Oh, and a letter come for you Ida—addressed to our house by mistake."

Ida takes the letter absentmindedly, still focused on the mysterious Harley. Wondering who could possibly be inside with Cello.

The house feels like a men's club—male laughter, the odours of beer and cigar smoke, "Conquistador" on the stereo. Ida sets the box of cannoli on the kitchen counter.

In the living room, Marcello lounges in an easy chair with one long leg thrown over the armrest, a stripe of pale skin across his forehead and nose marking where the bandage had been wrapped. The rider sits on the couch across from him, meaty arms resting on his knees as he doubles over with laughter, dressed in black leather pants and a sleeveless leather vest that exposes arms that bulge like rising bread, tattooed with skulls and the words *Ave Maria*. His hair, curly and black like Marcello's, hangs to his shoulders in ringlets, held off his face by a red bandanna knotted around his forehead. Ida takes a sharp breath: Lina Agnelli was right, the man looks like a thug. But when Marcello sees Ida, he says with joy in his voice, "Ah, here she is now," and the thug turns and shows Ida his face.

The hair on her neck tingles and rises. She knows this man from somewhere. He looks like Marcello, if Marcello were prone to getting into knife fights. A thin silver scar runs from the corner of one large brown eye, along his cheekbone, to the corner of his lip. It must have been an ugly wound when it was fresh, but it has faded to make the man's face look like that of a stone angel, damaged by vandals or neglect. His mouth is wide and full, his cheekbones sharp above the stubble of a beard, his eyes a rich chocolate, thickly lashed.

"Ida, you remember my *paesan*, Rocco Andolini," says Marcello, who is clearly delighted that the man is here. Shoulder to shoulder, the two men look like brothers.

Ida takes Rocco's hand when he offers it, then turns her cheek to be kissed. The man even smells like Marcello. Of course, he would have to be an Andolini, one of Prima's many grandsons who were always running in and out of the house where Ida lived for a few days.

"Of course I remember you," says Ida, smoothly. "Rocco Andolini, the fighter."

Rocco grins. "Boxer, not fighter. It was almost worth having a house collapse on Cello so I could find him. And you."

Ida, for once, doesn't know what to say. Finally she manages: "This is your motorbike outside?"

"Yeah, but it's no bike—it's a chopper."

"I am sorry, I don't know the correct English words for so

many Canadian things," she says, waving her misaddressed letter in the air for emphasis. "It's a very, a very—attractive *macchina*. Speedy looking."

"I can take you for a ride later if Cello doesn't mind."

Marcello laughs. "I'd be afraid she'd want one for herself. Ida's just learning to drive the Chevy, and she's already talking about getting her pilot's licence."

Rocco raises his eyebrows. "That so? Well, well. Not many chicks would have the guts for that," he says, looking her over again with those soft eyes. "I like strong women."

Ida feels as though she's been dipped in melted chocolate.

"Rocco's on his way west," says Marcello. "I told him, stay for dinner."

"Only if it's no trouble," adds Rocco, dropping his head slightly as though asking permission.

Ida lifts her chin. "I would insist on it, if Marcello hadn't already. Just give me a moment to change out of my work clothes."

Ida goes into the kitchen, her face warm, unbuttoning her blazer. She thoughtlessly slips the letter Lina Agnelli gave her between the toaster and the wall, the handwritten name *Ida Umbriaco* magnified in the dome of the electric kettle. Forgetting about it immediately, she goes to the bedroom to change. She pulls out a pair of pretty flats, then decides to stay barefoot, suspecting that Rocco will find her pink toenails charming.

When Ida returns to the kitchen, she stops to fill a pot with water for *penne*. In the next room, the men speak in raised voices, louder than they realize. This happens all the time since Marcello's eardrums burst.

She hears Rocco say, "He won't stop until he finds you."

Marcello answers, "I'll get my lawyer to force him to agree to a divorce. Annulment be damned. That way he won't have any right to Ida, even if the Church thinks he does."

"Better hurry it up, brother. Until she's *your* property, he considers her *his*."

Ida has broken into a light sweat, even though she is standing stock still. She braces her back against the counter, staring at the modern kitchen fixtures in harvest gold and avocado green. *My fridge. My stove. My property.* It's just beginning to sink in that Cello and Rocco are talking about her. What do they think she is—an appliance?

"Ida isn't 'property,' Roc."

"I'm telling you what they think, not what I think."

She forces herself to slow her breathing and the wild tango of her heart. Senior still hasn't given up. Still wants her back. Still wants revenge. But they are not children anymore, she tells herself. Everyone in the neighbourhood knows and cares about them. And Cello's best friend Ed is a lawyer. How can anyone try to hurt them? She and Marcello are still—*come si dice?*—respectable.

And yet, Ida feels sweaty fear settling around her shoulders like a shawl. Their trespasses haven't been forgotten or forgiven in Shipman's Corners. She straightens her spine under her thin T-shirt before she goes back into the living room.

"Dinner will be ready in an hour," she says crisply, sliding out her Air Canada voice like a linen serviette from its wrapper. "What shall we have for *apperitivi*?"

Ida serves the *penne all'arrabbiata* with a little extra oregano—very good with the wine she is serving. After espresso and *cannoli*, the three sit sipping grappa that Ida has poured into cut crystal liqueur glasses. A little extravagance she picked up on sale at Eaton's.

"How's Pasquale getting along at Prima's?" asks Marcello.

Rocco clears his throat and stares down at the table. "She passed away last spring."

Marcello puts his hand on his heart. "I'm sorry to hear that, Roc. She was like a mother to me. How'd Pasquale take it?"

Rocco stares down at the table. "He doesn't know. He'd already run away by then."

Marcello's glass stops halfway to his mouth. "You're kidding. What the hell happened?"

Rocco shrugs, eyes still lowered. "Bad blood between him and Dad. That's why I'm headed west. Dad wants me to track him down and haul his ass back to the farm."

"I do not understand this. Why would your father want Pasquale back if they quarrelled?" asks Ida.

Rocco grimaces. Ida notices that he's still not meeting her eyes.

"The night the kid took off, he made a cash withdrawal from the Bank of Prima. Five hundred bucks out of her underwear drawer. The shock gave her a stroke. She poured her heart and soul into looking after the kid and look how he repays her. Dad's wanted to get his hands on him every since."

"Why do you think he went west?" asked Marcello.

"He said he was going to look for you two. He figured you were still on the run."

Marcello says, "We're done running, Roc. We just want to live a regular life. Get married. Have kids."

At the mention of kids, Ida glances at Marcello who refuses to meet her gaze. A sore topic between them, even now.

"If you didn't want to be found, Cello, you shouldn't have let a house drop on you," points out Rocco, refilling all their glasses with grappa.

After dinner, Rocco takes Ida for the promised ride on the Harley. She climbs on the back, straddling the wide saddle, following Rocco's instructions to slide hard against him and wrap her arms around his waist. With Ida sitting on the idling chopper, Marcello carefully places Rocco's spare helmet on her head, tightening the chinstrap. "Wouldn't want anything to happen to my little *testadura*."

"Ready?" Rocco yells, as he backs the Harley onto Barrie Avenue. Before Ida can answer, he guns it.

The rush of wind in her face, the sense of flying through empty space without the metal cage of a car or plane around her, is so exhilarating to Ida that for a few moments, her breath will only come in gasps. She clings tightly to Rocco, her face against the wall of his leather-clad back, her nose full of his Marcello-smell. She quickly learns to become one with him whenever he goes around a curve, moulding her body into the wall of his back and butt.

Rocco blasts along St. Clair to Oakwood, loops east to Bathurst, and south toward the lake, rocketing up the on-ramp to the Gardiner Expressway. They fly past massive billboards and tops of water towers and roofs of buildings. At one point, Ida realizes they're passing the spot where the boarded-up Seahorse Motel waits to be demolished to make way for a ten-storey apartment building. It's been a long time since she picked dandelions in the empty lots under the Expressway.

Eventually the Gardiner blends into the Lakeshore, and then into the highway. Ida begins to see signs reading QEW WEST. *He's not turning around; he's kidnapping me and taking me west,* thinks Ida. She knows she should thump a fist against the broad wall of Rocco's back, but instead she tightens her arms around him.

When they reach the city limits of Oakville, Rocco pulls onto a country road. They're flying past fields and barns now, the eye of the sun split open as it sets in the sky. Ida is both relieved and disappointed when Rocco slows and pulls onto the gravel verge on the side of the road. He straddles the bike with the engine idling, arms spread and head lowered, for so long that Ida finally shouts: "Is something wrong? Why are you stopping?"

Rocco shakes his helmeted head slowly, then looks up at the sinking sun.

"Just catching my breath," he shouts back.

He heel-toes the chopper back a few paces, then reverses direction, speeding back toward Toronto. Soon, Ida sees the city skyline on the horizon. She feels strangely let down.

When they finally coast back to Barrie Avenue, Ida sees Marcello in the driveway, grinning as the two of them roar in.

He helps Ida out of the helmet. "I wondered if you were ever coming back. What did you think?"

"I love it!" she says, pulling herself unsteadily off the saddle, her knees jellying beneath her.

"Don't get too excited, these things can be dangerous," cautions Marcello, gently cupping Ida's face with his hand.

Ida turns away. Why can't Marcello let her enjoy this small adventure without talking to her as if she's a child? She feels a prick of irritation, watching the two men crouch together in the driveway to examine the engine. Ida stands silently, holding the empty helmet, a bystander to the dangerous world of men. She can visit it now and then, but she can tell that Marcello prefers her safely at home. Even her career as a flight attendant has a tentative feeling to it, as if Marcello thinks of it as an interlude in her life, a short period of independence before they have children. If she can have children. Marcello's expectations unsettle her. She tries not to think about them.

It's decided that Rocco will stay the night. Ida gathers bedding from the upstairs closet and brings it downstairs. In the darkened living room, she pulls the cushions off the couch and Rocco yanks the folding bed from the frame. She busies herself making up the pull-out couch with the neat hospital corners Jeanie taught her at the Seahorse. When she straightens up, she sees that Rocco has taken his shirt off.

The two of them stand looking at one another. She feels herself sinking into those chocolate eyes again.

"That was fun, riding your chopper," Ida says. "I thought you were going to forget to bring me home."

"That was the plan. I just didn't have the stomach for it."

Ida stares at him uncertainly, the nape of her neck tingling again. "Plan?"

Rocco rubs his eyes. "Forget it. Bad joke. I just meant, I liked having you with me, on the back of my bike."

"Is that so?" says Ida, one of the couch cushions pressed to her chest.

"Yeah, it's so."

Ida steps closer to him. "Can I ask you a question? Something personal in nature."

Rocco crosses his arms and takes a half-step back. "I got nothing to hide."

Ida is not sure what she's doing, except that somehow she knows it's the right thing to do. A way to balance things between her and Rocco.

"Why do you feel shame when you talk about Pasquale?" she asks.

Rocco visibly tenses. She's struck a nerve, as Marcello would say. "What makes you think I'm ashamed of something?"

Because I know shame when I see it, thinks Ida, but says, "When you talk of him, I feel you had some part in his running away. For example, that he shared with you his destination after stealing Prima's money seems strange. That you search for him now seems like a guilty act."

Rocco steps closer to her. "It's not Bum Bum I feel guilty about. It's you, Ida. Okay, you asked, so I'll tell you how this was really supposed to go down. The chopper ride was not supposed to end with me bringing you back to Marcello. I was going to take you all the way home to your real husband in Shipman's Corners. Senior made a deal with me."

Ida's throat is so dry, she can barely ask, "What sort of deal?"

Rocco stands looking into the darkness of the room, but not at Ida. "One night, out on the farm, Senior caught me doing something that would've pissed off Dad. Bad enough to get me thrown out of the family. Senior said if I found you and brought you back to him, so he could teach you a lesson, he'd keep his mouth shut. In the end, I just couldn't do it. Forgive me."

The couch cushion falls out of Ida's arms. All this time, watching and waiting for someone outside, when the threat was waiting right here at home. Laughing with Marcello in her living room. Eating her penne. Drinking her grappa.

"You were going to betray me? Kidnap me?" she finally manages to say.

He lowers his head like a boy. "Don't tell Marcello till I'm gone, okay?"

Ida stares at Rocco in silence. No wonder he reminds her of a fallen angel. "Why would I not wake Marcello and tell him right now?"

Rocco lifts his chin to her, as if issuing a challenge. Suddenly the room seems very dark and he seems very large. "Because if you do, I'll tell him what I know about you, Ida. Why you married Senior. Why you came so cheap."

Ida steps closer to him. She can see a crown of thorns, tattooed onto his chest. Summoning all her strength, she hauls her hand back and slaps Rocco's face. His eyes flicker slightly.

"You should remember who your friends are. I could have taken you back to Bramborough by force and I didn't," says Rocco.

"Go before the sun comes up," Ida says, and turns her back on Rocco, her neck tingling as she walks up the stairs.

Behind her his voice rises softly, "Don't worry. Now we're all in the same boat. I have to get the hell out of Dodge too."

In the bedroom, Ida finds Marcello asleep with his glasses on, textbooks scattered on the comforter. She leans over and removes his glasses, placing the books on the floor. He isn't supposed to strain his eyes by reading, just yet. She clicks off the lamp and lies in bed, rigid as a statue, staring at car headlights washing across the ceiling.

A few minutes later, she hears the sound of the front door closing and a motorcycle engine cycling through its gears as it picks up speed. Rocco's shame has propelled him back into the darkness where he belongs. Ida rolls onto her side, away from Marcello, and lets her tears leak out without making a sound.

She wakes up the next morning alone. The empty sheets are washed by sunlight. She sits up and rubs her head. The previous evening has a groggy, unreal quality to it. Pulling on her robe, she patters downstairs to a silent house. The remains of breakfast litter the kitchen table. A message jotted on the back of a sheet of paper covered with equations, reads simply: GONE JOGGING. M.

Ida sighs. Jogging is part of Marcello's new health regimen, along with quitting smoking. And he does jog—miles, in fact, up to the St. Clair reservoir, around Casa Loma and back—straight to Esposito's for a post-jog espresso and a cigar.

Ida starts clearing the kitchen table. As she moves plates and cups to the sink, she notices the letter Lina Agnelli gave her yesterday, reflected in the kettle.

Ida pulls it out with one hand while she balances two dirty dishes in the other. When she reads the return address, the plates fall to the floor.

Gripping the envelope, she stands barefoot among the dirty shards, feeling as shattered as the dishes. Picking her way around the splintered mess, she gets a sharp knife out of the drawer and goes into the living room. Carefully, she slits the top of the envelope and eases out two pale blue sheets of airmail paper. It is some time before she can force herself to read the dense, precise handwriting she knows well.

First, he apologizes for driving her out of Italy.

Next, he states that it is time to put the past behind them and start anew.

He says their relationship is too important—"too fundamental" is the literal meaning—to let die. Or worse, to pretend it never happened. Which, of course, was what she had always accused him of doing. Regardless of the consequences, he wants to own up to his responsibility to her. His love for her.

I never knew how much I treasured you, until were you gone, he writes.

He knows that he should have said something before Ida flew away to Canada. He should have stopped her from going through with the ridiculous proxy marriage. But if we do not own up to our sins eventually, how will we be forgiven? How will we be redeemed? Can she forgive him after all this time?

Please write back.

He offers her all his love and signs his name, *Paolo*.

Ida's father never reveals how he obtained her address or learned her new last name.

When she finishes reading, she creases the letter neatly, slides it back into the envelope, and sets it in her lap. She has read an expression in books, *Crying as though her heart would break* (it was always a woman doing the crying and the breaking). It seemed a stupid way to describe sorrow, but she understands it now. For precisely a quarter-hour, Ida cries as if her heart will break. Then she goes upstairs, pulls a suitcase from the bedroom closet, and starts tossing clothes inside. When everything she owns has been stuffed into it, she sits down on the bed. She lies down beside her suitcase and stares at the ceiling.

What am I doing, running again? What will he do if he gets home and I'm gone? Should I wait and try to explain, then say goodbye? Or just leave?

Through the Venetian blinds, the morning sun stripes her overflowing suitcase with bars of light. If she leaves now, the years with Marcello will recede behind her as she rides off down the road, disappearing along with her other memories.

She thinks about the look of concentration on Marcello's face as he does his schoolwork, the muscles of his arms tensing as he turns a wrench in the Chevy's failing engine, the cadences of his voice when he tries to make her laugh, the way he strokes her face after they make love, or puts a hand over her eyes when they listen to some new record album, assuming that she will be as transported by the music as he is. If she leaves him, she'll eventually forget the hours they've spent listening to opera, sharing food and wine, arguing about politics while Ida cooks—or he does; lately she's started to suspect he's better in the kitchen than she is. And then there is the absolute, unwavering affection he shows her. She can lean into Marcello's broad chest and cry, or shout with indignation about some male chauvinist pig on the plane that day, or complain about how fat she feels with her period or how tired she is after a double shift, and he will always wrap her in his arms and say something to make her feel comforted. And there's that particular combination of smells he has: lemon soap, motor oil, basil, sweat. Sometimes Ida likes to stick her nose into his body and take a deep sniff, causing him to laugh, "What the hell are you doing?"

In short: she loves him. But she also loves the possibility that she can be reinvented, that nothing is written or defined for her, that her past is forgotten. Until Paolo's letter arrived, she didn't even have to think about where she came from anymore.

Marcello, on the other hand, wants security. A comfortable, predictable life looking after Ida and creating the large, loving family he craves so much. If only, thinks Ida, there was a way for her to give him all that and breathe the fresh air of changing times too.

She dumps the contents of her suitcase on the bed and begins to hang up her clothes again.

By the time Marcello returns from his jog, the kitchen floor is swept, the table tidied, the blue letter hidden in Ida's lingerie drawer under a stack of flannel nighties. She's even been next door to have a quick word with Lina Agnelli about what to do if any other misaddressed letters come for her: "No need to trouble Cello with them, just pass them over to me."

When Marcello runs up the steps, stinking of sweat and Cuban tobacco, Ida is sitting on the porch with a library book, her eyes masked by large sunglasses.

"Did you have a nice run?" she asks, putting down *Jonathan Livingston Seagull*.

By way of answer, Marcello leans down to kiss her. Ida takes his hand, leads him to the upstairs bathroom, and turns on the bathtub faucet. As hot water fills the tub, she strips off her jeans, shirt, panties, and bra, and steps into the water. Marcello takes off his clothes, too, and slides in behind her, his long legs surrounding her.

As the steaming water rises higher and higher around them, Ida unwraps a fresh bar of soap, and hands it back to Marcello who slowly, lovingly, begins to wash both of them clean.

Later, after they've washed, made love, and dressed, she will tell him about Rocco's treachery.

The painful letter, she will keep to herself. It contains more words of affection from her father than she's ever heard outside of a confession box.

10. HALF-COCKED

TORONTO, BARRIE AVE., OCTOBER 1975

BANG. A DOOR SLAMS and Benny opens his eyes to sunlight knifing through the windshield of the Chevy. He knows this car so well, it might as well have been his boyhood bedroom. In fact, it practically was. This car was his refuge on hot summer nights, the year Marcello befriended him, taught him to read, then abandoned him to Prima.

Now here he is again, sleeping in the Chevy, this time in Vera's dress. He's been disguised as a woman ever since showing up at Vera and Marco's door with Claire's baby, looking for a place to hide. For weeks, he's been wearing a long, curly black wig from Vera's stripper days. A little foundation and lipstick, and Benny makes a very passable woman. Vera tells him he looks like Cher, even with construction boots under his skirt because his feet are too big for any of Vera's shoes. The important thing is, he doesn't look like Claire's boyfriend anymore. The cops have been trying to find Pasquale "Benny" Pesce, a former employee of Gentleman's Hand Touch Car Wash, the prime suspect in a baby-snatching. Worse, they've managed to connect Claire with the missing pregnant teenage girl from Love Canal, New York. Claire's mother and stepfather have appeared on the news every night, tearily calling for the return of their beloved granddaughter. The *Toronto Sun* ran a photo of them under a headline blaring BRING BACK OUR BABY! Claire's mom, a puffy-faced, drugged-looking blonde, held up a Bible. The stepfather, a skinny car salesman with a bad dye job on his blow-dried hair, hid from the camera behind tinted aviator glasses. Benny hates both of them on sight; when they appear on TV, he hugs the baby to his chest, the sour-sweet smell of her newly hatched scalp filling him with a maddening protectiveness.

"Over my dead body will those two get their hands on you. No way, after what they did to Claire," Benny tells the baby, flat out. He thinks she understands. Her eyes, black as an oil slick, fasten onto his as she sucks furiously on the nipple of a bottle of formula, the fingers of one hand gripping Benny's thumb with the determined strength of the Incredible Hulk.

When a TV reporter asks about the baby's father, the sleazy stepfather stares at his shoes while Claire's mom says in her flat, Western New York accent: *Well, you know young people these days, they've lost their way. Could be any of the boys on the senior basketball team I'm afraid. But even though the baby was conceived in sin, Karl and I will bring her up in the spirit of the Lord.*

Once, Claire's brother showed up on screen in a wheelchair beside his parents, his thick blond head drooping to his chest. No wonder Claire didn't think he'd have to go to Vietnam.

With Vera's help, Benny's been looking after Noname in the back room where Marco forges fake IDs. He's provided Benny with a driver's licence identifying him as "Holly Golightly." He's working on a passport in Benny's soon-to-be real name— *Ben Pisces*—which Benny thinks has a certain glamour. It's the name he plans to go by when he escapes to New York.

Vera wanted to name the baby, right away—she suggested Charlene—but Benny said it was bad luck to name anything you weren't going to keep. Like Holly and her nameless cat. It was Marco who suggested "Noname," pronouncing it *No-nah-mee*. Which, they all agreed, was a pretty name for a baby girl, even if temporary.

"Once you give her a real name, I'll forge her a nice birth certificate as a gift," volunteers Marco.

Benny and Vera came up with a way to get baby supplies without attracting attention. While she distracted the sweating, pimply-neck pharmacist in the College Street Rexall with questions about vaginal lubricating creams, Benny loaded up a hockey bag with disposable diapers and Similac. He bottle-feeds the baby while rocking her in an old La-z-Boy of Marco's, then puts her down to sleep in a dresser drawer they've converted to a bassinette. The baby eats voraciously, shits copiously, and seems healthy, as far as the three of them can tell.

Today, Vera and Marco are looking after Noname, but it's clear the arrangement can't go on much longer. With all the news stories about the missing baby, they're nervous that the police will knock at the door and hear her cry. Not that Noname cries much—she's what Vera calls, "a good baby." Smart, too, thinks Benny, her deep black eyes following him knowingly, everywhere he goes. He's convinced she can read his mind, as if she's from Vulcan. He wishes Mr. Spock had fathered Noname instead of that douchebag car salesman.

The cops have already been to Scott's house and ruled him out as a suspect, although not before taking him in for questioning. Scott pretty much freaked out when Benny showed up at his house the next day and proposed his plan to give the baby to Monica.

"Are you out of your fucking mind?" was the way Scott put it.

Monica had left Scott when the zoo story came out in the *Star*—making the plan even better, in Benny's opinion. He didn't really want Scott hanging around the baby. Monica was a woman and therefore trustworthy. Once she saw Noname, she'd no doubt fall in love with her, just as Benny had. Better to have Scott out of the picture altogether. But when Benny tried to explain this, setting out his arguments in a logical, Spock-like fashion, Scott freaked out all over again.

"Get the hell out before I call the cops," he threatened. This, from a guy out on bail for cruelty to animals. Benny was pretty sure that the cops were the last people he'd call.

With Monica and Scott and Vera and Marco out of the running as parents, Benny needs a Plan B. He can't stay in disguise forever. Eventually, the cops will track him down. Besides, he's decided that his destiny is to start fresh in New York City. Instead of picking up guys in nightclubs the way Holly Golightly did, Ben Pisces will work the discos, hustling bankers and movie stars. Now he just has to convince Ida and Marcello to agree to raise Noname.

When Benny realized the woman in the uniform on TV was Ida—and the man trapped under the house, Marcello—it was as if one of the old dead gods had gifted him with the perfect plan, one even better than the Scott-and-Monica plan. But first, Benny wants to make sure that they are still the heroic man and kind woman he remembers them to be. What if Ida has turned into a bitch and Marcello a prick? Benny wants to know what's under their fingernails before entrusting them with Claire's baby.

With Noname in a buggy that Benny quietly stole off a front porch two streets away, he took the subway and streetcar to the neighbourhood known as the Corso Italia. The *Toronto Star* said that Marcello and Ida lived on Barrie Avenue. Figuring out their house number was a cinch: he just watched the flow of housewives arriving at the door with casseroles and trays of lasagna. For a week, he'd had the place under surveillance but was only spotted once, when Ida saw him hanging around in the parkette. Benny was pretty sure she didn't recognize him in his dress and wig. As far as he could tell from his walks up and down the street, Marcello and Ida were well-liked by their neighbours and their habits were routine. Peeping through their windows at night, he was happy to see signs of affection between them. Kisses, hugs, lovemaking, the works. And there were a lot of books in the house. All proof that they deserved to be Noname's parents.

Benny decided that he would simply walk up to Marcello and Ida's front door with Noname in his arms and knock, like Ed

MacMahon appearing at a sweepstakes winner's home with a giant cheque. *Congratulations, you have been selected!* But before he could push the buggy across the street, Rocco roared up on a chopper. That was a bad surprise. What the hell was Marcello doing, hanging around with Rocco? Maybe Marcello wasn't quite the Mr. Wonderful everyone thought he was.

Benny couldn't be careless about this baby's future, the way others had been careless with his and Claire's. He took Noname home, coming back today before dawn to see what Rocco was up to. Judging by the absence of the chopper in the driveway, the asshole wasn't there anymore. That was a relief. Maybe Marcello had sent him packing.

He considers bringing Noname back in a bassinette and leaving her at the door with a note, the way his *nonna* said they used to do with orphans in the old country, but it was kind of chilly to leave a baby outdoors even for a short time. Yawning, he finally decides to sack out in the old Chevy and think things over. Like Marcello always said: *When you go off half-cocked, you're bound to do something stupid.* Words to live by. Benny takes out his set of lock-picks, jimmies the door of the Chevy, and crawls into the back seat to snuggle under an old blanket that smells of mould and mothballs. Before he can make a single intelligent, well-considered decision, he falls asleep.

He wakes up with a start when the car door bangs. It's daylight—shit, how long has he been asleep?

Peering out from under the blanket he can see the back of a head covered in black curly hair—damp, as if freshly washed. It's Marcello, for sure. He reaches over the seat to toss a baseball bat in back; Benny stifles a groan when it cracks him in the shin. Marcello flicks on the radio, turning it up full blast. He slams open the glove, pulls out a pack of Rothmans, tamps one out, lights up, and sticks the key in the ignition. The car coughs once, twice. The engine reluctantly turns over and Marcello

Marcello wheels out of the driveway. Fast. He's muttering to himself. Benny hears the words, "Fucking Rocco." *No guff,* thinks Benny.

He lies absolutely still, trying not to let the dusty blanket makes him sneeze. Through the window, he sees telephone poles and street signs fly by. Soon, they're accelerating past the tops of buildings and billboards suspended in the sky. They must be on the Gardiner Expressway. Where the hell is Marcello going, all pissed off?

When he sees a sign reading QEW WEST NIAGARA, Benny knows. Marcello is driving either to Bramborough or Shipman's Corners, taking Benny right back to where he started. Driving toward Senior, the one guy Marcello should avoid at all costs. Benny decides he can't wait any longer. He sits up in the back seat and yells: "STOP!"

Marcello turns his head, sees him, almost veers into the next lane, curses, and pulls into the breakdown lane. "Who the hell are you?" he shouts.

"It's me, Benny. I mean, Pasquale."

"Why're you dressed like a woman?"

"Pull off at the next exit and I'll tell you."

Marcello exits at Lakeshore, pulling into the parking lot of the boarded-up Seahorse. They sit side by side, both in mild shock. When Marcello finally reaches out to him, Benny is at first alarmed—is he going to get socked? But Marcello pulls him into his arms in a bear hug. "It's good to see you, man," says Marcello. "But what the living hell is going on?"

For a half hour, they sit smoking and talking below the overhead roar of the Gardiner, getting one another up to speed on the past six years. When Benny explains the circumstances of Noname's birth, Marcello asks, "Why don't you just bring her to Children's Aid? They'll find a home for her. People are always looking for babies to adopt."

"No fucking way," states Benny. "Number one, the first thing they'll do is give her to Claire's family. Those creeps should never, ever have this baby. Number two, if Claire's parents don't get the baby, I want to know who does. What if she gets adopted by maniacs? Or ends up in foster homes for the rest of her life?"

"Okay, okay, I get it," allows Marcello. "So who's gonna look after her?"

"You and Ida," says Benny.

"Come on," says Marcello. "Are you serious?"

Benny nods. "You and Ida. I'm serious."

Marcello says nothing for a few minutes. "Ida lost a baby in B.C. Little boy. He was stillborn. Messed her up for a long time."

"That's why she'll want this one," encourages Benny. "You should see her, Cello! She's cute, smart, and healthy as hell. Hardly even cries. You're not going to find a better baby than this one."

"She's a baby, not a puppy," says Marcello, lighting a fresh Rothman off the end of the old one. "Anyway, I can't think about this now. Senior's waiting to see me. We're gonna have it out. Once and for all."

"He's *waiting* for you?" Benny stares at Marcello. "Waiting to kill you, more like. You telling me that you actually talked to him?"

Marcello nods. "Rocco showed up last night. I thought it was a social call but turns out, Pop sent him to kidnap Ida and take her back. He just won't give up on her. Enough is enough. We agreed to meet at the Andolinis. Neutral ground."

Benny barks out an angry laugh around his cigarette. "The only Andolini who's on your side is Prima."

Marcello clears his throat. "Prima's dead."

Benny thinks about Prima's five hundred dollars, now pissed away in rent and food and useless vitamins for Claire. He stifles an impulse to make the sign of the cross. "Sorry to hear. But, listen, Cello. Senior *doesn't* want Ida back. He wants *revenge*."

"He's gotta listen to reason some day," answers Marcello.

"What're you planning to say to him with that baseball bat?" asks Benny.

Marcello shrugs. "Might encourage him to sign the annulment papers."

Benny stares at Marcello, scarcely believing how stupid he is for a smart guy. He considers pressing his hands to Marcello's face in the Vulcan mind meld. Anything to get him to turn around and drive to Robert Street. He decides to try a combination of shame and logic.

"For about a week, I've had your house staked out. Watching you. You've already got everything a guy could want. Friends. A home. Work. Shelves full of books. You got *Ida*, for Christ's sake, even if she's legally married to Senior. Big fucking deal. It's 1975. No one cares about that shit anymore. Nobody's gonna touch you—not even Senior. He'd be afraid, now that everyone knows what a big hero you are. You should just go home, stop worrying about the fucking annulment, and live your fucking life."

Marcello checks his watch with obvious impatience. "You coming or staying?"

Benny won't let it go. "Kill your father or *be* a father. You can only do one with a baseball bat. For the other, I can help you."

Marcello takes a deep breath. "I want my own baby. One Ida and I make. Not the spawn of some sleazy car salesman and his holy roller wife. *Capisci?*"

This shocks Benny. It's not the kind of thing Marcello would have said in the old days, when he was saving Benny from parents as awful as Claire's. Maybe Marcello *has* turned into a prick, after all. Impatiently, Marcello reaches into the glove and pulls out a pack of matches and a pencil. "Okay, I'm wasting time here, for Chrissakes, what's the fucking address?"

"Huh?"

"Where you've got the baby hidden. I'll finish with Senior and meet you later."

"After the bloodshed, you mean? After you've beaten your father's brains in, you're going to drop by and kiss the baby?"

Marcello rubs his eyes with thumb and forefinger, as if he's getting a headache. Good. Benny can see that's he's finally getting through to him.

"What's Ida think of all this? The part where you kill your father and try to get away with it, I mean."

"I didn't have a chance to tell her. She's at a women's rights demo today. A march or protest or something."

"You should've told her," says Benny.

Marcello, hands on hips, spits into the dirt. "Ida doesn't need to know everything."

Benny weighs whether to take a swing at Marcello. He probably has fifty pounds on Benny, but Benny could still do some damage.

Don't go off half-cocked. Work with what you got, Benny tells himself, trying to calm his fury. Marcello may not be good enough to be Noname's father but he's the only choice Benny's got. He grabs the matchbook and pencil from Marcello, scribbles the Robert Street address, and tosses the matchbook at Marcello's feet. Turning, he heads for Lakeshore Road.

"Where you going?" calls out Marcello.

"The fuck away from you," answers Benny.

As Benny dips his thumb into the flow of eastbound traffic, he hears the sound of the Chevy engine, coughing its way to the Gardiner on-ramp. A gleaming silver Cadillac slows and pulls to the curb in front of him, a middle-aged guy in a suit peering at Benny through the windshield. When Benny trots up to the passenger side window, the man calls out: "Where you headed, miss?"

The guy looks safe enough, decides Benny. And if he tries something funny, he could probably take him. You gotta consider these things when you're hitchhiking as a woman. "Anywhere along Spadina would be great."

The man shakes his head. "I can get you close, but Spadina's closed for that protest march. Bunch of women's libbers burning their bras. How's Bathurst?"

Benny opens the door and slides in. "Close enough, man. Close enough."

11. AMBUSH

TORONTO, HIGH PARK AVE., OCTOBER 1975

IDA PUTS ASIDE "DOWN WITH" and paints "FREEDOM TO CHOOSE NOW," pondering the meaning of the words. Jasmine comes outside in a long, faded skirt, her braless breasts bouncing under a tube top. She's carrying a placard that reads "STOP THE SPADINA EXPRESSWAY NOW!"

"We can paint over this one and reuse it," she advises Ida, looking over her shoulder at the sign. "Darling, what's with this 'freedom to choose'? You need to be more direct: 'ABORTION RIGHTS NOW!' And you and I should talk about passive resistance."

Ida picks up a fresh brush and dips into can of white paint. She starts painting over SPADINA. "You already told me, Jasmine: sit down on the ground and go limp because it is hard for the cops to carry a dead weight. I know this but I do not plan to be arrested."

Jasmine snorts. "No one plans to, darling. But it happens. Things get out of hand."

Ida turns back to finishing her FREEDOM sign, silently disagreeing. This is Toronto. If there's one place where things don't get out of hand, this is it. Sometimes it seems like a city full of sweater-clad old *nonnas* constantly fussing over people's drinking and gambling and love lives, while at the same time slyly electing this playboy of a prime minister again and again, along with the rest of the country.

Marcello has absorbed a bit of that Canadian diffidence too, although when she told him of Rocco's treachery, he became so enraged that he leapt out of their bed, ran downstairs, made a phone call, came back upstairs, dressed, and left the house without speaking to her. When she followed him out to the driveway, and asked him where he was going, he shouted, "I'll tell you when I'm back."

Blowing off steam over Rocco, no doubt. Probably spending the day at Esposito's.

"Dinner at seven," she said, watching him pull out of the driveway like a mad fiend. Ida didn't even have a chance to remind him she was going to the women's march.

On the other hand, why would he care? She'd be back in plenty of time to make the risotto.

Before the demo, Ida needs to finish her shopping. She walks into Bertinelli's, list in hand: *Asiago* cheese, Arborio rice, basil fresh-not-the-dried-stuff.

Almost hidden in the narrow aisles of the store is Angela So-and-So—so called, because for a long time people didn't know whether she was married to her brother-in-law Tony Lo Presti or was his housekeeper. Angela is a tiny ghost of a woman, probably in her mid-twenties, who never comes out of the shadows. The story going around is that back in Italy, Angela was forced to marry Tony by proxy after the sudden death of her sister here in Toronto. She was sent to cook and clean for Tony, presumably to sleep with him, and to wipe noses and teach prayers to her niece and nephew. Ida's heart is always slightly wrenched by the sight of her, a thin, young woman who is already starting to look middle-aged. She's lived here a year but has never been able to get the hang of English. Ida suspects she doesn't want to, as if being able to speak the language will trap her here forever.

Once, looking out the window of the house on a Sunday morning, Ida was shocked to see Angela walking behind her husband, head bowed and shoulders stooped. At first she just thought Angela was trying to catch up with Tony but it became obvious that this was the way they walked together: Tony striding ahead, Angela cowering behind. Tony has a reputation for being a bully; Ida wonders what happened to wife number one.

Ida walks down the aisle, basket on her arm, and smiles at Angela. "*Come stai?*" Ida asks her, gently touching her arm. "*Stai bene?* How are you? Are you well?"

Angela tugs her thin cardigan around her shoulders and gives a quick, sharp nod, not wanting to look at Ida straight on. That's when Ida notices dark patches on her pale cheeks, daubed with foundation. Cover Girl medium-light, Ida thinks, the same shade she herself uses to turn her face into a blank canvas for work. No wonder Angela stays in the shadows: that bastard Tony has been hitting her.

In Italian, Ida whispers, "Angela! Is someone hurting you?"

Angela looks at Ida now, eyes wide. The woman is clearly terrified. She shakes her head, quickly. "No, *signora*. I'm just tired."

Ida takes her hand. "*Mi chiamo Ida.* I'm called Ida. If anyone ever hurts you or you need help, you come to me. I'm your sister. You know where I live, yes? Next door to Agnellis."

Angela again gives a quick nod. "*Grazie, signora*, but don't say you are my sister. You don't want to be my sister. She's dead."

Ida touches Angela's hand quickly and goes about her business in the cheese section. She feels fury rising inside her, starting in her belly and overflowing into her chest like warm yeast. She thinks of going to the Lo Presti home to confront Tony but knows what Marcello would say: *Mind your business.* This is another thing about Canada: passionate emotion expressed in the form of physical and verbal confrontation is frowned upon. You've got to keep things bottled up and boiling under the surface. Maybe write a letter to the editor, or say something behind someone's back. Slapping Mr. Carlyle was one thing—he was an outsider after all, and it was an extreme situation—but slapping Tony Lo Presti would be lunacy. Like all good Canadians, Ida has learned to pick her battles.

Back at Barrie Avenue, Ida unloads the groceries, does some quick preparation for that night's meal, changes into her WOMEN'S RIGHTS NOW! T-shirt and a pair of jeans, and waits for Jasmine to pick her up. The plan is to drive to a parking lot near the one of the sweat shops at Spadina and Richmond, gather together with the other women, and march up the street. It should all be over by four o'clock, leaving plenty of time to make the evening meal. Jasmine is bringing the bullhorn and the protest signs; while she waits, Ida touches up her fingernail polish.

As she spreads a top coat over shell pink lacquer, Ida hears a knock at the door. Checking her watch, she sees that it's only noon. Jasmine isn't supposed to be here until one. She opens the door to Angela So-and-So, a shawl hiding her face.

"Please, *signora,* you say I could come here for sanctuary," she says, pulling the shawl back to reveal a large purple bruise spreading over one cheekbone, the eye socket turning black. Her one good eye brims with tears. Ida has the oddest feeling that she's looking at another version of herself.

"Come in," says Ida, but Angela doesn't move. Ida has to reach out and take her by the arm, gently pulling her inside the alcove. Angela looks around in wonder as though she's never seen the inside of any Canadian home but her own. It strikes Ida that this could well be true.

"You're hurt," says Ida. "Do you want me to take you to the doctor?" Ida hesitates, then adds, "Or *la polizia?*"

Angela's already huge bruised eyes grow even wider. She shakes her head vigorously. "My husband, he would kill me if I go to the police!"

"He's doing a good job of that right now, Angela," says Ida, at which Angela bursts into tears.

Ida manages to get Angela to sit down in the living room with a bag of ice on her face. Jasmine will be here in thirty minutes—less than that—but Ida is reluctant to leave Angela alone. *What if she gets frightened and goes back to Tony? No. Impossible.* The women's movement is supposed to be there for the oppressed. She'd rather have Angela close by where she can keep an eye on her.

Ida sits next to Angela, holding her hand. "I want to take you somewhere today. One of my—sisters—is coming to pick me up in a few minutes to go to a protest march for women's rights. Do you know what that is?"

Angela's one good eye rolls to look at Ida. She shakes her head uncomprehendingly. "Women's rights?" The words make no sense to her. *Well, why would they?* thinks Ida bitterly.

"Never mind. You're staying with me Angela."

Angela manages a small smile behind the ice bag. "Thank you, *signora*."

When Jasmine arrives in her old VW bus, Ida goes out to the curb to meet her and explain the situation. Jasmine raises her eyebrows. "Let me have a look at her."

Angela is huddled in a chair in the furthest corner of the living room, her shawl over her face, her body pushed down into the chair as if trying to disappear inside it.

"There, there, darling, let me see what the bastard did to you," coos Jasmine, reaching out to pull back the shawl, but Angela edges away, and pulls the shawl around her even tighter.

"She doesn't understand English," explains Ida, who gently moves the shawl away from Angela's face. Jasmine looks at the bruised cheek and eye with clinical interest.

"I think she should go to the police, then the hospital."

"I've tried," says Ida. "She refuses to do either. She says her husband will kill her."

"Probably true," mutters Jasmine. "What should we do? Leave her here until we get back?"

Ida shakes her head. "I don't think we should leave her alone. And she doesn't seem to have any friends in the neighbourhood. Maybe the church—I could try calling the priest."

Jasmine snorts. "Oh please. It's that kind of patriarchal sexist medieval institution that got her into this situation in the first place."

Ida starts to explain about the kindness of Father Dave Como, but stops. Jasmine isn't wrong. It was no doubt the priest back home in Angela's village who arranged the marriage and performed the proxy wedding. An entirely different breed from the educated, enlightened Dave, but still. To quote from Marcello's favourite movie about the glamorous mobsters, *they're all part of the same hypocrisy.*

"Maybe we should take her with us," says Ida. "The march is for her rights, too, no?"

Jasmine nods. "Right on, sister."

Ida explains to Angela that they are going for a walk with a group of Canadian women. This gets Angela out of the chair and into the back of Jasmine's car with the protest signs and the bullhorn. As they set off, Jasmine glances in the rear view, then says to Ida: "I don't mean to be ghoulish, dear, but your friend already looks like a ghost. Someone has to convince her to leave that brute."

Ida sighs. "We could try to call the police ourselves, perhaps. Make them talk to him."

Jasmine shakes her head. "Useless. Unless your friend makes the complaint, the authorities won't do a damn thing."

In the parking lot on Adelaide Street, they meet the rest of the group. Jasmine hands out protest signs and gives brisk instructions, while Ida stands with an arm wrapped around Angela's shoulders. Something about all the people and activity seems to have perked her up: "What are they doing, *signora*?"

"They are going to march to demand their rights. Yours too. See the signs? They are telling the government to start treating women equally with men. Do you understand?"

Angela nods. "It's like a church procession."

Well, not really, thinks Ida but doesn't try to explain further. She'll find out soon enough what a demo is.

They marshal with the other marchers—mostly labour union-ists, a few ancient Communist organizers from the old days on Spadina, some gay rights activists, and anti-nuke campaigners. The women at the head of the group unfurl a banner that reads "WOMEN'S RIGHTS NOW."

Ida offers the "FREEDOM TO CHOOSE" sign to Angela: "You don't have to carry it but you can if you want to." To her sur-prise, Angela accepts it. Ida picks up "ABORTION RIGHTS NOW."

The march begins to move up Spadina. Sidewalks are crowd-ed with onlookers, some of them applauding, others jeering, especially at the women.

"Come on you bitches, take your shirts off, and burn your bras for us!" someone shouts from the sidelines. "Show us your tits!" yells another.

Ida pats Angela's arm reassuringly; they're walking together, side by side, Angela holding up her sign like the others. At least Angela doesn't understand what the men are shouting. Looking at Angela's battered face makes Ida feel enraged again—not just at Angela's husband, but at everything, at the unfairness of life, at these stupid louts who can hassle them so freely. Where are the famous Canadian decency and politeness now?

On the bullhorn, Jasmine shouts: "WOMEN'S RIGHTS NOW! WOMEN'S RIGHTS NOW!" Her fist in the air, Ida shouts too until she feels something soft and wet hit her in the side of the face. She reaches up to touch it, then sniffs her fingers: it stinks. Someone is lobbing rotten tomatoes at the women marchers. Angela reaches out to dab Ida's face with her shawl: "*Signora*, why..."

And all hell breaks loose.

For reasons Ida is never quite able to make sense of later, everyone starts running. Ida links arms with Angela, trying not to be separated from her, but the sea of people wrenches them apart and washes them away from one another. Caught in a whirlpool of bodies, Ida is trapped in one place while

Angela is carried off by a different current, her head bobbing with the motion of the crowd, the FREEDOM sign abandoned on the ground. Forcing herself to pay attention to what is going on around her, Ida realizes that the crush of people is spiralling like water going down a drain or a toilet flushing. Ida has a brief moment of panic in the crush of bodies; she feels like she's suffocating, can't make sense of why they're all moving closer together instead of forward, until she sees the police in helmets and vests surrounding them, carrying batons and shouting "MOVE BACK! MOVE BACK!" She's too short to see much of anything else except people's backs as they try to flee. But there's nowhere else to move to. Ida remembers the instructions about passive resistance, but there's no way she can get down on the ground, and if she did, she'd be trampled. She feels a hand on her elbow and a strong pressure pulling, pulling her out of the crowd. Someone is rescuing her—Marcello? she thinks, but when she turns her head she sees that it's an older man, heavy, a tool belt slung under his the gut, a pair of wire cutters hanging from a loop. He grips her around the waist so hard that her feet drag along the ground as he pushes the panicked crowd aside. When Ida recognizes her rescuer, her bladder empties immediately.

"Let go! Let go!" she shouts, struggling to break free of Stan's grip. "I'm not that candy man's wife anymore!"

"You're not a wife, you're an unfinished business transaction. Just stay calm or I'll take out the wire cutters. Wanna lose the end of your nose?"

Ida looks around in desperation. Stan is moving quickly, pushing people aside, dragging her; in a moment, they will be free of the crowd. Not far away, the police are pushing women into black vans. Ida struggles, trying to kick Stan in the knee but he's gripping her at arm's length. "My Marcello will kill you!"

"Yeah? Hasn't he figured out what you really are yet?" asks Stan, turning toward her. Ida spits in his face.

With his free hand, Stan grips Ida's neck, crushing her windpipe. Her feet leave the ground. She can't breathe, but in the wildness of the crowd, no one notices that she's about to die. She still has the "ABORTION RIGHTS NOW" sign in her hand. Lifting it in the air, she brings it down on the back of Stan's head, the wooden stick of the placard giving a resounding *thwack*. A red bloom appears on his scalp.

"You goddamn bitch!" He swings at her face, the slap sending her to the ground, into a storm of running-shoed feet; Ida curls into a ball, trying not to be trampled. Struggling to get up, she sees Stan trying to push his way back into the crowd, toward her. But now there's something on his back. At first Ida thinks it's an animal—a dog perhaps—until she sees that the figure is clothed in a granny dress and construction boots, and is hitting Stan over the head with the FREEDOM sign: a tall woman with long black hair, roused to a fury. He flails his hands, trying to pull the Fury off his back; finally he wrenches her away and lifts one large fist to punch her but before he can connect, Ida sees a clear path and rolls across the ground, hitting him just below the knees, knocking him off his feet. Flat on her back, Ida looks up between the legs of a cop; he's standing directly over her, probably not even aware that she's there. "Move back!" he shouts, *thwacking* his club on a shield, and Ida suddenly sees the quickest means of rescue: seizing her sign, she jabs hard at the exposed part of the policeman, right between his legs. He topples like a sack of potatoes thrown from the back of a truck. Ida finds herself lying directly beside the groaning man, his baton rolling on the ground. Ida grabs it; if Stan comes for her again, she's now properly armed. A few feet away, another cop is peeling the Fury off Stan's back; she must have jumped him again when she had the chance. When Stan is finally free of her, Ida watches him disappear into the crowd.

Ida is lifted by her arms and dragged forward, the baton wrenched from her hand. Looking around, she is relieved to see Angela So-and-So, Jasmine, and the Fury being hauled away too.

It takes Ida's eyes a minute to adjust to the darkness. She and Angela have been pushed into some type of truck, black on the outside, black on the inside, packed with women. The two of them huddle together in the dim interior, the only light entering through a tiny window in the back door. "Where are we, *signora*?" asks Angela breathlessly.

"*Non lo so*. I don't know," answers Ida. Looking around at the other women, she asks, "Where are we?"

"Inside a Black Maria. A Paddywagon," says a woman's voice. "The pigs are taking us to jail."

"Jail? What did we do wrong?" Ida is shocked; Jasmine had assured her that the protest was entirely legal.

The woman barks a laugh. "We didn't do nothing wrong. The male chauvinists are trying to teach us a lesson. Put us in our place."

Ida suddenly becomes conscious of the smell of her own body, covered with rotten tomato, urine, and sweat. Her thigh is pressed against the woman next to her. Now that her eyes have adjusted to the light, Ida can see that she's a teenage girl improbably dressed in breeches, boots, and a dark riding jacket.

"Excuse me, but aren't you Ida Umbriaco?" asks the girl.

Ida peers at her. Although the rotten tomato on her jacket gives her common ground with everyone else in the wagon, her clothes make her look like royalty. "Yes, I'm Ida. Who are you, Princess Anne?"

The girl laughs. "I'm Cindy Carlyle." She waits a moment, waiting for Ida to recognize the name. When she doesn't, the girl adds: "Jonathan Carlyle's daughter."

Mr. Cake! thinks Ida. How much worse can her luck get? "But why did they arrest you?"

"I came down for the demo. Daddy thinks I'm at Sunnybrook

Stables for my riding lesson." Ida hears her sigh deeply. "So much bourgeois crap."

"I always wanted to ride horses," says Ida, despite the ridiculousness of bringing this up now. "It is one of my dreams."

The girl perks up. "Really? I'd love to take you. It would completely freak out my father."

The processing at Don Jail is tedious. Ida sits on a bench between Cindy and Angela, her clothes still damp with pee and tomato pulp, needing to empty her bladder again. On the other side of the room, the Fury sits beside Jasmine, hands behind her head, her construction-booted feet stretched out in front of her. She's a pretty woman, but a remarkably large and powerful one.

"Thank you for your help, Miss," says Ida to the Fury. "I'm Ida. May I know your name?"

The woman acknowledges Ida's thanks with a nod, as if saying, *It was nothing.* "Holly," the Fury says huskily, then falls into silence.

"We'll be out of here soon," says Cindy. "They're just trying to scare us for being uppity. It's not like they can charge us with anything."

Each woman's information is typed onto a form by a policeman who scarcely bothers to look at them. Ida asks for and receives permission to make a phone call. She calls Georgia at Ed's house, who gets on the line and tells Ida to stay put until he gets in touch with Marcello.

Stay put? What else am I going to do? wonders Ida.

Ida, Jasmine, Angela, Cindy, and Holly sit side by side in the holding cell, Angela's head in Ida's lap, Cindy peeling nail polish off her thumb, Jasmine softly humming "We Shall Overcome," Holly sitting with her legs spread under her dress, elbows to knees, when Ed arrives wearing a suit jacket and blue jeans. He stands outside of the cell, arms crossed, looking in at the five of them. "Well, this makes a pretty picture."

Ida looks at him through the bars, then down at Angela, who has fallen asleep in her lap. "If there were justice in this country, the police would arrest this one's brute of a husband, not us."

Ed's eyebrows shoot up. "What the hell is Angela Lo Presti doing here?"

"She came to our house looking for sanctuary," says Ida, stroking Angela's hair. "I didn't want to leave her so I brought her along on the march."

Ed sighs, rubbing a hand over his face. "When Tony finds out, things are going to be even worse for her. You know that, don't you?"

Ida feels a spike of anger at Ed so intense that she can barely speak. "Oh *yes*? *You* know about Tony and *everybody* knows about Tony, about how he *beats his wife*? And you do *nothing* and tell me this *makes things worse*?"

The other women in the cell glare at Ed and nod.

"Give it to him sister," mutters Cindy.

Ed drops his eyes. Clears his throat. Adjusts his tie. "I'll see if I can find out when they're planning to release her. Maybe I can get Dave Como involved. To act as a go-between between her and Tony."

"*What?*" says Ida. " You're going to send her back to him?"

"Where else is she going to go?"

Ida lifts her chin. "I'll take her home with me."

Ed clears his throat again. "You're not going home, Ida. At least not right away. They're charging you with assaulting a police officer."

"Oh baby," says Cindy, putting her arm around Ida's shoulders. "You've gotta stop hitting The Man."

"I thought the *fascisti* lost the war, Eduardo," says Ida acidly.

"Don't worry about it, Ida," says Cindy. "My father's going to pull some strings and get the charges dropped for all of us. With you and me both in here, he's worried about more bad publicity."

Ed looks at her skeptically. "And who would you be?"

Cindy stretches out her long, riding-booted legs and puts her arms behind her head, leaning back against the wall of the cell. "I'm The Man's daughter."

True to Cindy's word, strings are pulled and cell doors are opened. Everyone is released without charges.

Dave Como, waiting at the entrance to the jail, says he's come to take Angela to a women's shelter run by Italian-speaking volunteers. "Mrs. Lo Presti won't be the first woman in the parish I've had to take there, unfortunately. It'll give her a safe place away from Tony, for now."

From the steps at the front of the jail, Ida scans the crowd of women for her rescuer, Holly, but the black-haired Fury has vanished.

With her car still parked in the lot on Spadina, Jasmine hails a cab for Cindy, Ida, and herself. Ida asks to be dropped off, not at home, but at Spadina and Bloor.

"I want to walk a bit, breathe the air," says Ida. "It feels good to be free again."

Exhausted yet exhilarated, Ida strolls along Bloor, past Hungarian restaurants and porno movie houses and second-hand bookshops. As she nears the circus lights of Honest Ed's department store, someone falls into step beside her, slipping an arm through hers—the black-haired Fury.

"Holly! I'm glad we meet again. I didn't have a chance to say enough my thanks," says Ida. Arm in arm, Holly's unusual height is more noticeable. It's not unlike walking with Marcello.

"I've gotta talk to you, Ida," Holly says.

There's something odd about her voice. It's too deep. Her face has changed, too, the bristles of a five o'clock beard beginning to poke through the surface of her makeup. That's when Ida realizes that Holly is a young man. Ida tries not to show her surprise. She is a woman of the world, after all.

Holly nods in the direction of a stone church on Bathurst Street, its bell tower tolling the hour. Six o'clock. "Let's go into St. Peter's."

Ida laughs, and shakes her head. "I'm not one for church."

"Me neither, but it's a good place to talk without anyone hearing us."

Ida pointedly checks her watch. She's grateful to this woman—person—but far too tired for a conversation. "I have to get dinner on. Perhaps another day."

Holly shakes her head firmly. Almost angrily. "No. Now."

Ida tries to gently extricate her arm. "I must go home. My husband will be wondering where I am."

Holly gives a deep, bitter laugh. "By now, Marcello's probably either dead or in jail."

Ida stops walking. "How do you know his name?"

For one horrible moment, Ida thinks that Holly is another of Senior's thugs. She tries to yank her arm away but Holly is holding her in a firm grip. She's about to start screaming when Holly drops her voice into an even lower register and whispers urgently into Ida's ear: "Ida, it's me! Bum Bum. Pasquale. Benny. Whatever you call me, I'm on your side. But you have to come with me now."

In the pews of St. Peters, a scattering of penitents bow their heads. A cross is lit over the door of the confession box, indicating that someone is pouring sins into a priest's ear. Ida hasn't been to a church service since her proxy wedding in Italy, where she exchanged vows with a hired groom, stinking of wine and mothballs. He turned out to be the real groom's brother. As part of a package deal, the marriage broker had loaned him a suit, and threw in a priest, a bouquet, and a dingy wedding dress two sizes too big for Ida; she had to be pinned into it. The proxy wedding meant she was legally married to a man in Canada she had never met: Senior. A horrible day.

Benny and Ida slide into a pew screened from the rest of the church by a rack of devotional candles.

"Why do you say Marcello is dead or in jail?" she whispers.

"He's gone on a vendetta to get Senior to sign the annulment. Either his name goes on the paper, or his brains," Benny whispers, as he pulls off his wig and wipes a sleeve across his face. "Man, this thing gets hot."

With his wig in his lap, Benny talks. Ida listens. When she learns why and how he escaped from the Andolini farm, Ida puts her arm around him and leans her head on his shoulder in sympathy. When she hears of Claire's death, she starts to wipe tears. When they get to Benny's liberation of Noname from Doctors' Hospital, Ida rises abruptly. "Enough. We go now."

At Benny's knock, Vera opens the door. "Benny, thank Christ. Your friend's been here for two hours, tying up the goddamn phone. Trying to call his wife. Marco's got business to do, he can't have customers getting nothin' but busy signals." Vera glances at Ida. "Who's this?"

"The wife," says Benny.

In the back room, under a laundry line holding a string of fake IDs for college students from Buffalo, Marcello sits in the La-Z-Boy with Noname in his arms and the phone pressed to his ear. When he sees Ida, he gives a shout of relief, waking the baby, who chirps her displeasure.

As Ida and Marcello embrace, Benny tosses his wig on Marco's desk. "Kill anyone today?"

Marcello shakes his head. "I paid my respects to the Andolinis, visited Prima's grave, had coffee with Frank, and left. They didn't know anything about a meeting between me and Senior. He was a no-show."

"He just wanted you to go off half-cocked, so Ida'd be alone when Stan came calling," says Benny. "You got a lot to learn about vendettas, brother."

Ida gazes down at Noname, whose oil-slick eyes stare back. She feels a strange sense of recognition, as if gazing into a bottomless pool that mirrors a familiar face.

"She's beautiful. She has your eyes," she tells Benny. "You could be her father."

Benny shrugs. "I must've given her my looks by sleeping with my arm around Claire every night."

"Inherited traits don't get passed on that way," says Marcello, as Benny lifts the baby out of his arms to quiet her.

Ida rolls her eyes. "Marcello goes to university now. He thinks he knows everything."

Benny lays out his proposal to Ida and Marcello with the same logical, Spock-like arguments he tried on Scott. Having spent the last two hours bonding with the baby, Marcello needs no convincing. Ida agrees without hesitation. She knows Noname's possible future by heart and already aches to rewrite it, just as she's trying to rewrite her own. They're all outcasts—Benny, Marcello, Ida, and Noname—members of the same pagan tribe of lost children. A family in everything but blood.

Always practical, Marcello asks: "How do we explain where she came from?"

Ida and Benny exchange looks over Marcello's lack of imagination.

"We say that we adopted her and the papers just came through. Or, she's a cousin's child from back in Italy with no one to look after her," Ida rattles off, waving a hand in the air impatiently. "We think of something, Cello."

"But what about papers—birth certificate, medical records, that type of thing?" asks Marcello, still fretting. "We can't have anyone connecting her with the Love Canal baby."

Marco pats Marcello's shoulder. "Don't worry Papa. It's on me. All you gotta do is give her a name."

Marcello wants to call her Sophia, after his mother. Benny pushes for Claire—appropriate, but risky. Ida mentions that she's always liked the name Zara.

Finally, Marco gets out an old set of craps dice and they play for the naming rights. Benny rolls a four and a two. Ida, a three and a one. Marcello rolls boxcars—a pair of sixes. The baby will be christened Sophia Claire Zara Umbriaco, with Benny, Vera, and Marco as a trinity of godparents.

"No priests or holy water, please, let's just baptize her with a friendly drink," suggests Vera, and everyone agrees. She twists open a bottle of Baby Duck sparkling wine and fills five juice glasses.

After they toast Sophia's health, Marco gets out his tools and starts forging the birth certificate. From under the glare of a gooseneck lamp, Marco grins up at Marcello, who watches him work with interest. "Beautiful, eh? With the right papers, this little girl can be anyone she pleases."

"How hard is it to forge church documents?" asks Marcello.

Marco raises his eyebrows with interest. "You mean, like baptismal papers or a marriage certificate?"

"No, I mean, the document for annulling a marriage," answers Marcello.

Marco shrugs. "Piece of cake. Thought you were going to give me something interesting."

He slides open a drawer and slips out a printed sheet, placing it on the desk in the front of him with a professional flourish. Marcello recognizes it as the same form he received from the diocese with Senior's refusal.

"When can you get me the signature?" asks Marco.

Marcello silently pulls out his own annulment form—the one with Senior's signed refusal—from his jacket pocket and places it on the desk.

Marco looks up in surprise. "You carry this with you everywhere?"

Marcello grins down at him. "Only when I'm planning to ram it down someone's throat."

12. A BRIEF HISTORY OF LETTERS

FIVE GOOD YEARS. That's more than many married couples have, reasons Marcello. He and Ida were married in a small ceremony at St. Lucy's. Marco's forged annulment papers fooled both Father Dave and Ed Ceci. Marcello and Ida know the truth—that their marriage is a fraud, at least in a legal sense. But with Sophia to consider, the end justifies the means, as Canadians like to say.

Frank Andolini makes the peace with Senior, in exchange for Marcello's presence at business meetings—a strong, silent figure in a suit standing next to Frank, something the Andolinis have needed ever since Rocco's banishment.

"Rocco was not the son—not the man—I thought he was," says Frank mournfully, his hand on Marcello's shoulder.

In his first year of teaching, Marcello receives telephone calls in the staff room, several times a month, requesting that he make an appearance in Bramborough to help Frank negotiate the sale of the family farm to developers planning to throw up row upon row of subdivisions. In this way, Marcello keeps Frank happy, who in turn keeps Senior and his attack dog Stan muzzled. And so life goes on in the Umbriaco family in a strangely peaceful way. What Marcello doesn't know—and won't know, until much later—is the drama unfolding by mail.

The second letter appears almost exactly one month to the day after the first. Misaddressed, it arrives at the Agnelli house

in an onionskin airmail envelope, blue tinted, addressed to
UMBRIACO, *Ida*.

The address is always wrong. Confusion about which
semi-detached belongs to the Agnellis and which to the Umbriacos means the letters end up in Lou and Lina's mailbox
at 15 Barrie, rather than in Ida and Marcello's at 17. You
might expect the mail carrier to put things to rights, slipping
the letters in with the Umbriacos' hydro and phone bills. But
no. Perhaps confused by the airmail envelope and foreign
stamp—Lina and Lou receive mail regularly from overseas—
the carrier always places the letter firmly in the Agnellis'
mailbox, as he will all the other letters that fly across the
ocean addressed to Ida.

When Angela Lo Presti moves into the vacant flat upstairs—
where she will live for several years, learning English and
looking after the baby while Ida works and Marcello finishes
his degree—the mail situation gets even more complicated,
with letters for Angela sometimes jumbled up with the Umbriacos and the Agnellis. When that happens, Angela discreetly
passes on the misaddressed letters to Ida without a word.

At first, Ida hides these new letters with the first one, under
the nighties in her dresser drawer. Eventually she bundles them
together and slips them behind the old record player in the
spare room closet. She still remembers that warm night after
the women's lib meeting, when she and Marcello made love
to the records on that player, over and over again. It seems
as good a place as any to hide the central fact of her life.

This is one of several reasons why Marcello didn't know
about the letters for such a long time.

Years later, when he can't sleep and finds himself sitting with
Ida's letters spread out before him on his espresso bar at two
a.m., he wonders why Lina or Lou or Angela never mentioned
them, never handed any of them to him over the back fence:
Ecco, Cello, a letter for Ida come to our house by mistake.

It just never happened.

The mailing dates of the letters are widely distributed over time (the first, September 22, 1975, the last, July 10, 1982). For Marcello in the year 2000, it is clear that each letter must have passed directly from Lina's hands to Ida's. Lina always brought in the morning mail, Lou always leaving for some distant job site—Mimico, Mississauga, Burlington—long before the postman showed up at their house.

But it's odd that in all the conversations Marcello ever had with Lina over the years, about cooking, vegetable gardening, the care of infant skin, the death of three Popes and election of two, and Lou's heart condition (diagnosed in 1989), Lina never once mentioned Ida's letters. Neither did Angela, who stayed in touch even after remarrying and moving to Woodbridge. Which makes Marcello believe that it was a deliberate sin of omission.

There must have been an agreement between the three women to keep the letters a secret among them. Ida's secrecy, as much as the fact of the letters themselves, makes Marcello shake his head in disbelief almost thirty years later.

Why didn't you just show me, Ida, just explain everything to me? It doesn't seem like such an awful secret that I wouldn't have understood.

Ida's voice always interrupts him. *Excuse me, Cello, but you are thinking like a twenty-first century man. Thirty-five years ago, people thought differently. Including you. I kept this secret for your own good.*

For his own good.

13. TERMINAL VELOCITY

JULY 11, 1982

SOPHIA OPENS HER EYES to the poster on the wall opposite her bed: two rows of smiling men in white shorts and blue shirts, arms crossed: the Azzurri, the Italian National Soccer Team. She loves looking at them. Her eyes settle on her hero, the beautiful Paolo Rossi. She adores the footballer almost as much as she does her father. The two of them even look a little bit alike.

It's going to be an exciting day. She can feel it.

The steamy night heat has left her smelling like curdled milk but no one is going to make her take a bath because she won't be going to church, even though it's Sunday. Her father took her to Mass last night so that they would have the whole day free for football.

She slips out of bed and barefoots her way into the kitchen, the soles of her feet slapping the floor. Her father doesn't like her dirtying her feet. He's always telling her to put her slippers on. But he's asleep. It feels good to just do whatever she wants, for a change.

She climbs up on a kitchen chair, gets down the Kellogg's Corn Flakes and Nestle's Quik, takes a jug of milk out of the fridge, and spreads everything out just-so. She pours milk on her corn flakes and dumps in powdered cocoa straight from the box, mushing everything together into a pleasantly disgusting mess. If her mother saw Sophia do this, she'd kill her. But she's asleep, too. The morning sun hammers down on the kitchen table through lace curtains, casting a web of light over the cereal bowl in the shape of a goal net: *a sign from God*, reasons Sophia. Making a man out of her fingers, she kicks in a corn flake and sings softly to herself, "Goal, goal, goal!"

Today, Sophia and her father will go to the social club and watch the game with everyone else in the neighbourhood. The place will be packed with men but her father will stand out like the sun around which everything else revolves. Sophia chews slowly, dreaming about the day ahead. If the Azzurri beat the Germans (and they will!) this is going to be the best day of her seven-year-old life.

The alarm clock goes off in a blast of music. Groaning, Marcello slams his fist down on it, then hoists himself to the edge of the mattress. Ida reaches out to absent-mindedly rub his back. "Why do you set the clock when you intend to sleep in? Lie back down."

"I need the bathroom."

"Go pee and come back. Okay?"

"Okay."

In the hallway he can hear Sophia singing to herself at the kitchen table. He pops his head around the corner to where she flips through her FIFA Player Guide.

"'Morning, sweetheart. What day is this again?" yawns Marcello.

"World Cup final! When are we going to the club?"

"In an hour or so. I'm just going to get a little more sleep first." He runs his fingers through his daughter's tangled hair. It could use a comb.

"How can you sleep when the Azzurri are getting ready to play?" shouts Sophia. "Olé, olé, olé, olé!"

Lying in bed, waiting for Marcello to return, Ida listens to her daughter's cheers. If the Italian team loses to Germany (which Ida thinks is likely) the girl is going to be crushed, along with the rest of the neighbourhood. Every Azzurri win has sparked spontaneous street parties, shutting down traffic on St. Clair West and College Street. At first the police tried to impose order, but, faced with the vast number of overjoyed revellers, they finally gave up and let the party spill from street to street. Now the authorities simply stand back and allow the Italians to have their fun. This staid Victorian city, Ida senses, is finally learning how to roll down her girdle, sip a glass of wine, and relax a little.

When Marcello returns to the bedroom, he's smiling. "I've never seen that kid so excited."

"Did you tell her not to come in?" asks Ida pointedly, pulling her nightie over he head.

"She knows."

Marcello drops his robe and slips under the sheet, caressing Ida's belly, letting her direct his hand. Here, and here, and here. Finally she climbs on top of him. As he nears his climax, he groans and turns his face on the pillow.

Afterwards, Marcello sprawls across the bed, sweaty top sheet on the floor. Maybe this year they should spring for an air conditioner.

"You're wearing me out," he murmurs.

Ida smiles at him. "My book says lovemaking is very health-ful for the man."

Marcello rests his hand on her breast. "You want to make love every day, sometimes twice a day. And you're doing it for my sake?"

Ida groans and pushes his hand lower. "Of course my darling."

Afterwards, Ida dozes. She's still drowsy when Marcello comes in damp from the shower and says, "I'd better take *signorina* to Esposito's or she'll explode. Are you sure you don't want to come?"

Ida yawns. "I come by later. I have things to do. A little shopping."

"Shopping on a Sunday? What's open?"

"I go to Chinatown to buy cuttlefish from the little grocery."

Marcello pulls on his running shoes. "You'll have to take the bus. The Dart is still in the shop."

"I take the Chevy."

"I'd rather you didn't. It can't take much wear and tear anymore."

Ida sighs. The nervous old Scotsman is back.

"This is why you spend every Saturday lying underneath it, hitting it with a wrench and swearing? So it can sit in the driveway?"

Marcello runs his hand through his hair; at thirty-two, he's already got a patch of grey above one eye, as though he's been daubed with paint. "I'm just trying to keep her from falling apart. She's for looking at, not for driving."

Ida snorts. "You are too sentimental, Cello. Always thinking about the past."

Marcello pushes Ida's bangs away from her face. "With the energy crisis, she costs a fortune to fill up and there are no lap belts. I don't want you riding around in her with Sophia. I'll get you your cuttlefish at Loblaws tomorrow."

"But Cello, I want to make *polenta con seppie* today. Is just a quick trip, down to Dundas."

"No," insists Marcello. "Obey your husband, for once."

Annoyed, Ida rolls away when he tries to kiss her, then shouts after him: "Get that filthy girl to bathe and comb her rat's nest!"

"Yeah, yeah."

"And you eat something before you go."

"I'll get Mike to make me some eggs," Marcello calls back. "*Calmati.*"

Ida listens to the sounds of leave-taking, impatient for her husband and daughter to get out of the house. She has more to do than beat cuttlefish until they give up their black ink. The previous week another letter arrived, via the Agnellis: the first one in almost two years. This time, from Riccardo, her brother. Holding his letter, she feels a stab of guilt and another emotion she tries not to feel: a longing for the past. *Live now,* she constantly tells herself, but, unlike some others, Rico does not deserve to be forgotten. Ida has decided to write back. With Marcello out of the house for the afternoon, it's the perfect time to compose a letter.

She gets out of bed and stands naked in front of her full-length mirror. Even though she's only in her fourth month, she can already see the darkening areolas of her nipples and the swelling basketball in her lower belly. *I don't look so bad,* she observes, then moves her hand to touch where Marcello has just been. All she can think about these days is sex; her pregnancy book says that it's got something to do with the rush of hormones. She was shocked to discover she could get pregnant at all; apparently, that doctor back in the clinic Jeanie sent her to didn't know his business as well as he thought he did. A few years after they adopted Sophia, she stopped taking the Pill—what was the point in spending the money if she couldn't conceive?

Before she knew it, she'd skipped a period, then another. Her breasts became tender and sore. When she mentioned these symptoms over the phone to Angela, her old friend started laughing. "Wake up—you're pregnant, Ida! Too bad I don't live upstairs anymore to help with this one, eh?"

Ida takes a cool shower, then pulls on a thin rayon dress that the shop lady at the Eaton Centre described as "Yorkville Hippie 1969." It's the kind of thing Jasmine used to wear. Perfect for a pregnant woman on a hot summer day, thinks Ida.

In the spare room closet, she rummages behind Marcello's old phonograph and pulls the bundle of letters from its hiding place. She'll re-read the latest one while she eats, then write and mail her response right away. She doesn't want Marcello to ask who she's writing to—although she has decided, finally, to tell him everything. He will be surprised by the story and perhaps hurt that she kept these matters a secret all these years, but times have changed. What would have once been considered scandalous is now simply shameful and embarrassing. Besides, it will feel better to get things off her chest, as they say. Another English expression she finds amusing.

At the breakfast table, she spreads out the pale blue pages. Riccardo explains that he is writing, in part, on Paolo's behalf, who apologizes if he has upset her with his letters. He realizes now that her lack of response was a signal that she did not want to hear from him.

Riccardo has only one request: could she, please, write back just this one time so that he can reassure Paolo that she is all right?

You are so headstrong, Ida, I worried that you did not understand the situation you were entering. Just one word of reassurance and Paolo and Zara will be content and so will I. All of us will leave you in peace. But as a point of information, I have a bit of money now. With Zara retired, I sold the pensione and came here to London to work in a fine dining establishment—did you see my address? They are rather trusting in England; I told them I had "professional qualifications" and gave Zara as my reference. Imagine what she said—you would think I had trained at the Cordon Bleu! It's troubling, how smoothly our mother can lie. Of course, I am much better at the stove than even the so-called "master chefs" here who know nothing more than how to fry a potato. They never suspected I've done nothing more than work in the kitchen of the pensione. Good enough training for the English, I suppose!

I hear of Canada often here and always think of you. Toronto seems not so far away from London. I could make a trip to see you, perhaps arrange for Paolo to join me...

Ida shakes her head at that one. *No.*

From Marcello's office, she fetches paper, a pen, and an envelope. She writes:

Caro Riccardo:

I am so happy to hear from you. But please understand I am only responding because it is you writing this time and not Paolo!

First, let me assure you that I am very happy. I am married to a good man who I love very much, Marcello Umbriaco, a teacher of mathematics. In some ways, Rico, he reminds me of you! As I suspect Paolo knows, given that he has always addressed me by my correct married name, this is not my proxy husband: I left him long ago. We have a seven-year-old daughter and another on the way.

You will be glad to know that Zara's investment in my training was not wasted after all. I was a flight attendant (Air Canada) for a number of years. Now I train girls for them. It's a good job, and I'm no longer away from home often. Sometimes I miss the travel.

She pauses. Taps the pen on the sheet.

Finally, she writes: *Do not come see me, Rico. Especially, tell Paolo and Zara not to come. Perhaps, one day, I will bring my family to meet you. I still haven't explained things to them. One day soon, I will, and then perhaps we will come to see you.*

She signs it and seals it, addressing it carefully. What in the world, she wonders, would entice Rico away from Venice, up to England? Such a long way!

She smiles, thinking how far she herself has come.

When Marcello and Sophia arrive at Esposito's, the tables are already full of people in blue jerseys and Italian flags are everywhere. With the six-hour time difference between Toronto and Spain, the game starts early. Mike Esposito has set up a huge TV screen with a satellite feed—an extravagance, but it attracts customers, even from outside the community. Today it will probably more than pay for itself in food and beer.

Marcello sits with Sophia on his lap, waving her flag and yelling *Ros-si! Ros-si! Ros-si!*

"Where's the *Contessa?*" asks Mike, dropping a plate of eggs and toast in front of Marcello.

A man at a nearby table slaps Marcello's back and laughs. "She's probably home cheering for the *tedeschi.*"

"Watch it!" warns Marcello, glancing pointedly at Sophia, but she hasn't heard a word. She's too focused on watching the game and eating Marcello's eggs.

After writing and sealing her letter, Ida finds a handful of stamps on Cello's desk and affixes all of them—she's never sure about postage. She hides the bundle of letters back in the closet, pulls on her sandals and heads off to the corner mailbox. In the distance, she can hear a blare of music; seconds later, a convertible pulls into view, packed with men waving a huge Italian flag. They're shouting and singing as one of them dances on the back seat. *Those* idioti *are going to kill themselves if they're not careful,* thinks Ida, heading for home.

Now she is ready to turn her attention to the cuttlefish. Getting to Chinatown on a Sunday by bus—*beh*. She'll have to catch one bus along St. Clair, then switch at Spadina, then switch again to go south from Bloor. Who needs it? As she walks back to the semi, the refurbished chrome grille of the Chevy seems to grin at her, the car gleaming in the driveway with its fresh coat of cherry red paint.

Ida crosses her arms and stands in front of the perfectly good car, thinking: *He loves you more than he loves me.* The Chevy would take her down to Dundas Street and back so fast, Marcello would never even know she'd been gone. Never know she'd "disobeyed" him.

She fetches the keys.

When she goes to unlock the passenger side door, she is surprised to find it open; it isn't like Marcello to forget to lock up. Sliding behind the wheel, she notices something on the floor: a tattered, badly stained book. *I, Robot* by Isaac Asimov. Opening it, she sees a stamp reading *Bramborough*

High Library and the name *Marcello Umbriaco Junior* carefully written in dark-blue cursive script. Did the book get pushed under the front seat years ago, only to be found again when Marcello was overhauling the car? She is surprised he didn't bring such a valuable memento into the house to show her. Like the Chevy, the book is exactly the kind of touchstone with the past that Marcello treasures. The kind of thing that proves how far he's come.

Tossing the book on the passenger seat, Ida slides the key into the ignition. She can tell that the car has been recently tuned—the engine roars to life with more vitality than she remembers. As she pulls out of the driveway and accelerates, then slows again at the end of the street, she notices a sponginess when she applies pressure to the brake. The car stutters to a stop as though grinding through heavy mud. For a moment she considers turning around—perhaps Marcello was right—then thinks with irritation about *obeying* him. She's used to the power brakes in the Dart; this is probably nothing more than forgetting the "feel" of the Chevy. She hasn't driven it in years. Besides it's just a quick trip, traffic is light on a Sunday and everyone is home watching the game.

She heads west to Spadina, then swings south near Casa Loma, the road dipping over the edge of the Escarpment ("the shoreline of the giant inland sea that used to cover Toronto," Marcello has pedantically explained to her many, many times in his teacher's voice, as she rolls her eyes and thinks to herself, *you only tell me about the Escarpment five hundred times before, beh!*).

As the Chevy descends the steep hill, Ida finds herself picking up speed even though she hasn't touched the gas. Tires squealing, she winds past Walmer Road, still heading south, and presses the brake. This time she senses nothing at all beneath her foot. The car is not responding.

She grips the steering wheel. As she approaches Bloor, she sees that the stoplight immediately ahead is turning from yellow to red and that same convertible, jammed with men, is nearing the intersection, their giant flag snapping. *Goal, goal, goal,* they're shouting as they race toward the green light. When she realizes that a collision is inevitable, Ida cries out and throws her arms over her head, bracing hard against the steering wheel, as she's been taught to prepare herself for an airline crash. She also makes a brief (and, she suspects, pointless) appeal to God.

What she does not expect—what, later, the police report will point out—is that the force of the crash will knock loose the ignition wires, which the husband will freely admit to having tampered with in the past. No point in being caught out in a lie. He will confess to hotwiring the car when they interrogate him.

"Why the hell would the guy jump his own ignition?" one officer will ask another, as they watch Marcello weeping on the other side of the two-way mirror.

"Doesn't quite pass the sniff test, does he?" the other will agree.

In the classroom, Marcello always enjoys creating hypothetical situations to demonstrate physical laws.

Assume that: two objects are moving towards one another on a frictionless surface. One object, a 1959 Chevy, is moving at a speed of sixty miles per hour (according to estimates from two eye witnesses). The other object, a 1970 Ford Fairlane convertible, is moving at sixty-five miles per hour (give or take). Using vector transformations, calculate their Relative Speed at Impact (RSI).

The answer is eighty-eight miles per hour. Even taking into account the friction of the road, at that speed, fatality is probable.

Like one of Marcello's math problems, the forces of the two cars meet and combine. The Fairlane convertible slams into the Chevy, causing it to spin and collide a second time and rupturing rust spots in the older vehicle's gas tank.

A chain reaction ensues. Energized by the car key, sparks from the exposed copper ignition wires create an electrical charge that speeds through the twisted car frame to the spilled fuel. The resulting fire scorches away any evidence of rubber skid marks from the road surface and burns off what remains of the fuel.

Little will be left for the police to investigate. Without skid marks, there is no way for them to conclusively determine speed and direction, or to test whether the gas had been tainted with an accelerant or the brake fluid siphoned off, crimes that the husband, out of his mind with rage and grief, keeps insisting must have happened. The investigator listens patiently to his wild theories, even going so far as to follow up on his accusations against two men in the Niagara Region: Marcello Trovato Senior and Stanley Mancuso. Both have solid alibis: they spent the day with fifty other men in a sports bar in Thorold, watching the World Cup.

The investigator can see no motive for mechanical tampering unless the husband did it himself. They bring him in and question him, but it's hard to believe the man's intense grief isn't genuine. As one detective says, "If he's faking it, someone should give him an Academy Award." In the end, the investigator can find no motive for the husband to go to such lengths to kill his wife and unborn child.

More to the point, a pedestrian crossing Spadina Road that Sunday morning witnessed the woman running the red. The investigator suspects the accident is what it appears to be: a housewife in a hurry to get to the grocery store. Sad, sure, but what can you do?

"Typical woman driver," the investigator says behind closed doors to his assistant, shaking his head as his secretary types up the report. "Maybe they shouldn't get behind the wheel when they're pregnant. The hormones make them crazy. Considering that a guy in the other car broke his neck, we might've had her up on charges, if she'd lived."

"Speaking of crazy, what'll we tell the husband?" asks the assistant.

"That he's off the hook. The husband might be a bad mechanic but he's not a killer. The report will say he lost his wife in a speed-related accident, answers the investigator. He's going to have to accept that and move on."

14. TEST

SOPHIA UMBRIACO HAS FAILED a math test. Again. She knew she would fail. Although her father sits with her most evenings, drilling her on integers and algebra and all that number stuff he loves so much, it just doesn't go in. He's always patient, he's used to having to explain things over and over to his students. He never loses his temper or gives up on her. He keeps telling her that there are patterns in the numbers, just like in music.

Sophia *wants* him to give up. She hates math. Her father can't understand how this is possible. "You're my daughter. There's no reason for you not to be good at math."

"Was my mother good at math?"

At the mention of *my mother*, Sophia's father pauses, rubs his eyes, and carries on: "Your mom was good at everything. Now, Soph, let's go over this again..."

At sixteen years of age, Sophia is a serious-looking girl, with large black eyes and long legs. Her reddish-brown hair curls loose to her shoulders, making her look like a Renaissance angel. One thing that strikes people about Sophia: she's solemn. She doesn't laugh easily or make friends quickly. She practices the piano every night, but plays joylessly. It's like an athletic event for her. Put your fingers here, here, here, faster, faster, faster, finished.

"Yes, Dad, I practiced," she tells her father, but like numbers, the music never goes into her heart.

Sophia's heart is in sports, her trophies and medals turning the basement into a shrine to hockey, soccer, and basketball. She enjoys watching the long graceful arc of a football leaving her father's hands and the satisfaction of snatching it out of the air and drilling it back at him with a spiral that Dad says reminds him of Brett Favre's. "Too bad ladies can't play football," he likes to say, just to get a rise out of her. She always responds with an imperious look: "That's discrimination, Dad. And it's 'women' not 'ladies.'"

They go for long runs together, sprinting down and then charging back up steep hills, challenging one another; these days, Sophia's father can just barely stay ahead of her.

Sometimes, at night, she rummages under her mattress and pulls out the squishy packet of letters that she found stashed in the spare room closet. Ida's Magic Words. She likes to sleep with them under her pillow, as if the dense, handwritten paragraphs will drift into her head while she's asleep, giving up her mother's secrets. She makes sure the letters are back under her mattress in the morning so that her father doesn't find them. She wants the letters to remain a secret because any mention of Ida can send him into a dark mood that imprisons him for days on end.

Sophia was eight when she discovered Ida's Magic Words during a game of hide-and-seek with her friend Pasqua. As soon as she saw the name *Umbriaco, Ida* she knew who they belonged to. Ida wanders on the fringes of Sophia's memory, a pale, powerful presence rich with the mingled fragrances of garlic, onions, basil, and oregano—everyday kitchen smells that Sophia associates with home and loss. Every bite of home cooking tastes like her mother. Sophia has been living in an atmosphere of grief for so long that it surprises her when a friend's house simply smells of cat pee or cabbage or dirty laundry.

When she and Pasqua were little girls, they pretended that Ida's letters had been dropped from heaven, a magic charm for them to untangle. Ida was like a fairytale princess, except there was no poisoned apple to cough up and no prince handsome enough to wake her with a kiss, not even Sophia's father. Pasqua and Sophia imagined that, if they could figure out how to crack the code, Ida would come back to life and break The Spell of Eternal Sadness that kept Sophia's father in its grip.

Most of Ida's Magic Words were written in Italian in an elaborate looping script that Sophia found hard to decipher. By sixteen, she had had enough Saturday morning Heritage Language classes from the Board of Education to recognize many phrases. Strung together, they came out sounding like a corny Italian love song— *amore, cuore, tristezza, memoria, dolore, mi dispiace, mi manchi, ti voglio bene.* Love, heart, sadness, memory, pain, I'm sorry, I miss you, I love you.

Two letters were even more mysterious, written by a different hand, in an unrecognizable language, each one starting: *Draga moja kći, tvoj otac i ja smo toliko zabrinuta za tebe,* and ending with the signature, *Zara*—intriguingly, one of Sophia's middle names.

Sophia stared and stared at the words. Regret and loneliness wafted from the pages, but the meaning of the sentences refused to knit itself together for her. Even though she didn't believe in charms and spells anymore, she couldn't shake the feeling that the day she finally understood the letters, her father would come fully to life again, like a prince waking up from a dream. Eventually she moves the letters from under her mattress to inside her desk, making it easier to study them when she should be doing homework.

Sophia's father spends a lot of time alone, even though he has many friends: Ed the lawyer, Mike who runs the social club, Lou next door, and Dave who used to be a priest and now sells hockey equipment. Even when Dad's with these men, Sophia can see that he feels alone. He's always looking somewhere else in the room.

When the Spell of Eternal Sadness falls over her father like a heavy black blanket, only one friend is powerful enough to lift it: Uncle Benny. He drives up from New York every couple of months and sleeps in the spare room. When he arrives, the first thing he does is ride over to Blockbuster to rent a bunch of movies. He and Dad like to watch James Bond best. Sometimes they'll turn on a hockey or football game; when that happens, Sophia will curl up between them, pretending to be a cub between two lions, comforted by the deep masculine rumble of their voices.

Benny used to be in the entertainment business. That's how Dad describes his job to Sophia, although every time he does, Benny grins in a way that suggests this is not quite true. These days, Benny owns a bookshop in Greenwich Village, sometimes selling comic books that people make themselves. He brings copies to Toronto for Sophia and Marcello. One, a comic book called *Maus*, is one of Dad's all-time favourite books.

Benny is good-looking, even more so than Dad. He's younger, too, which makes it surprising that so many of his friends have died. One, a man he calls Scott, was a writer Benny knew in Toronto who moved down to New York to be with Benny. That's when he got sick, Benny said, and eventually died in a hospice. From what Sophia understands from overheard conversations, Benny was worried about getting sick, too, until he took a test and found out he was okay. Now he says he's playing it safe.

Some of the dead friend's novels are on their bookshelf. Dad hasn't read them yet. Benny says that Sophia shouldn't read them until she's older.

"They're a little raw," says Benny. "Adventure sci-fi stuff from the seventies. A lot of fantasy stories about this superhuman guy called Giro. Some of it gets violent."

Benny is one of the few people who talks easily about Sophia's mother to her father. At times, Benny sounds confused, accidentally calling Mom by another name—Claire.

"Sorry," says Benny, tapping his head when Sophia points this out. "Senior's moment."

Sophia sits at her desk in math class and feels the numbers swim out of her head. All the little rules and tricks and memory aids that Dad gave her that made so much sense are gone. She sits and stares at the questions and makes a few attempts. It's hopeless.

The following afternoon, Mr. Lennon hands back the marked tests. Sophia is not surprised by her failing grade. There is a notation beside it: *Please get your mother/father to sign and return tomorrow*. It's a standard note all teachers write on a test they want a parent to sign, but it always seems to Sophia that that's exactly what she's got: a *mother/father*.

She puts the test in her backpack. Her father will be disappointed when he sees it. Deeply so. Not angry: he never, ever gets angry. Just disappointed. Sophia decides to take the failed test straight upstairs to the third floor of Our Lady of Lourdes Secondary School where Dad teaches the senior students, to show it to him and get him to sign it right away. Then she can get the disappointment part over with before dinner. It's better if he hears it from her rather than in the staff room. Since Dad is the head of the math department, there's the uncomfortable business of the teacher who failed her technically answering to Dad. Sophia often wishes she had gone to a different high school but her father wouldn't hear of it.

Up on the third floor, one of the music teachers sees her and calls out, "Sophia! Are you looking for your Dad? I just saw him in the science lab."

There's a little storeroom where the science teachers keep all the beakers, Bunsen burners, and pipettes. If you enter the lab through the storeroom, you come out of a door at the front of the classroom, as if appearing from heaven. This is how she finds herself in the storeroom, her father's voice drifting from the classroom through the adjoining door.

"I'm sorry, Barbara. You have to understand that I have other priorities."

"Oh, I'm getting that," a woman's voice answers. "I'm trying to figure out what they are. Half the time I think you like being with me. The other half, you barely speak to me. If this is going nowhere, I'd just as soon know now."

Barbara is Ms. O'Leary, one of the chemistry teachers. She's a very thin, tall woman with unconvincing red hair, who wears large, complicated-looking earrings and a cloyingly fruity perfume. She and Dad have gone out a few times.

"I have my daughter to think about. She has no one else. I have no other family and neither did my late wife."

"So you're telling me that there's no way I could be a mother to Sophia?"

Sophia's heart speeds up, as if she's just left the blocks for a hundred-yard dash. *Be a mother to Sophia? Oh my God.*

"Sophia doesn't need a mother; she's got me. She knows she can depend on me one hundred percent for the rest of her life. That's the way I want it. Just her and me."

Sophia suddenly feels as though she's being pulled down into the earth by a heavy rope. She can see her whole life before her. Her father will continue to look after her, for now. Eventually, when he's older, Sophia will have to look after him. She is never, ever going to be able to leave home. Or him.

Quietly, so that they don't know she's back there listening to their lover's quarrel (if you can call it that—Sophia suspects her Dad doesn't love Ms. O'Leary), she opens her backpack, removes the math test, lays it on the counter, and sets a beaker on top of it.

Then she starts walking. She doesn't know where she's going. She's just going.

From the front entrance of the school, she runs down the long winding cement steps to the street. For the first time in as long as she can remember, she has no plan or direction, no idea what's going to happen next.

She comes to a familiar corner where two high-rise apartment buildings stand side by side. Her friend Patrick lives in one of these buildings; she remembers walking him to the door once. She goes in, locates CHEN on the board, and presses in the code she sees next to the name. There's a click on the intercom and she hears Patrick's voice, "Yes"?

"Patrick, it's Sophia."

There's a pause. "Who?"

"Sophia! Your friend from school?"

There's another pause. "What's the password?"

Sophia has forgotten that Patrick is a latchkey kid. Sixteen years old and he's still not allowed to let anyone in unless they know the password. His parents are even more protective than her father.

"Patrick, come on! How would I know your password? Look, it's me! We eat lunch together every day! You know my voice, right?"

There is another long pause. "What's the funny name Sophia calls her dog?"

Sophia realizes what he's trying to do. Smart.

"His real name's Astro but I call him Astroturf," she answers.

"Come in."

The buzzer sounds.

Patrick lives on the seventh floor. The elevator creaks its way up as though it's not sure it can make it without having to stop and cough something out of its gears. On the second floor, the doors grind slowly apart to let in a woman in a long black dress and headscarf, carrying an overflowing laundry basket. A group of children enter with her; the two boys are in striped T-shirts and jeans, wearing small, round hats on their heads; the girls are in headscarves and long dresses like their mother, but with running shoes on underneath.

"You go down?" the mother asks Sophia.

"No, up."

The mother shrugs. "I go for ride," she says, resigned.

One of the kids—a boy, of course—presses all the buttons on the panel. It's going to be a long ride up, stopping at every floor. The little boy smirks triumphantly at Sophia as if saying, *Just try and stop me being bad!*

"*Tzk, tzk, tzk!*" the mother chides him.

When she gets to Patrick's apartment, he peeks out at her through the peephole, then opens the door with the chain still on, and sticks his eye to the crack. "Hi Sophia. What are you doing here?"

"I just thought I'd come for a visit. Maybe we can, I dunno, watch a little TV."

Patrick unchains the door and lets her in. "I'm playing pong right now, but we could watch afterwards."

"Cool," she says.

Patrick Chen is almost as tall as Sophia. He has a round, sensitive face that has recently broken out in an explosion of acne. Patrick pours glasses of juice for both of them and sets out a tray of cheese and bread. The two of them settle down in front of the pong game and start hitting the tiny white ball back and forth across the screen. The room is quiet except for the game noises, and the distant sound of rap music several floors away.

Cooking smells are starting to waft through the apartment door. Sophia is not sure what she's smelling, but it isn't any of the things her father makes.

"Where are your folks, anyway?" asks Sophia, to be sociable.

"Working."

"Both at the same time?"

"Yup. Game over! Okay let's see what's on the tube," he says, obviously copying something someone at school said. Patrick's speech is heavily accented; the Chens came from China just a couple of years ago.

Sitting on the floor in front of the TV, Sophia is suddenly blissfully happy.

Just try to make me not be bad, she thinks to herself.

Marcello is working on new math curriculum guidelines. The draft is due tomorrow. He stays at his desk until five o'clock, packs up his work, and leaves his classroom, just as the music teacher walks by lugging a cello case. "Did Sophia find you?"

"Sophia? No. Was she looking for me?"

"I told her you were in the chemistry lab. Maybe she couldn't find you and went home?"

"Maybe," says Marcello doubtfully.

On impulse, he goes back to the lab and enters through the back storage room. That's when he sees Sophia's math test sitting beside the sink, under a beaker, marked with an "F" and the note: *Please have your mother/father…*

Marcello suddenly thinks he knows what might have happened. He pictures Sophia coming into the room while he was talking to Barbara. Damn it all. What did he say, exactly?

Feeling as though he should have been home an hour ago, he rushes out of the school.

At home, Marcello calls out Sophia's name several times but only Astro the dog comes waddling out to meet him. He stands in the middle of the house, heart thundering. He's having trouble breathing. *Where is she?* Maybe a friend's house? She's never gone anywhere without permission so Marcello doesn't have phone numbers for any friends she might visit. He always drives her and picks her up. Why would he need phone numbers?

He sits on the couch, trying to calm himself. It's almost six o'clock. She'll be getting hungry by now. Where is she? And how long can he wait before he calls the police?

There is nothing he can do. Can't work, can't listen to music, can't read. Time will stand still until Sophia gets home. By seven, Marcello can't stand it anymore. He calls 13 Division and is put on the line with an Officer MacKay.

"Well, she hasn't been gone that long, sir. Are you sure she didn't just go to a friend's house? Have you tried calling around?"

"Not coming home is out of character for my daughter. She wouldn't wander away without telling me."

"Was she upset about anything? Any arguments, that type of thing?"

"She failed a test. But she knows I wouldn't get mad over that."

"Look, I'm taking the particulars but I think we should give it a little more time," says MacKay. "Most sixteen-year-olds turn up eventually. If I were you, I'd search around, see if you can find names and numbers of friends you could call. But if she doesn't get home in the next hour, call me back."

The officer gives Marcello his direct number, who jots it down with a shaking hand. Surely God wouldn't punish him by allowing Sophia to be hurt. Surely not.

But what will he do if a terrible tragedy has happened and he never sees his daughter again? He can't lose his wife and unborn child *and* his daughter and be expected to keep living. Over the past ten years he's become amazed by his body's stubborn persistence, his heart continuing to beat stupidly in his chest. If Sophia never comes home, he'll end up a shadow-man. He decides to appeal to God, but what comes out of his head is more like bargaining than praying: If Sophia comes home safely, I'll make up for everything I've done wrong in my life. As if in response to his prayer, he hears a knock.

Sophia forgot her key again, he thinks, hope soaring. But when he opens the door, it isn't Sophia but two police officers, a man and a woman, their squad car parked at the curb.

"Mr. Umbriaco? I'm Officer McKay," says the male officer. "This is Officer Oleski. You sounded so worried we thought we'd better talk now."

Sitting on the living room couch, Oleski flips through her notebook while MacKay's walkie-talkie, strapped to his belt, keeps squawking. Marcello feels uneasy in their presence. He can never completely shake that feeling of being wanted for questioning. Do the police still suspect he's Kowalchuk's murderer and Ida's kidnapper? It's been so many years. And he's legally changed his name. Of course, there's also the matter of Sophia's forged birth certificate. If the police asked to see it, would they be able to recognize it as a fake? Maybe use forensics to connect her to the missing baby from Love Canal? He's seen things like that happen on a new TV show, *Law and Order.*

"I want to make sure I've got your name right," says Oleski. She spells Marcello's full name, first and last. "You're a teacher, where?"

"Our Lady of Lourdes."

"And you last saw your daughter, when?"

Marcello walks Oleski through the series of events: the music teacher seeing Sophia in the hallway; the test sitting in the storeroom of the science lab; his suspicion that she had overheard his argument with a colleague.

"Colleague?" says McKay.

"She's also a former girlfriend," admits Marcello.

"Are you separated? Divorced? Is it possible Sophia is with her mother?" asks McKay.

"I'm a widower. Sophia's mother was killed in an accident over ten years ago."

No matter how many times he says this, it still ratchets open the crack inside his heart a little wider.

"Maybe the conversation upset Sophia, and she's hiding somewhere," suggests Oleski, looking down at her notes. She taps them with her pen. "There's something about your name. It sounds so familiar."

Marcello braces himself for what she will say next: *Aren't you the guy we interviewed about that accident during World Cup? The one who said his wife's car had been sabotaged?*

"Aren't you that guy who got stuck under a house, back in the seventies? Some type of explosion?" asks Oleski. "I remember seeing you being rescued on TV when I was a kid."

"Yeah. That was me," he answers warily.

"Small world," says Oleski. "Do you have a picture of Sophia? Something recent? A school photo, maybe? Or a yearbook?"

Marcello tries to quiet his breathing. "Give me a minute."

Going into Sophia's room, he pushes through the clutter on her desk, searching for the envelope of school photographs. Finally he pulls open the top drawer where he sees a smiling Sophia in her school uniform, her face repeated again and again and again.

When he pulls out the sheet, he notices a bundle of letters underneath it, the top one hand-addressed to *Ida Fabbro Umbriaco*.

What the hell is this?

He yanks off the ribbon holding the bundle together. There must be, what—ten letters here? All addressed to Ida. He pulls one out at random and skims it. The dense Italian script is full of phrases he recognizes instantly: *I love you, I miss you, I wish you hadn't run away* ... it's a love letter. Signed by someone named *Paolo*.

The letter is dated 1977. A love letter, to Ida.

Ida was writing to someone back in Italy and keeping his letters to her, bundled lovingly with a ribbon. All that time they were together she was keeping secrets from Marcello, who loved her so much he would have gladly taken her place behind the wheel of the Chevy. If it weren't for Sophia he would have found a way to join Ida long ago. Pills, the Falls, car exhaust and a hose through the window. Something.

Perhaps—and this thought is so poisonous that it crawls over his mind like a spider—Ida never loved him. Maybe she kept meeting up with the other man when she was a flight attendant. What would stop her from taking a lover on a stopover?

He's often felt Ida with him, touching him, talking to him, trying to comfort him. Now even that hope has winked out like a dying picture tube. It's all just a voice in his head. A stupid wish that once, he loved and was loved. He feels his heart slowing down and giving up.

He places the letters back in Sophia's drawer. The paper feels as soft as butter. It's been handled a lot, the letters read and re-read. Cherished.

Calm, calm, he tells himself. First things first. He's got to find his daughter. As he scissors around the border of a photo, he hears the phone ringing in the next room.

Sophia and Patrick are watching *Law and Order* when the door of the apartment opens to the length of the chain. Patrick runs to unlatch it.

"It's my Mom, back from her cleaning job," he tells Sophia. "Don't tell her we've been watching TV all evening, or she'll be mad."

Sophia grabs the remote and reluctantly turns off the TV. Mrs. Chen comes in, a small woman in battered Adidas and a pink wool coat that looks far enough out of fashion to be second-hand. Patrick and his mother trade words in Chinese; his mom sounds exhausted.

Mrs. Chen smiles wearily at Sophia and says, "Hello, girl. You do homework with Patrick?"

"Sort of," mumbles Sophia.

"It late," chides Mrs. Chen. "Mommy want you home?"

"I only have a father."

"You call him now, pick up," urges Mrs. Chen, taking off her pink coat.

"Dad? I'm sorry, I forgot to call. I'm at my friend's. Can you come pick me up?"

At the sound of Sophia's voice, the clock inside Marcello's heart, frozen for the last three hours, starts marking time again.

On the ride home from the Chens, Sophia wipes tears. Marcello says nothing. At the first red light, he reaches out and puts his arm around her shoulders. Sobbing, Sophia explains that she can't do math and that maybe she should switch to the remedial program that Mr. Lennon has been pushing, even though it is kind of embarrassing when your own father is the head of the math department. She also wants to quit piano and choir and spend more time at friends' houses.

Marcello listens and tries not to talk. At last, he says, "Everything but choir. Please stay in the church choir for one more year."

"Okay," she agrees. "I'm sorry about scaring you, Daddy."

When they get home, he thinks about asking Sophia about the letters, but he can't. She must know by now that her mother was involved with someone else.

He can go back into Sophia's desk and read the letters on his own, another time. Maybe when she's at choir practice. If he can bear it. But what would be the point of tormenting himself further? He's read enough to know what the letters are, what they mean.

Marcello doesn't sleep that night. He stares into the darkness and thinks about Ida, the letters, Senior, Kowalchuk, and the incomplete curriculum outline, draft four, due tomorrow, sitting in his briefcase.

The next morning, he signs Sophia's test. "Tell Mr. Lennon I'll talk to him about the remedial program. And stop worrying."

In the staff room the next morning, Marcello sits slumped at a work table, trying to wake himself with very strong, bitter coffee, when Walt Kipps walks in. One of the older math teachers who was passed over for department head in favour of Marcello, Walt is working with him on the new curriculum. Walt also has the thankless job of being the liaison between the committee of teachers and the Board office.

Walt sits down across from Marcello and gets right to the point: "Did you finish the draft? I've got the Board breathing down my neck."

"I need a little more time," answers Marcello wearily.

"I thought ... you said you were working on it last night!"

"Something came up last night."

Walt snorts. "What, did Barb come over so you could play hide the salami?"

Marcello stands up, leans over the table, grabs Walt by the knot of his tie with one hand, and punches him, hard, in the face with the other. He hits him again, and again. The blood is fearsome. Walt's face turns into Kowalchuk's, then Senior's, then the faceless lover in Ida's letters. When Marcello finally realizes what he's doing, he lets Walt drop to the floor.

Walt is screaming. Marcello staggers back and sits down in his chair. He even closes his eyes. Maybe this will turn out to be a dream. He'll wake up, find himself in bed and this will be over.

The music teacher runs to the fridge and gets a can of pop, which she holds to Walt's nose to try to stop the bleeding. The principal calls 9-1-1 and requests an ambulance and a police car. Thirteen division.

The officers who answer the call are not MacKay and Oleski. Marcello is grateful for that, at least. They cuff him and walk him to the squad car, passing quite a few of his students. Marcello can feel their eyes catching on him as he passes, the cuffs on his wrists, the blood on his shirt. Strangely, he feels nothing. No shame, not even embarrassment. All that will come later.

When they get to the Don Jail for processing, the intake officer asks him if he knows the phone number of a lawyer off by heart and is unsurprised when Marcello says yes. Ed Ceci appears at the jail an hour later in a blue suit, dressed for court.

"You in trouble, brother?" he asks Marcello.

Marcello looks up at Ed. His exhaustion is so great that all he does is nod.

15. AMOR AND PSYCHE

MARCELLO'S CAFE (FORMERLY ESPOSITO'S SOCIAL CLUB), 1992

MARCELLO'S FINGERS SLIDE along the grain of cherry wood, sweet-smelling and smooth to the touch. The lumber is young, fresh, and light in colour. Over time, it will age to the deep reddish-brown of Sophia's hair.

Brushing sawdust from his overalls, he steps back to look at his work: a double-curved bar with a zinc countertop undulating along one side of the café. He designed it to suggest the shape of a reclining woman propped on her elbow, one hip thrust seductively forward. The empty bar stools are tucked tight against her like children.

He loves working with cherry wood. The bar is his wooden woman, created with his own hands. An eternal, unchanging Ida who will never die, or hoard love letters, or have an unfaithful thought. Projecting again. His doctor has warned him not to do this, but it pleases him to turn the bar into Ida, or Ida into the bar, even if it's bad for his mental health.

The carpentry started as therapy, part of the treatment that followed the court-ordered psychiatric assessment that kept him out of jail. Although diagnosed with depression, the assessment noted that Marcello Umbriaco may also have experienced a psychotic break during the attack on Walter Kipps. In answer to a question about whether he ever heard voices, he admitted that occasionally he conversed with his late wife.

At first, his psychiatrist, Dr. Athena Drakopolous, suggested art therapy, but the paints and clay made Marcello feel like an overgrown child. Then music therapy; Marcello explained to her that if listening to music could cure him, he would already be the most mentally healthy man in Toronto. Finally, she suggested trying something more physical. And she was right: pounding nails and sawing two-by-fours quieted his mind. At least he felt like he was doing something a man was supposed to do.

Dr. Drakopolous took getting used to. Ever since he had started teaching, every younger person except Sophia had addressed him with an honourific. Even Sophia's friends called him *Sir* or *Mr. U.* He wasn't sure whether times had changed or this was just how therapy worked, but in the doctor's office, he was simply Marcello. The psychiatrist, on the other hand, never invited him to call her anything but Dr. Drakopolous. This helped him feel younger than his forty-three years, making it easier to go back in time. That seemed to be the whole purpose of therapy, to take him back, and back, and back. To figure out what had happened in the past to make him crazy.

Not that Dr. Drakopolous ever used the word "crazy," but Marcello was no fool. It was crazy to grieve for his wife for ten years, crazy to feel a black-mouthed void yawning beside him, sometimes threatening to swallow him whole. Sometimes the void shrank to a tiny lead dot at the end of a pencil eraser; at other times, it canyoned into a gullet into which people fell and never came out. He often dreamed of climbing down the dark throat; hearing Ida call his name, he would reach for her fingers, as familiar as his own, and start to climb, pulling her up behind him. But when he reached the mouth of the void, he would turn and see that his hand was empty.

"Why do you turn?"

"To see if it's really her."

"You think you've taken the wrong woman's hand?"

"I'm not sure if it's Ida or just someone who feels like her."

For the first time in his life he was on medication, a new drug called "Prozac," which, he reluctantly admitted to Benny, made him feel better, then guilty about feeling better. But one side effect of the drug was that he could no longer hear Ida's voice speaking to him.

"Maybe that's not such a bad thing," suggested Benny. "Maybe that means you're getting better."

"If that's 'better,' I'm not sure I want it," answered Marcello. He weaned himself off Prozac after six months.

Where do you think your guilt comes from, Marcello?

How do you feel about Sophia growing up and leaving you?

The aggression toward your colleague—was it directed at him or do you think you trying to attack someone else? Your father, perhaps?

Dr. Drakopolous asked a lot of questions but never answered any of them. She always wanted to know what *he* thought.

Once, as he was leaving the office, he said, "Psychiatry seems like a pretty soft racket, Athena. You make me do all the work."

A tiny smile softened her lips. Triumphantly, he returned to calling her Dr. Drakopolous.

The only other time her mask slipped was the day Marcello described falling in love with Ida when she first arrived as his father's proxy bride. Pausing in his story, he heard Dr. Drakopoulos mutter a single word to herself: "*Oedipus.*"

"What's that?" asked Marcello, turning his head in her direction from where he lay on the couch.

Dr. Drakopolous looked up in surprise, as if she hadn't realized she'd spoken. "Oedipus. A tragic hero from Greek literature. I assume you've heard of him."

"I studied math and sciences. I didn't read many of the classics, even in high school. Or if I did, I don't remember. What does this guy have to do with me?"

Dr. Drakopolous hesitated, then proceeded. "He was a king who killed his father and slept with his mother. Unknowingly. It's where the term 'Oedipus complex' comes from."

Marcello swung his legs off the couch and sat up to look straight into the psychiatrist's eyes. "Let's be clear: Ida wasn't my mother. And I didn't kill my father. Although I'd like to."

"Let's move on," suggested Dr. Drakopolous, dropping her gaze.

Of all the questions Dr. Drakopolous put to Marcello, he answered only one without thinking about it. "You're a relatively young man. Do you want another relationship?"

Marcello almost laughed. *What would be the point? What woman wants to sleep with a dead man?*

A silence ensued. Marcello was surprised to find himself crying. "Sorry. Where the hell did this come from?" he mumbled, wiping his eyes with his sleeve.

The silent woman handed him a box of tissues.

Despite Dr. Drakopolous telling him that he *still had work to do*, Marcello wrapped up therapy after the one year mandated by the court. Instead of returning to the classroom, he bought out Mike Esposito. Now he could run the café—and continue sanding, smoothing, and perfecting his Ida-shaped bar—full-time.

At their last session, Dr. Drakopolous handed him a book: Ovid's *Metamorphoses*. "There's a myth in it about a great Greek tragic hero. One of the classical stories your ancestors stole from mine."

"Oedipus again?" frowned Marcello, flipping through the book.

"No, not Oedipus. Orpheus, son of Apollo. He loved his wife so deeply that after she died, he went to the Underworld to bring her back."

"Did he pull it off?" asked Marcello with interest.

"Find out for yourself. I know you didn't care for art therapy. Think of this as reading therapy."

"*Grazie*, Athena."

"*Parakalo*, Marcello," she answered and bestowed a smile on him.

16. SHOWDOWN IN SHIPMAN'S CORNERS

QUEEN ELIZABETH WAY, 1992

HE PICKS AN AFTERNOON in early December. Snow starts lashing the windshield as he crosses the Burlington Bay Bridge, the steel mills of Hamilton welcoming him with their grubby grey towers and catwalks. Passing through Bramborough, he keeps his eyes on the road. The Andolini farm is now lost in a tangle of subdivisions. At Shipman's Corners, he takes the Niagara Street exit off the Queen Elizabeth Way. In minutes he can see the high dome of the Ukrainian Catholic church. A few more blocks and he's on the street where he grew up.

He's shocked by his old neighbourhood on Canal Road. The decline in what used to be an ordinary, working-class neighbourhood is something he should have expected, given what's happened to the factories and the decline in shipping through the Seaway. It's a ghost of a street with little left of the old immigrant families who lived and worked here, raising kids, and burying their first generation. Most of the houses are empty, and the few still occupied are surrounded by weeds and junk. The roadbed is cracked and deeply potholed.

He parks in front of Kowalchuk's flower shop. The windows are dark, the concrete stoop crumbling. He peers through the front window, but all he can see are the bright feral eyes of an animal scuttling away inside. For a moment, he thinks he hears the sound of voices, but it's just the rising wind.

Wet snow is falling thickly now, piling into soggy drifts. Lake effect snow. Typical of Shipman's Corners, almost unknown in Toronto. Nearby Buffalo must be getting hammered. He should have worn boots.

He turns to look across the street at the wreck of the candy store. The main floor window is boarded up, the scorched *Italian Tobacco & Sweets* sign barely readable. He's surprised to see the second floor is inhabited. There's a light in the window.

He goes to the side of the building and climbs the rickety fire escape. At the top he comes face to face with a windowless grey steel door, the kind seen in institutions, looking new against the building's blackened wooden walls. He hesitates, listening; he can hear the rise and fall of voices inside.

He knocks. No response. Knocks again. Nothing. Just as he starts to turn to leave, the door opens. Voices pour out as Senior stares at Marcello without recognition.

He has shrunk into a skinny, sagging tortoise, his hair completely gone. The only things Marcello recognizes are his large, slightly protruding eyes and the stink of rye and body odour. Inside the flat, a television blares.

"Pop?"

Senior furrows his brow. "So, you come back, eh? She kick you out?"

Marcello opens his mouth, then closes it. What the hell is he doing here? "Can I come in?"

"Free country," mutters Senior and steps aside.

The furnishings in the flat have not changed in twenty-three years. The only additions are a small microwave oven sitting on top of the burners of an old Moffatt stove and a portable television. On the screen, colour images waver, pulled in by a pair of rabbit-ear antennae. As the music swells, a gaunt woman dripping jewels and clutching a highball glass implores a man in a suit and tie to make a deal with someone named Victor.

"You come right at the start of *The Young and the Restless,*" Senior complains, sitting down on a chesterfield. He immediately turns his attention back to the screen.

Marcello stands, uncertainly, in the middle of the flat. He

feels as if he's eighteen again and has just run up the stairs from the store to check where Senior wants the guys to unload a delivery. He sits down on the couch next to Senior, trying to put together some sort of opening question when Senior asks, "What you do with my wife?"

"She's gone."

Senior turns toward Marcello. "She run away on you, too?"

"No, she was killed in a car accident. A long time ago."

Senior nods. He's smiling now. "God's judgment."

Marcello stares at the screen. A tall man with a mustache is gripping a blonde woman by the shoulders and shouting, *What did you do with the baby, Nikki?*

"I need to ask you something," says Marcello.

"I got no money or jobs, if that's what you're here for," says Senior.

"I don't need money or a job, Pop. Just information. What do you know about Ida's life before she came to Canada? Was there a man, back home? Someone she was running away from?"

"The father," grunts Senior, staring at the show.

Marcello hesitates at this news. "I thought Ida's father died in the War."

Senior is seized by a coughing fit. It takes a second for Marcello to realize that he's laughing. "Her father was no soldier. He was a priest, and her mother was a *puttana!* This is why her blood is bad, why she run away. *Beh!*" He gestures at the screen. "She almost as bad as this one, Nikki, who take her baby and run off from her husband."

Marcello looks at Senior in astonishment. Ida's parents, a priest and a prostitute? For a moment, Marcello is so stunned he can't decide what to do or ask next. One thing is clear: Senior will answer any question, just to get him to shut up and let him watch his show. Marcello forces himself to wait for a commercial break.

When a Tide ad comes on, he asks: "Was the father's name Paolo?"

Senior shrugs. "Somethin' like that. Why the hell you ask me? I read about him in one of those Italian gossip papers we sell back in the sixties. What you call it?—*Oggi*. That how I find her."

Marcello stares at Senior. He doesn't seem all there. Surely he must already have known Ida was dead. Especially if he had a hand in it. Dementia? Maybe.

"Pop, did you kill Ida? Rig her car?" asks Marcello. He tries to keep his voice steady.

Senior barely reacts. "Not me," he answers, without emotion. Unexpectedly, he adds, "Stan figure it out on his own."

Marcello tries to stay calm. There's no sense in doing anything to Senior anymore. Time and old age are doing a good job of finishing him off. "Where's Stan now?"

"Grantham Gardens. Old folks' home downtown." Senior taps his forehead. "He had a stroke. Can't talk so good no more."

Marcello gets off the couch and buttons his coat, looking down at this father who dumped him on the Andolinis like a sack of potatoes. "You said once that I wasn't your son. Is that true?"

Senior doesn't look up. The show has started again.

"Well?"

"Your mother show up here with you. I got no idea who your father was," grunts Senior. "You probably *un' figlio d'una buona donna.*"

Son of a good woman—by which Senior really means *son of a whore.* Marcello feels the old anger at Senior building, poisoning his brain, infecting his blood. "Go fuck yourself, Pop."

"You wanna fight, come back after my show," mutters Senior, not looking at Marcello. "Otherwise, go to hell."

Senior's attention remains on the television. Marcello feels a sudden desire to kick the screen in. Instead, he walks out the door and runs down the fire escape. Beneath his feet, the rusty metal stairs tremble. *Ida, Ida, Ida!* they shout as Marcello descends.

There was no deception, no violation of the heart, just shame. Ida was as true as the curve of the café bar that he'd plotted and sawed and sanded so carefully. He's so relieved that he hardly notices he's up to his ankles in wet snow.

Marcello drives downtown —the "good" section of Shipman's Corners. It always seemed a world away from Canal Road, when he was a kid. Now it's just another seedy street, a ten-minute drive from the candy store. Where once there were tearooms and china shops and bookstores and a small but serviceable Woolworths, the main street is now mostly boarded up storefronts. A couple of adult video stores flash out their attractions on pixilated screens. Even the old movie theatre has been turned into a second-hand furniture store.

Grantham Gardens turns out to be easy to find, right off the main street, built into what used to be an elementary school. The sandblasted yellow brick façade greets him with an air of antiseptic indifference. When he walks through the sliding glass doors, he finds himself in a small lobby full of elderly men and women staring at a TV bolted to the wall. They are watching the same show as Senior, *The Young and the Restless.* A dusty artificial Christmas tree squats beneath a sagging banner reading BUON NATALE / HAPPY HOLIDAYS, a few unconvincingly wrapped gifts scattered around to suggest the false cheer of a family gathering. Care providers in brightly-coloured sweats and scrubs call out to their charges at the tops of their lungs. "Hello, Mrs. Benedetti! How are we today?"

Murdering Stan lives *here*?

A ponytailed blonde in running shoes and an emerald green track suit spots him and smiles brightly. "May I help you, sir?"

Marcello glances around, as if trying to decide whether to stay or go. "I'm looking for someone. Not sure he's even living here. Guy named Stanley Mancuso."

Ponytail giggles. "Of course he's here. He's everybody's boyfriend."

Marcello looks at the woman in amazement. "He doesn't sound like the same Stan."

"Come on, dear, I'll show you to his room," says Ponytail. "He'll be thrilled. Doesn't get many visitors."

The hallway smells of urine, mashed potatoes, and disinfectant. Elderly men and women with walkers and wheelchairs watch them pass, occasionally calling out *Lindy* to the woman, who assures them she'll be back soon with their meals and meds. She explains to Marcello that Mr. Mancuso is having a good day after a bad bout of pneumonia. He even managed to eat some solid food for lunch.

"The ladies fight over who gets to feed him," she confides. "There aren't many men his age in the home. He the cock of the walk."

Marcello says nothing, struggling to decide whether to describe to this woman the kind of man she's keeping alive, like making a pet of a rabid animal. When they arrive at the room she sings out, "Look what I've brought! A visitor!" he sees an emaciated man strapped into a wheelchair, his head resting against a brace that keeps it from flopping over. One side of his face sags, the paralyzed eye partially closed; the good eye rolls in Marcello's direction.

The son of a bitch is still alive in there, thinks Marcello.

"If you're here at five, I'll bring a tray for you, too. Now I'll leave you two boys to your fun," Ponytail says and walks away, her crêpe-soled shoes sucking against the linoleum.

Stan's cold blue eye studies him.

"You know who I am?" Marcello asks.

"No." The word comes out like a breath. *Nuh*. But at least Marcello knows he understands.

"Marcello Umbriaco."

"O'yeh. Zhun'er."

Oh yeah. Junior.

"There's stuff I want you to tell me. And I don't want to be lied to."

Stan is watching him, the mobile side of his face collapsing into folds as he struggles to speak. He's angry, thinks Marcello.

"I want you to admit you killed Ida."

The right side of Stan's mouth twists into something like his old sneer. "Geh te heh!"

Go to hell.

Marcello stares at Stan, trying to gauge how to pull information out of the old bastard's brain.

Stan shifts his head slightly, one side of his mouth working. He's getting excited. "Plan yur wyfs akstent, tha bich. Dindoit. Ahranched it."

I planned your wife's accident, the bitch. Didn't do it, arranged it.

Marcello's ears are full of the sound of his own heartbeat. "You're a murderer."

"Suk kee me."

So kill me.

Marcello closes the door and pushes an easy chair against it, jamming the back under the handle. He's alone with the man who killed his wife and his unborn child. The villain is helpless, his skull as thin as an eggshell. Marcello will be the avenger, St. Michael the Archangel swinging his holy sword, wielding divine justice. Stan's breath starts coming in ragged pants.

C'mehn, c'mehn, c'mehn!

On the unmade bed, a silver handrail shines among the rumpled sheets, the brightness catching Marcello's eye. He can see his own reflection in its surface, a man with a patch of white hair and glasses, middle-aged, bereaved, enraged. He picks up the rail and weighs it in his hand. It's a length of steel pipe, longer than a baseball bat, heavy enough to support a man's weight.

If Marcello is the x axis and Stan is y, then the handrail is the lever that will shift the whole goddamn world.

"Guh uhn," urges Stan, one blue eye fixed on Marcello.
Go on.

He *wants* me to do it, thinks Marcello, gripping the handrail. "Do eh. Do eh. K'menh. Dun 'oo haft a guss?"

Do it. Do it. Come on. Don't you have the guts?

Marcello imagines himself beating Stan to death and beyond, rendering him down into gristle and blood and bits of brain, nothing left of a human being at all, just stains and offal. But before he can strike, the image in his mind changes.

Not this way, Marcello tells himself.

He tosses the handrail back onto the scrabble of bed sheets where it hits a bedpan, giving a hollow metal ring. Marcello places himself directly in front of Stan and wraps his hands around the man's neck, a thin stick of cartilage and sagging flesh. One blue eye, wide open and staring at him, starts to tear up.

Stan gurgles. From the hallway comes the shuffle of feet, the squeal of rubber wheels, the call-and-response of patient and caregiver.

Lin–deeee?

Com–ing!

Stan's face is darkening to the colour of ink. He hears Ida's voice. *You're doing him a favour! Stan welcomes death—so let him live! Besides, they'll lock you up and then what happens to Sophia?*

Marcello closes his eyes. Just let me finish it.

Ponytail's voice, high and frightened, is shouting, "What's blocking the door? Sir? *Sir?*"

Marcello releases his hands from around Stan's neck. He steps back and yanks open the door, face to face with Ponytail, her trolley beside her. She has brought two dinner trays. Marcello picks up one of them and hurls it at the wall over Stan's head. The old man sits slumped in his wheelchair, head flopped forward like a dead man, but flinches when the metal tray clatters to the floor. He's alive.

Marcello pushes his way through the crowd of onlookers peering in at the door. Caregivers, residents, even a janitor with a pail watch Marcello pass. No one bothers to stop him. Stan becomes just another mess to clean up while Marcello returns to the world.

17. A SHOUT FROM GOD

LILY GAVE UP on religion long ago, but when her mother's illness overwhelms her, she goes to Holy Martyrs. They have the best music of all the churches in Toronto's west end. None of that modern stuff; it's traditional all the way, with a pipe organ and a four-part choir.

Her only other escape is physical. As her mother's body breaks down, Lily builds hers up: weights, crunches, running. Yesterday, one of the trainers at the gym took her aside: "Lily, you're overdoing it. Maybe you should see your doctor?"

Lily goes to Saturday evening Mass instead. A torrent of notes cascades out of the organ loft like a shout from God. Lily pauses at the back of the church, trying to let the music drown out her grief. On this particular winter's night, even Bach's Fugue in G Minor isn't working.

Earlier that day, at the nursing home, Lily had spread out some pictures: family snapshots, portraits of friends from the old days, even a photograph from the Oka standoff that won Lily a photojournalism prize.

Mamére's fingers tremble over a Kodachrome of Lily squinting in sunlight as she rides piggyback on a man's shoulders. His big hands grip her ankles hanging over his chest. Her running shoes are different colours.

"Remember, Mamére? You took this one at the Seahorse. I would've been what—eight years old? Nine?"

Her mother's fingers brush the snapshot. For one breathtaking moment, Lily thinks Mamére actually recognizes someone in the photograph. She has to remind herself that the movement is likely a trick of her mother's torn and tangled nerve endings. Her frozen eyes might as well have been staring at a bedpan. Lily slips the photograph back into the leather portfolio.

Mamére is only sixty-seven; Lily, eighteen years younger. Almost as close in time as sisters.

Soon I might be you, Lily thinks. If she's inherited the Huntington's gene from her mother, she'll get the disease. Paralysis, dementia, all of it.

Her doctor urges a genetic test. Lily refuses. Knowing her destiny would be like waiting for years to be in a car wreck, watching as her body tears itself apart in slow motion. No amount of healthy living will make a damn bit of difference.

Lily picks an almost-empty pew near the back of the church, where she can listen to the music without feeling like she has to take part in the Mass. She especially wants to avoid giving the sign of peace to strangers.

A man sits at the other end of the pew, bulky in his winter coat; he doesn't look at her when she slides in. She suspects he's not the sign of peace type, either.

At the altar, Father Silva lifts his hands and says, "Peace be with you."

"And also with you," the congregants respond. They trade kisses and handshakes.

Lily glances at the man at the end of the pew. He's looking at her now, too. His eyes appear to be deeply bruised. A white patch on his tangle of grey hair makes him look as though he's been daubed with paint.

"Peace be with you," he says. He doesn't offer his hand.

"You, too," Lily responds.

When Mass is over, Lily remains in the pew, listening to the choir sing the processional. The man hasn't moved. He's sitting with his head bowed and hands clasped in prayer. Lucky him.

Lily hasn't been able to pray for years, ever since she realized that she was talking to the empty sky.

She glances at him again. *Robust,* her mother would have called him, with the broad body of a boxer and the High Renaissance profile of a stained glass martyr. St. Sebastian, after the Romans got finished with him. She imagines the man looking down at himself in surprise, his winter coat bristling with arrows.

Lily stifles a laugh but one note escapes up into the nave. She pretends she's clearing her throat, but the man is on to her, trying to decipher the joke. He has to be at least sixty but looks younger when he smiles.

Lily smiles back. "Do you like the music?"

"Very much. My daughter joined this choir in high school." Lily can hear the cadences of a long-lost accent in the man's voice.

"Really? What part?"

"Soprano."

She looks up at the choir loft where two dark-haired women, a soprano in her twenties and an alto about Lily's age, gather sheet music. The older woman tucks in the younger one's blouse, a tender gesture that reminds Lily of Mamère. The soprano and alto are obviously the bruised man's wife and daughter. That's why he's waiting.

"Your daughter has a wonderful voice. I enjoy hearing her sing duets with her mother," says Lily, searching for her gloves.

The man gives Lily a puzzled frown, then glances up at the choir loft. "No, no. Those two aren't mine. My daughter Sophia is away." The man hesitates, before adding, "Her mother is dead."

Oh, great. All Lily wanted was a quiet moment alone, and now she's stumbled into someone else's grief. As if she needed more. "I'm sorry for your loss," she says. It's the correct phrase, all that's required.

But before she can slide out of the pew, he says: "Thank

you, but I lost her a long, long time ago. Not that you ever really get over it."

Lily stands awkwardly with her coat half-on, trapped in this stranger's tragedy. Surprised by his naked show of emotion, she's tempted to confide in him.

My mother's dying. Very, very slowly. I have to grieve while she's still alive.

Instinctively, she knows this level of intimacy would open a discussion about the misery of witnessing a slow death versus the shock of a sudden one. *No, thank you.* Looking for a way out of the conversation without seeming rude, she offers: "Raising a little girl on your own must have been a challenge."

He smiles as if she's paid him a compliment. "Now that she's grown up and gone off to work for her uncle in England, I don't know what to do with myself. This'll be my first Christmas without her."

"England! How nice. Have a good night, then."

"You too," he says, still not moving from the pew.

Lily pulls on her gloves. The man's solid presence is starting to attract her like a big planet pulling a smaller one into its orbit. She finds herself wanting to touch that white patch of hair. It reminds her of a blaze on a tree, marking a way through the woods.

Behind them, in the narthex, the organist hustles her way out the door with her arms full of sheet music, the choir members huddled close behind her, singing out their displeasure at the blast of wind.

Lily and the man are alone in the church. She sees now that his eyes are shadowed, not bruised. The mark of a fellow insomniac. Someone who lies awake nights, thinking about people who aren't there any more.

Oh, what the hell, thinks Lily. *I'm alone, he's alone, we're grown-ups.* Pretending to rummage in her purse for car keys, she says, "Would you like to join me for coffee? There's a place near here I've been meaning to try called Marcello's."

The man laughs, the sound of his voice echoing in the hollow space above them.

"Yeah, sure, I know it," says the man. "I own it."

Sitting in the passenger seat of Lily's Honda, Marcello says he prefers walking to Mass, even on blustery nights like this one. He says he used to love driving but, these days, enjoys it less and less. Lily resists the temptation to ask why. As she pulls to the curb across from the café, a Future Bread delivery truck rumbles past, its sign reading: *The Future Is Coming!*

A chill runs through Lily as Marcello unlocks the front door of the café. She glances around at the neighbouring groceterias, dollar stores, and wedding and Communion dress shops, all asleep and dreaming.

"Not enough business in this weather to stay open late," Marcello says, holding the door for her. "How about I make a couple of cappuccinos and we take them upstairs?"

Unbuttoning her coat to let in the warmth, Lily watches Marcello steam milk and pour espresso into thick cups, a gold band on his hand catching the light as he places biscotti on a plate. For a big man, he handles the food with surprising delicacy.

Balancing a tray, he leads her up a stairway behind the bar to a flat. An upright piano shines against one wall; a wood-burning fireplace dominates another. A few greeting cards are propped on a table. Otherwise, he hasn't decorated for Christmas. Not that it's any more festive at Lily's place.

Over the mantel, a solemn-looking, dark-haired girl stares out of a painting—the daughter, obviously. Next to her are several black-and-whites of a woman with large, serious eyes, chin resting on her clenched fist. She looks directly at the camera, not smiling, but with noticeable emotion. She dearly loved whoever was taking her picture, thinks Lily.

"Your wife?"

Putting a record on the turntable, Marcello nods. "Ida. I took those the year before she died."

As the Flower Duet from the opera *Lakmé* fills the room, Lily examines the photographs. Ida looks no more than thirty. Wide, dark eyes, a pointed chin, full mouth, blonde hair. Her expression is watchful, alert. And something else: slightly alarmed. Despite the passion in her eyes, there's a certain tension in the set of her mouth. Perhaps she didn't want her picture taken. Or she was guarding a secret she was afraid the camera would expose. Lily has seen that expression in some of her subjects. The look of someone with something to hide.

"You have a good eye," Lily says.

Marcello acknowledges the compliment with a nod and waves Lily to the couch. When he offers biscotti, she shakes her head. He raises his eyebrows at Lily's refusal to eat.

She crosses her legs. "What was weighing on your mind tonight, Marcello? I could feel you thinking from the end of the pew."

He shrugs, soaking a chunk of biscotti in the coffee. "Sometimes I just like to sit quietly and talk to God. To Ida, really."

"What was tonight's conversation about?"

"I've been thinking about becoming a priest," he mumbles through a full mouth.

Jesus!, Lily thinks, tugging down the hem of her skirt.

"A rather late-in-life decision, isn't it?" she asks, carefully.

Marcello grins. "Now you sound like Ida. She thinks I'm crazy to even consider it. You'd be surprised how many guys join the priesthood after their wives die."

The offhand way that Marcello mentions his late wife makes her seem alive. Lily feels almost guilty about being alone with her husband. Oblivious to the effect of his words, Marcello starts eating Lily's untouched food.

"What about you? Why were you there?" he asks, dunking her biscotti in his cup.

Lily considers whether to tell him about her mother's illness and her own fears of getting sick. She decides: *No.*

"The usual for a lapsed Catholic. I like the music."

They sip their cappuccinos, Lily watching Marcello over her cup. *Drink up and go,* she tells herself. Early tomorrow, she has to return to the nursing home with its antiseptic washes never quite covering the odour of dirty diapers, the *crrrkk* of privacy curtains, the ring of a catheter hitting stainless steel while a voice sings, "Good girl, Ms. Daigle!" Lily never witnesses the siphoning of her mother's bladder. She stands outside the curtain and waits. Waits for the neurologist, the nurse, the physiotherapist. Waits for the first signs of Mamére's disease in herself. She's so tired of waiting.

"Marcello, if you haven't yet taken a vow of celibacy, I'd really like to sleep with you," she announces.

He stops gathering their cups, his eyes wide. "You don't even know me."

"I don't want to, except in a Biblical sense."

"But I could be anybody!"

"You're an attractive man. I want to go to bed with you. That's really all there is to it."

He opens and closes his mouth, as if struggling with how to tell her something. Finally, he says: "I'm sixty-three. Too old for a young woman like you."

Lily laughs. "I'm forty-nine. I'd hardly call that young."

"Lily, it's flattering to…"

"Do you have condoms?" she interrupts.

Marcello shakes his head.

"That's okay," says Lily, rummaging in her purse. "I do."

She places two Sheiks on the table.

Women have changed, Marcello thinks in awe. *So have you,* Ida reminds him.

Lily is lovely but she's *sfacciata*, thinks Marcello. That's the word Ida would use. Nervy.

I was nervy, too, says Ida. *Or have you forgotten?*

Marcello closes his eyes. I haven't forgotten anything. That's the problem.

Finally, something we agree on, replies Ida. He can almost hear the sarcasm in her voice.

His bed has been more or less empty since Ida's death. A few relationships here and there, but the women always drifted away. One of them even said Marcello's bed felt too crowded. When he asked what she meant, she said, "There's you, there's me, and there's your dead wife lying between us—and I don't think she cares for me very much."

In fact, that wasn't far wrong. But he senses that Ida wouldn't mind him being with Lily.

You have a body, yes? she would say with her usual exasperation at Marcello's cautious nature. *So use it! Subito! What you waiting for?*

Marcello moves next to Lily, close enough to pick up a flowery scent on her skin and something strangely sharp and clinical—an antiseptic, perhaps. He takes her hand. Lily moves it to her breast and kisses him. A puddle of clothing collects softly on the floor. Ambushed by desire, Marcello takes her hand and leads her to his bed.

Lily's body surprises him: her muscles are hard as rock and she is almost completely hairless. He strokes and enters her, bringing her to climax, although his mind is unhappily aware that they're having sex, not making love. An ugly Italian word pops into his head—*gigolo*—but he swats it away.

Marcello gentles her face with his hand, the gesture so unconsciously intimate that Lily recognizes it as muscle memory. His body thinks she's someone else.

"Can I get you a sandwich? A glass of wine?"

"Thanks, no." Lily suspects that Ida must have liked a little something after lovemaking.

"Just thought you might be hungry," Marcello murmurs.

Lily yawns. Funny, how she can't seem to put her body in motion. *Is this an early symptom of Huntington's?* It takes a heartbeat to realize that she's simply too comfortable to move her body away from his.

Maybe I should tell him about myself, she considers, then imagines the look on his face, the concerned tone of voice: *You could get sick? Can they do a test?* His eyes would brush her with pity, painting out the woman, sketching in a victim. It's happened before.

She searches the covers for her bra. "Time for me to go, Marcello."

He rubs his eyes. "Ah, I forgot. You don't want to know me. Except in a Biblical sense."

She's hurt him, the last thing she wanted to do. Trying to lighten the mood, she says, "After what you just did in bed, I think you'd be wasted on the priesthood."

Lily hopes for one of his embarrassed smiles. Instead he looks distressed. "You're right. I'm not even a particularly good Catholic anymore."

Lily shakes her head, confused. "Then why become a priest?"

Marcello's hands try to pull an explanation out of the air. "Because I need to be forgiven."

Lily turns on her side to look at Marcello.

"Forgiven for what?" she asks slowly, remembering that faintly alarmed look on his wife's face in the wall portrait.

Marcello rubs his eyes. "For Ida."

Lily feels time slow down as everything in the room—the bed, the discarded condom, even Lily herself—moves slightly out of true. What does she really know about this man? He claims to love his wife, yes, but now admits to doing something bad enough that he needs to take holy orders to be forgiven. Lily edges to the side of the bed and reaches down to pick up her panties from the floor, the hair on her neck prickling as she turns her back on Marcello.

Only then does she notice the clatter of sleet against the window. Marcello swings his legs over the side of the bed and twitches the curtains aside. Under a streetlight across the street, her car glitters inside a thick coating of ice.

As she stands at the window, an explosive sound shivers the

panes. A flash illuminates the bedroom as the streetlights fizzle out. The hum of the bedside clock radio stops dead. All the ambient electronic sounds in the room vanish. The only thing Lily can hear is a muffled buzz in her ears.

"Transformer must've blown nearby," says Marcello, turning from Lily to rummage in the bedside table.

"I'd better leave before it gets worse," she says, scanning the darkness of the bedroom for the rest of her clothes.

"You can't go home in this. Driving will be treacherous."

She looks out the window again. Across the street, a dangling power line sends a zip-line of sparks across the roadway. Toronto is turning into a city of fire and ice. If something happened to her on the way home tonight, who would go to the nursing home to check on Mamére tomorrow?

Marcello sweeps the bedroom floor with the flashlight. When he finds a crumpled robe, he picks it up and sniffs it.

"Pretty sure it's clean," he says, wrapping it around Lily and belting it tightly. He scrounges under the bed and pulls out a pair of crumpled jeans and a sweatshirt.

Marcello's lack of self-consciousness fascinates her. Unlike Lily, he's confident in his body, the heavy muscles of his shoulders, the unfashionable tangle of hair travelling from a crosshatch of scars on his chest, down a belly softening with age, finally nesting around his dangling cock. It's a body he's at peace with. *Does the job,* she can imagine him saying with a shrug.

He opens the bedroom door. A noticeable chill has settled into the living room. Marcello hands the flashlight to Lily, motioning for her to light the way.

As Marcello builds a fire in the hearth, Lily tries to call the nursing home. Her mobile phone is dead. She tries Marcello's landline and finds it dead too.

"You trying to reach anyone important?" he asks, too casually.

Lily can tell that he's wondering about the possibility of a husband or boyfriend out there in the city somewhere, worrying about where Lily might be. "My mother. I wanted to see if the power is still on at the place where she lives."

She can read the relief on Marcello's face.

Bundled in the thick robe, perched on a stool by the fire, Lily watches the rhythm of Marcello's hands as he prepares food by candlelight.

"So, are you going to tell me?"

"About what?"

"About Ida. What happened to her? And why you need forgiveness so badly?"

Marcello lets Lily's question hang in the air for a moment. "Do you know what a proxy bride is?" he asks.

She nods. "Like a mail order bride, except that she was married to her husband before she met him."

"That's right," says Marcello. "Ida was married by proxy to my father."

"How did she end up with you?"

Marcello says nothing for a moment, as if trying to figure out how to put together an explanation. "I guess you could say that I stole her from him." Filling juice glasses with wine, he continues: "My mother died when I was a kid. When I was nineteen, Pop married Ida by proxy. His uncle stood up for him in Italy and had her sent to Shipman's Corners, where we lived. Ida was twenty. Beautiful, like you, Lily. I fell in love the moment I saw her. I tried to stay away, even slept in my car. But she kept calling me in for meals—you know how it was in those days. Women cooked, men ate. Every time I sat across the table from her, I fell more deeply in love."

"Did your father know?"

"All Pop saw was the soup in front of his nose. Ida had told him, 'Give me a month to get settled, then I'll share your bed.' She never did. Instead, the two of us became lovers. We'd sneak out at night in my car. Park in the farmers' fields. Eventually we ran away together." Marcello stops to stare disapprovingly at Lily's untouched plate. "*Mangia*, Lily, that's good cheese!"

To appease Marcello, Lily nibbles on a chunk of asiago. She can feel a chill coming off the window behind her, the clatter of freezing rain only inches away from this cozy space. Marcello's story is hazily familiar. As if she'd seen it a movie or read it somewhere, long ago. Or dreamed it.

No, not a dream, but a bedtime story that started as Mamére's gentle explanation for two friends who had lived for a time at the Seahorse. Eventually, she turned their story into a fairy tale she called *Dreamboat and the Proxy Bride*.

It's all there: the mysterious young wife. The young man, eaten alive by a forbidden love. The cuckolded father. Lily feels as though she's fallen into an opera. Perhaps, a temporary distraction from the misery of Mamére's illness. She's owed at least one night of forgetfulness, isn't she?

In the distance, she can hear the *zing-pop-bang* of another exploding transformer, as the city's electrical grid collapses under the downpour of ice.

Lily says, "Even if the storm lets up, I'll stay here tonight and listen to your story in exchange for another glass of wine. Deal?"

"Deal," agrees Marcello. "But wine on its own is bad for the digestion. You have to eat, Lily. I have a beautiful artisanal cheese and Calabrese bread."

Nibbling an olive, Lily watches Marcello's face in the candle-light, trying to turn him back into the young man whose photo sits in a portfolio on the back seat of her ice-coated car. He pours more wine and settles in to tell Lily about him and Ida.

She senses that she could be here listening to their story for a very long time.

18. EVEN VENETIAN COWGIRLS GET THE BLUES

CHIESA SAN ROCCO, VENEZIA, JUNE 30, 1969

FROM THE OTHER SIDE of the door, Ida hears the hoarse whispers of a man unburdening himself. She tries not to listen; his sins are usually boring anyway. He's moaning now, his tears stimulated by his recounting of his filthy lustful act. She's in the box often enough to know that there's a point at which this man likes to cry out, sometimes in despair, occasionally in anger or frustration. That's the reason the man comes every Saturday: to have a priest clean away the one very bad sin he's not sorry he commits every Friday between 10:00 and 10:30 a.m. in his neighbour's flat. Certainly, he fears dying with a mortal sin on his soul; what would happen if a block and tackle collapsed over him on his walk home from work, a grand piano being winched into the second floor of a *palazzo* hurtling down on his head like in one of the American cartoons? Better to sin and confess and be forgiven, knowing you'll sin again, than to go to hell for the sake of a little fun.

He can't be bothered confessing small sins like taking the name of the Lord in vain or the occasional eye cast at thy neighbour's wife. Now, *taking* thy neighbour's wife, legs in the air under her gold brocade counterpane while the old man's away at work, that's a different story. Then, *boom,* the two of them head to San Rocco for confession. Sometimes the adulterers even sit at opposite ends of the same pew, tempting one another with their guilty, smouldering glances. It's all part of the seduction, according to Zara, who says she has seen everything in her line of work.

What phonies, thinks Ida in disgust.

She's already decided that she will never let herself be ruled by passion, neither a man's nor her own. She will never allow herself to fall senselessly in love, the way Zara did. She will be free, a woman of the world, a cowgirl riding the range with a palomino and a six-shooter like her heroine, Dale Evans—or better yet, like Blondie, the man played by Clint Eastwood in her favourite film, *Il Buono, Il Brutto, Il Cattivo.* At seventeen, her heart has never been touched, not once. Occasionally, yes, her hand or her leg and even, once, her breast when some old *ubriacone* who used to come to the Gilt Rose in the old days mistook her for a *cortigiana.* Zara gave him a smack in the face for that!

The Church claimed Zara's business was immoral. In 1958, they successfully pressured the government to close down La Rosa D'Oro and all the other brothels in the country. Not that switching from servicing men to the tourist trade has been bad for Ida's family; the *americani* and the *inglesi* get a thrill thinking about what scandalous things used to go on in these rooms eleven years earlier. Zara occasionally unlocks a closet full of special furniture and devices from the old days for the appreciation of paying customers. One of the favourites is a *ciuladura,* a specially designed velvet chair that helped old men with bad backs finish their business in comfort.

The clientele at Ca'Rosa, like that of the old brothel, is, as Zara likes to sniff, *high end*: well-heeled American and British couples, anxious for the authentic Venetian experience. Yet many of them turn up at the door with their own tea bags, instant coffee, and other foodstuffs. Once, a couple from New England, a professor and his wife, insisted on something for breakfast called *porridge*; anticipating that such a delicacy didn't exist in Italy, they brought their own, even coming into the kitchen to show Riccardo how to prepare it. Ida can still remember her brother, wide-eyed with disgust at the bubbling beige mess in his good iron saucepan, *Signora* Campbell showing him how to cook it while simultaneously admiring his muscular forearms. Like Ida herself, Rico is popular with guests of both sexes.

Signora and *Signore* Campbell were at the Ca'Rosa for an entire week, yet never came to understand that their hosts, young Ida included, understood every word they said. Once, when Ida was serving their coffee, Signore Campbell said, "Mornings must have been quite sybaritic when it was still a brothel! No wonder Peggy Guggenheim loves this place. Venice is all angels and whores, isn't it?"

"Like this one," agreed Signora Campbell, jerking her tightly-permed head at Ida. "No doubt there are a few Austrian captains of the guard in that family tree!"

She glared at the woman but kept her English to herself, instead offering a wide-eyed "*Che?*" when the *Signora* asked for their porridge.

Ida went into the kitchen where the steaming bowls sat waiting, Rico smoking over them with a grin on his face. They let the dog have a lick from *Signora's* bowl before Ida brought it to the table.

On the other side of the box, the man is finishing up. She can hear the rhythms of his Act of Contrition and Paolo's voice, deep and reassuring, as he mops up the man's sins with a light penance: just two Our Fathers and one Glory Be to the Father for all that noisy guilt. *Beh!* If Ida were the priest, she'd give the man ten Hail Marys and a boot in the ass.

The velvet curtain and wooden walls are so bloated with the whispered sins of five hundred years that she can *smell* the guilt, she can *taste* it. But the confession box is the only place she's allowed to talk freely to her father. Which, of course, is crazy. Just one of many reasons why she must leave this preposterous place for the green, rolling hills and open skies of America.

When the door finally slides open, the luminous dial of the priest's wristwatch glows through the screen as he gives the opening blessing. Ida gets to her knees, the cracked leather snagging her nylons. She places her mouth close to the screen and whispers fiercely: "Bless me Father for I have sinned. But not half as much as you!"

The blessing stops.

"Ida?"

"I've come to say goodbye."

A silence. "You're really going, then?"

Does she hear a note of regret in his voice? More like relief, she suspects. Once she gets on the plane to Toronto, Paolo can go back to his holy life without the inconvenience and embarrassment of an illegitimate, half-breed teenage daughter.

"Yes, I'm going to Canada. The part of America where they worship the Queen."

"You are too headstrong. Is this wise, to marry a man you haven't even spoken with?"

"Was it wise to fall in love with my mother, you a seminarian, and give her Rico and me? Was it wise to confess to that damn *giornalista* who just wanted a good story for his magazine about the old brothels? Besides, I am married already. I have my tickets. This time tomorrow I will be living on a ranch."

Paolo gives a little cough. "Why must you torture me, Ida? I am to be punished for my admission of paternity. They're sending me to the chaplaincy of a prison."

"I didn't know."

"Well, now you know. I suffer too. As I'm sure your mother does. How is Zara?"

"Go ask her yourself," suggests Ida meanly.

She wants to storm out of the box and go to where Paolo sits concealed in his role as God's intermediary, throw open the door and pull him into the light. *Our Father.* Instead she stays on her knees and waits to see what he will do to prevent her from leaving.

He tries to calmly reason with her: "The airline ... they'll forget all about it in time. *Everyone* will forget. To them, it's just a story in the paper. Tomorrow, they're on to something else."

"Oh yes? The airline says, because of all the publicity, I can't fly again for a year, so that people have time to forget. *One entire year!* Another year at home with Zara and the old folks, fighting and fighting, another year of Signora Bellini yelling insults at me on the street, the other girls looking down at me, another year of coming here every week to talk to you in this damn box..."

"Ida," says the priest by way of warning. "I am still your father. God hears you! Obey the second commandment!"

Ida sits back on her heels in astonishment, anger expanding inside her chest like a balloon about to burst.

"You want me to respect you?" she snorts. "Do other fathers speak to their children only in darkness, surrounded by sins and lies? That's it! Close the door."

Paolo hesitates. She can see, very faintly, his profile outlined by a faint light. His face is in his hands. *He feels bad. Good!*

"*Aspetta!* Wait. Don't go. You know nothing of this man you marry."

"On the contrary, I know a great deal about him! His name is Marcello Trovato Senior," says Ida. "A widower. A rich businessman with a ranch and a little boy for me to look after, also named Marcello. Marcello Senior and Junior. That's my family now. That's where I go tomorrow."

"God forgive me," whispers Paolo.

"Close the door," orders Ida again. "A sinner is waiting for you on the other side."

Paolo mumbles a blessing and slides shut the door.

She can't believe he actually did it. He closed the door in her face. She sits in stunned disbelief. He loves her so little that he will simply let her go without a fight.

That settles it. *La donna é mobile.* She is moving.

As she leaves the box, an old woman kneeling in the pews gives her the eye. *What took you so long?* When she sees Ida, she lowers her head and fingers her beads.

Everyone knows her face now. She's "the priest's girl"—that was the headline in *Oggi* a month ago. Something intriguing and amusing and a bit scandalous for the Italians to enjoy along with their morning espresso. A priest, a brothel-keeper's daughter, and their beautiful child, a knock-out, a stewardess, no less—could there be any better combination for a titillating story? It's almost a comic opera.

There was a photo of her in her trainee uniform, another of Paolo at his ordination, a third of the *pensione*, formerly The Gilt Rose, the article explained, until the Vatican made the government change the rules, pulling the rug out from beneath their feet. Now the girls walk the streets and lurk in alleyways, and Casa Rosa loosens its robes for silly tourists instead of lustful men.

Zara and the old lady who owned the place were embarrassed by the news story, and Paolo's bishop is furious. But Ida is humiliated to the point of self-banishment. She must escape, she insists to Rico, and become someone entirely new. *I will re-invent myself in the New World.*

Rico says nothing. He knows she can do it.

Ida stands in the middle of San Rocco. Tintoretto masterpieces everywhere you look. A baptismal font that has anointed the infant heads of composers, courtesans, artists, assassins, even Ida herself, over the shrill criticism of Signora Bellini. So much history, you could choke on it.

She stares at the confession box. Paolo is still in there, giving ear to the penitents, while out under the apse his daughter stands disrespectfully, her back to the altar. She leaves without genuflecting or dipping her fingers into holy water to make the Sign of the Cross. Once outside, she pulls off her ugly black headscarf and stuffs it into a trash barrel beside the *scuola*.

At home, she packs her bag. The red skirt, white blouse, and best shoes go in last. As she has been taught to pack in stewardess school, the thing you wear next is the thing you pack last.

Next door an argument is raging between Zara and the old lady, as usual. She's already said her goodbyes to them both so now they're tearing into one another. "Why does she go? The guests like her. And this stupid newspaper story—it's all good publicity! It's just another thing to bring them to Ca'Rosa."

"Why are you shouting at me? I'm not the one sending the girl away!"

"No, no. We only have your priest to blame for that!"

"Paolo and I have always loved one another. Can I help it if he has a calling?"

Et cetera. Et cetera. The generation gap again, thinks Ida. Surely the older ones are totally crazy. It's up to her generation to change these ridiculous attitudes toward love and sex and religion.

She has one last place to go.

Downstairs, she enters the kitchen. As blonde as Ida, but tall like Paolo, Rico stands at the stove, his broad shoulders in a white shirt, slim hips in black pants. When he turns to look at her, Ida's heart melts a little. Her handsome brother, sweet as sugar. The only one she'll miss.

"I'm ready," she announces.

Rico wipes his eyes with his sleeve. He's chopping onions but she can see that he's also crying a little.

"I'll take your bag to the station."

At noon, Rico carries her white suitcase to Stazione Santa Lucia. From here, her ticket takes her to Milano where she will spend the night, then on to Malpensa Aeroporto for the flight the next morning. Everything all set up and paid for by her husband in Canada, even the chaperone, an old woman hired to guard her from the advances of men on the train and to see her safely on her way. It wouldn't do to have the virgin bride lose her purity before she meets her new husband! His people have also supplied doctored papers that add five years to her age. Ida shrugged at this suggestion: she finds no advantage in youth, so why not? From this day on, she will say she was born in forty-seven, not fifty-two.

Ida tries to imagine what her husband looks like. At the proxy wedding the previous Saturday, in an ugly modern church in suburban Mestre, a rumpled old man turned up to act as proxy groom, smelling of wine; she assumed he was her husband's uncle or great-uncle, but he turned out to be his brother. Well, of course, the real husband, the one in Canada, might have started out as a rough-edged *abruzzese,* but clearly he's hit it big in the New World with a ranch and an Oriental cook. Ida tries to comfort herself with these thoughts but doubts keep crowding in; she decides against sharing them with Rico. He's already worried enough. Besides, if things don't work out, she has a little money of her own—enough, perhaps, to provide her with a means of escape, should she need it.

"I'm thinking of leaving someday too," confides Rico, taking her hand as they wait to board the train. After satisfying herself that Rico was really Ida's brother, the old chaperone has already embarked to ensure that their seats are spotless and free from the eyes of curious men.

"Come with me," Ida says to her brother.

He shakes his head. "Not yet. I can't let Zara and Paolo lose both of us at once. And anyway I'm thinking of *Inghilterra,* not America."

"England, why?"

Rico shrugs. "I hear the restaurants like Italian cooking and the women like Italian men."

"I suspect this is also true in Canada," offers Ida.

"What sort of a name is 'Toronto'?" asks Rico, dubiously.

"An Indian name."

Rico laughs. "Of course! For you, of course, it would have to be an Indian name."

"But this is just the landing point. My husband will pick me up there and takes me to Shipman's Corners."

Rico frowns. "Sheep-a-man Corona?"

"Yes, yes. A town in the countryside. Like those pretty villages in Tuscany! Very good horse country. No doubt where he has his ranch. Perhaps I will live there with the little boy while he works in the city."

"You, a *mamma*. Hard to imagine." Rico puts his arms around her. "Leave this husband in the lurch. Stay here another year, then go back to Alitalia when all the publicity settles, you will still see the world...."

"No." Ida is firm. "In one more year, I'll be dead. It's too much Rico. I want to start again. Without Paolo, without Ca'Rosa, without Signora Bellini singing out insults at me every time I walk by her hanging her laundry."

"Everyone will forget. The airline will forget."

"Rico, they said to me, 'We only take good girls. Alitalia doesn't want scandal.' They won't forget and I won't forget."

Around them a crowd of hippie tourists, fresh off the train, shout to one another in English, Swedish, German, mouths gaping—*Oh wow!*—as they gaze at the unbelievable storybook city spread before them, already visible from the square fronting Santa Lucia Station. The canals, the cathedrals, the gondolas, the *palazzi!* Ida doesn't even take a last look.

Rico places the white suitcase on the top step of the coach, where a porter picks up it up to take to Ida's seat. The stone-faced chaperone reads her prayer book. Ida pushes past her to sit by the open window and look out at her brother. Their eyes meet, blue on blue.

Too many things to say, brother, thinks Ida. *So say nothing at all, eh?*

As the train starts moving, she waves, her hands in demure white gloves, the ones they gave her in stewardess training.

Rico has one last glimpse of his sister's beautiful, pale face, watching him, waving to him, before she turns her eyes to the west.

ACKNOWLEDGEMENTS

I gratefully acknowledge the support of the Ontario Arts Council Writers' Reserve Program for financial assistance in writing *Once Upon a Time in West Toronto*.

My heartfelt thanks go out to my editor Luciana Ricciutelli and publicist Renée Knapp at Inanna Publications. I also want to thank friends who took the time to read early drafts and give feedback: Diane Bracuk, Chris Caswell, Eufemia Fantetti, Izzy Ferguson, Glen Petrie, Kris Rothstein, Heather McCulloch, and Maria Meindl. Special thanks to Lisa de Nikolits for her friendship, and to Rick Favro and Izzy Ferguson for technical advice about car crashes and house collapses, and to my language experts Guingo Sylwan and Annalisa Magnini (Italian), Andy Drakopolous (Greek), and Marianne and Ana Marusic (Croatian).

A different version of the chapter, "A Shout From God", originally appeared as a story in the 2011 Diaspora Dialogues anthology *TOK 6: Writing the New Toronto*. Thank you, DD, for the valuable mentorship of David Layton.

Finally, to my husband and creative partner Ron Edding: thank you for your love, encouragement, and sense of humour. *Ti amo*.

Terri Favro is a novelist, essayist, storyteller, and graphic novel collaborator. *Once Upon a Time in West Toronto* is the sequel to her award-winning novella, *The Proxy Bride*. Terri is also the author of the novel, *Sputnik's Children*, co-creator of the "Bella" graphic novel series, and a CBC Literary Prize finalist in Creative Non-Fiction. Her short fiction and essays have appeared in numerous literary magazines and anthologies. Terri grew up in the Niagara area and now lives in Toronto.